HIGHLANDER'S HOPE

Called by a Highlander Book Two

MARIAH STONE

"Hope" is the thing with feathers -
That perches in the soul -
And sings the tune without the words -
And never stops - at all -

— Emily Dickinson

PROLOGUE

Dunollie Castle, Scotland, 1296

"*CRUACHAN!*"

Marjorie groaned. She must be dreaming. Why else would she hear her clan's war cry?

The straw mattress scratched her skin. The room was quiet and smelled like dust from the drapery that hung from the canopy. Was she alone? She tried to lift her heavy eyelids, but then she remembered...

If she opened her eyes, she might see *him*. And he'd want to strike her again.

Or take her again.

No more pain, please. No more humiliation.

She wanted dark, numb oblivion. She allowed it to take her away from the aches in her whole body. Something odd caught her ear, and she clung to the sound like to the edge of a cliff. The noise came from outside and below. Cries of pain. Metal ringing against metal.

And then...

"*Cruachan!*" The sound was louder now, coming closer. It was a chorus of many men.

Was she imagining it? Was she so desperate and broken that she was dreaming of home?

The air smelled faintly of smoke. Footsteps pounded against the stone floor outside the room she was being kept in. The door opened with a screech, the iron handle grating. Then it closed.

This sound, of this door, meant one thing.

He's back.

And if he was here, there would be pain.

Quick, heavy steps approached. He breathed heavily and paced around the room. His chain mail clanked softly. He hadn't touched her yet. Maybe he hadn't come for her.

But then why is he here?

Outside, the cries intensified. Something heavy battered against wood.

"*Cruachan!*"

They have come.

Hope blossomed in her chest, giving her strength. She opened one eye—the other was swollen shut—and turned her head to the light of the slit window.

Alasdair MacDougall paced along the wall of rough, dark rock. His nostrils flared, his eyes wild, his curly, dark hair unruly under the chain mail covering his head and shoulders. He tapped the flat side of his sword against his hand.

He glanced at her and froze for a moment, his face blank.

"Ye awake, wee bitch?" He covered the space between them in three steps.

Even without any strength left in her body, Marjorie pushed against the bed to try to drag herself as far away as possible from him. The blanket fell off, and her bare thighs with dry, caked blood flashed white and reddish brown. She wanted to cover herself, but she was too weak. His scent, one she was all too familiar with by now, reached her. He reeked of sweat and his male musk. He dropped his sword, and it fell with a loud *clank*. Grasping a handful of her hair at the top of her head, he lifted his other arm and slapped her.

Blinding white pain shot through her head. Then another hit came on the other side. Her eyes must have burst inside her skull. She didn't even cry. He brought her face close to his, and she smelled his bad breath—a mixture of ale, alcohol, meat with onion. "Ye happy now, precious princess? Ye thought ye were too good for my proposal, but now everyone will see what a worthless whore ye truly are."

She sucked air into her lungs. "What are ye talking about?" she managed to say.

"Yer clan of Cambels are knocking at our doors. But as long as I have ye, I have the power."

Him saying her family had come for her was different from her thinking it, or imagining it. It was real.

They had come.

She smiled and then openly laughed in his face. She gathered saliva in her mouth and spat right in his face. Her spit was bloody, and she laughed even harder. It hurt, but it was also cleansing. She'd fight a battle in here while her clan fought for her out there.

"'Tis over, ye raping bastart," she said. She continued laughing, even though his face paled and she might be dead in a moment. He slammed his fist into her temple, and she sank into a dark fog. Through that fog, the image of two men and their swords clashing floated in and out of view.

"Ye will die, ye maggot!" someone shouted.

Steel clashed and flashed in the shaft of light coming through the window. Cries of pain tore her mind. Then came a scream—deadly and desperate—and a loud *thud* of something heavy falling to the floor. She woke up to a familiar voice calling her. A dear, dear voice she'd known all her life.

"Marjorie."

Someone stroked her head, but it felt like knives cutting her skin. She struggled to open her eyes and managed to lift one lid just a little. It was Craig. Her brother. Bloody and covered in bruises, he knelt by her bed. He was smiling, his eyes red, his dark hair disheveled. Tears blurred her vision and burned. He was here. That meant Alasdair was no longer a threat. Craig would take care of her. He'd take her home.

Relief flooded her. The echo of gratitude and love filled her chest. Despite her cracked-and-bruised lips, she managed a smile.

"Brother," she whispered.

The door was flung open, and their cousin Ian stepped in. His red locks were sweaty, his face was covered in cuts and bruises, but he was alive.

"I found her," Craig said.

"Good. Let us go. The way is clear."

Craig gave her a little nod. She knew he was promising her that all would be well. He carefully wrapped her in a blanket and picked her up. Pain shot through her. As he carried her from the room, she saw Alasdair's dead body on the floor, a pool of blood around him. She would have smiled and laughed, but she was empty.

Craig walked to the landing of the wooden stairwell, where their clansmen stood waiting. Their stern faces were illuminated by the torches as Craig carried her by. Ian went down the stairs before Craig, checking around the corners for danger, his sword atilt. But as Craig walked down the steps, the fighting stopped on the lower floor as well. Her father stood on the next landing, his face distorted with pain as he met her eyes. She tried to smile reassuringly to show she wasn't angry at him for not protecting her or coming sooner. Craig carried her farther away, and she saw her uncle Neil and his sons. Sorrow and fury shone in their eyes.

As they exited the tower, she saw John MacDougall, chief of the MacDougall clan and Alasdair's father, held by her two clansmen. He jerked helplessly, his pasty face twitching in silent rage, no doubt realizing that his son must be dead if Marjorie was in Craig's arms.

MacDougall should never have allowed Alasdair to kidnap her and treat her like he had. He should have stopped the madness and sent her home. Everything that had happened to her, had happened under John MacDougall's watch. As far as she was concerned, he was as guilty as his son.

Craig finally stepped out into the clear daylight of the courtyard surrounded by stone curtain walls, and Marjorie closed her eyes. Many men had died today to save her, and she couldn't bear seeing evidence of it. Not right now.

Craig walked for a while and then sank to the ground. She opened her eyes. Their grandfather, Sir Colin Cambel, lay on the reddish grass. There was a deep wound near his heart, but blood didn't flow from it. His eyes were closed, and his skin was pale. He was completely still, only the wind played with his white hair.

Craig took their grandfather's hand in his and squeezed it. Ian stood beside them and laid his hand on Craig's shoulder. Craig whispered something to their grandfather, and a tear fell from Marjorie's eye. Then her brother stood and walked with her to the horses and carts.

"We have a cart for ye. 'Tis full of furs and blankets. Ye'll be home soon." He laid her down and covered her in blankets, and warmth began returning to her.

She felt safe.

And free.

She was free, aye, but the humiliation, the pain, and the feeling of being unworthy corroded her heart. It still held her prisoner. She curled into a ball and began to cry.

"Oh, Marjorie, sweet, dinna." Craig patted her side. "Please, dearie. I'm sorry I didna come earlier. As soon as we kent who took ye, we came."

She couldn't stop her sobs. Craig sat next to her on the cart and hugged her, covering her like a heavy, protective blanket.

When she finally did stop crying, she lay still and tried to adjust to the light sensation of freedom in her chest that felt alien.

What would it feel like to be around people again? To go from room to room? To go out into the sunlight? To ride a horse again? After two sennights in captivity, she'd thought she'd never do any of those things again. She opened her eyes and stared at Craig. He looked concerned, and pain and fury fought in his eyes.

"What can I do?" he said.

She shook her head. "Nothing," she whispered. "Ye saved me. Ye avenged me. Ye killed the bastart. There's nothing more that ye can do."

He squeezed her hand and nodded. "Now we will work on healing ye. Ye'll be yer old self soon."

She inhaled sharply and closed her eyes. As much as it hurt to admit it, that would never be true. She was a stone inside now—cold and hard. She'd never let a man touch her. She'd never marry. And she'd never let anyone do what Alasdair had done to her ever again.

CHAPTER 1

L ands near Loch Awe, Scotland, 2020

THE BEST THING ABOUT A GUY TRIP THROUGH THE SCOTTISH
Highlands was the absence of technology. Even after seven
years of civilian life, Konnor Mitchell's Marine training kicked
in, and he had no problem orienting with or without a map,
fishing, cooking on a fire, and sleeping on the ground.

Actually, the best thing about the whole man-against-
nature thing was that it occupied his mind, leaving little time
to think of his life back in Los Angeles or his past. With no
cell phones, no TV, and no electricity, he had nothing to rely
on but his brains, his muscles, and his best bud Andy.

"How much longer to the Keir farm?" Andy looked up at
the sky. "The clouds are coming in darker than your best
mood."

A leaden sky hung above the dark-green pines and ashes
like an iron ceiling. Nature around them stood still, as if
waiting for something. Branches didn't rustle, and grass didn't

MARIAH STONE

waver. The air was humid and warm, full of the scent of forest and moss and something strange...lavender, though Konnor didn't notice any around.

He glanced down at the map in his hands, and a flicker of a movement caught his eye. Something green flashed between the trees. He blinked but saw nothing out of the ordinary. Must be all the whiskey he'd consumed during the last week.

"We're probably going to be soaking wet either way," Konnor said. "It'll take us until the evening."

He and Andy had hiked along the loch up north towards the farm. The map showed there was a small ruin at the bottom of the glen behind them, and if they made their way back towards Loch Awe, they'd come to the ruins of Glenkeld, a medieval castle.

They'd interrupted their whiskey tour with what was supposed to have been a three-day hike. But due to their relaxed pace and drinking the samples of whiskey they'd acquired from several distilleries, this was their fifth day out already. Between setting campfires, assembling and disassembling the tents, cooking hot dogs on an open fire, and fishing in Loch Awe, they'd gotten carried away and lost track of time.

The trip was kind of a long bachelor party for Andy, who was getting married to Natalie, his girlfriend of eight years and the mother of his child. After the kind of childhood Konnor had experienced, he hadn't thought it was even possible to be so deliriously happy, but Andy was a good man, and he deserved every happiness in the world.

Konnor was happy for Andy. But he had no idea how his friend did it. Perhaps others possessed the secrets to a happy relationship and how to be a good husband and a good dad.

He certainly didn't.

Andy frowned at the sky. "It might still pass," he said, though with no conviction.

Konnor said, "Let's hit the road. I need to call my mom."

As much as he was enjoying this hiking trip, Konnor

needed to get back to civilization. He knew how a thirty-three-year-old man needing to call his mommy might sound to some, but his best friend knew better than to make jokes about it. Konnor supported his mom financially, and it was most important to him that she knew she was safe and protected, that he would never let anyone hurt her ever again. Right before they'd gone hiking in the wilderness, he'd told her he'd leave the cell phone in the hotel but call her in three days.

Andy hurried after him. "Come on, bro, you've left her alone before. You were in the Marines for Christ's sake."

Having the most perfect folks in the world, Andy had no idea how it had been for Konnor and his mom. He'd never had to watch the closest person in the world to him be beaten to a pulp and not be able to do a single thing about it.

Konnor's stepfather was dead, but he'd taught Konnor a valuable lesson that he lived by to this day. He could never let his guard down, never trust that those he cared for would be safe without his protection. As a child, he hadn't been able to protect his mother, but he could do it now.

"Leave it alone," Konnor said.

Andy nodded but didn't look impressed. "If you say so, brother. You know, when we get back to LA, Natalie has a friend she wants you to meet."

Konnor groaned. *Here we go.* At least every six months, Natalie wanted to set him up with someone.

"Andy..." Konnor said by the way of warning.

"I'm with you, man, but will you please go, just this once? Or she'll drive me crazy."

Konnor scoffed.

"Word on the street is you're a catch. Successful business owner and apparently *man candy*." He put air quotes around that. "Put me out of my misery, man."

Konnor scoffed. "You'll be more miserable if I go out with her once and never call her again, then Natalie will kill you. I'm not looking for a relationship. Never will be."

Why would he? Every relationship he'd been in had ended up bringing pain to the women because of what they'd all called his emotional unavailability.

Andy clasped him on the shoulder. "After all these years, I still think you're a puzzle."

"There's nothing puzzling about me. I'm simple. I have no intention of getting married or having a girlfriend. Ever."

They walked in silence for a while. A soft whisper of leaves and branches rustling went through the woods, and the sky darkened even more. A small shiver ran across the back of Konnor's neck.

Andy shook his head. "I will say one last thing. You're miserable, and you know it."

"I'm fine," Konnor growled. "I'm great. I have everything I ever wanted."

Thunder rolled in the distance, and they both glanced up to the dark-gray sky.

"Let's get a move on," Andy said. "Come on."

He sped up, but Konnor didn't. Seeing his friend moving off in the distance, he realized he needed a break from him for a while.

"You go on, Andy. I need to take a leak. I'll catch up with you."

Andy stopped and glanced at him with suspicion in his eyes. "Are you sure?"

Konnor sighed. "I'm sure the summer rain won't melt me."

"All right."

Andy hurried down the track. Once he was out of sight, Konnor took in a lungful of air and breathed out. He didn't really need to piss. The cold wind picked up, and the scent of lavender and freshly cut grass rushed by him.

Suddenly a woman's voice broke the silence. "Help! Help!"

Instinctively, Konnor reached to where he usually kept his gun. But of course, it wasn't there. The only weapon he had was a Swiss Army knife in his backpack.

He looked around. Andy was nowhere to be seen. Trees swayed, hissing in the wind, and leaves and branches flew by. One narrowly missed his eye and scratched his cheek. Thunder rolled closer, and the granite sky flashed with lightning. The storm was almost right over him. Was the woman stuck somewhere?

Rocks crumbled from somewhere behind him. Konnor squinted back down the trail but couldn't see anyone. The wind brought the woman's scream again. Or was it just trees moaning as the emerging storm assailed them?

The scream came again, and his pulse accelerated. It was coming from behind him, up the trail. He sprinted in that direction as fast as he could with his backpack on.

"Help!"

Trees and bushes flashed by as he ran. Twigs cracked, and pebbles rolled under his feet. The scent of lavender and freshly cut grass grew stronger. The voice was louder now, so the woman must be somewhere nearby, but he still couldn't see who was calling.

"Down here!"

The voice came from behind the trees and bushes. Through the gaps, he saw the edge of a cliff. He stepped through the undergrowth and looked down a ravine that was about two hundred feet wide. It was as though an ancient earthquake had cracked the ground in half here. There was a steep, rocky slope of about twenty or so feet right in front of him. A few pines grew straight out from the rocks. The ravine was shielded by a steep slope on the other side. A creek flowed along the grassy bottom below. It looked fertile and cozy, like a small, secluded piece of heaven. Something about it was magical and mysterious and unreal.

There was a woman down in the ravine. She was sitting on a small pile of rubble and holding her shoulder.

"Are you okay, ma'am?" Konnor called, trying to shout over the wind.

She looked up, and even from here, he could see a bright smile. She had long red hair and wore a medieval-looking green dress.

"Oh, lad, can ye help me?" she said. "I hurt my arm and canna go up."

The wind picked up, and the next gush stole Konnor's breath. He looked the slope over. It was really steep, but he could more or less see a path down. The question was whether he could bring an injured person back up.

First, he needed to get down there and see what was wrong with her arm.

"Don't move," he said. "I'm coming."

"Oh, bless ye, lad!"

Thunder shook the world, and lightning split the sky in half. Thick raindrops began to hit Konnor's face. He needed to hurry.

He laid his backpack on the ground and began making his way down the slope. Rocks and rubble crumbled under his feet. He hung on to bushes and the occasional pine that grew in between the hard rocks. Heavy raindrops fell faster now, and he had to blink rapidly.

His leg slipped, and he tumbled down. Earth and sky flashed. His military training kicked in, and he kept his arms close to his body to avoid his organs being hit. Something smacked against his ankle, and red-hot pain blinded him. He got a hard blow to his head, making the world explode.

Finally, he stopped rolling and lay still. He felt like he'd been put through a meat grinder. Willing the dizziness away, he opened his eyes. Raindrops fell from the leaden sky, and he blinked. His left ankle hurt like hell. Was it broken? With a groan, he sat up. When he moved his leg, fire shot through his veins. Goddamn it. His first aid kit was up in his backpack.

His wrist ached, too. No doubt, there'd be a bruise there tomorrow. His Swiss watch, a gift from Andy, had a hair-thin crack on the glass. Thankfully, it was still working. It was waterproof and as reliable as a German car. He'd hate to lose it.

He looked around. There was a heap of rubble and gray mortar nearby. The woman sat and stared at him with an emphatic grimace. Rain fell heavily all around them, but while Konnor's clothes were getting soaked, the woman didn't look wet.

Weird.

"Does it hurt?" she said.

Suppressing another wave of nausea, he swallowed. "You bet. I have bad news for you. I don't think we're getting out of here without help, not with me like this, and not in this storm."

As though to confirm this, lightning flashed and thunder cracked above them.

Konnor cursed. "I don't suppose you have a phone?"

She bit her lip and widened her eyes. "I dinna have a phone. 'Tis the one thing from yer time that scares me."

He blinked. Had he heard her right, or had he whacked his head so bad he was having audible hallucinations? "What's your name, ma'am?"

"They call me Sìneag."

"Sìneag. I'm Konnor Mitchell. Nice to meet you. We need to find some sort of a shelter until the storm passes, and I'll need to take a look at your shoulder."

"Oh, aye. Mayhap here by the ruin." The heap of rubble formed an alcove where it connected with the cliff. An ancient oak tree grew there, its thick crown forming a sort of a ceiling.

"Yeah," Konnor said. "That'll do."

He tried to stand, but the pain in his ankle was excruciating. She jumped to her feet and rushed to him. She put his arm around her shoulders and lifted him up with strength that surprised him. Was she in any pain at all? As though he weighed nothing, she helped him towards the small shelter and then let him slide down the wall of the cliff by the rubble.

It was a relief to be out of the hammering rain and wind. The ground here was cold and dry. The air was thick with the scent of rain and wet ground, but the predominant smell was lavender and cut grass. It seemed to be coming from Sìneag.

She sat next to him, and now that raindrops weren't making him blink every second, he studied her. She pushed back a strand of hair from her heart-shaped face. Her eyes were large, and she had a strawberry-shaped mouth, and freckles dotted her milky skin. Her hair was red and played in the small gushes of wind that reached her. She looked like Red Riding Hood, except her hood was green, and she had no basket.

"Your shoulder is fine, isn't it?" he said.

A guilty expression crossed her blushing face. "Aye. But I can help ye."

Konnor grimaced. She'd lied and put his life at risk. For what?

"I almost broke my neck trying to help you." he said, his voice ringing with restrained anger. She must have a good reason for the ruse, and he didn't get a dangerous serial killer vibe from her. He hoped Andy would come back to find him once the storm passed. He should see the backpack by the track easily enough.

Sìneag managed to look both sheepish and a little upset. Her green eyes darkened and became as hard as rocks. "Ye dinna have love in yer life, do ye?" she said.

Konnor blinked. He must have smacked his head really good, because this conversation was unbelievable. "What?"

"Do ye have someone? Love someone?"

Shit. He had to be reading her wrong. "Look, I'm sorry if I gave you the wrong impression, but I'm not looking for anything here. I'm just on a guy trip with my friend."

She laughed, the sound sweet and pure.

"Oh, nae!" she said. "'Tis nae what I meant with the question. Forgive me. I canna be with a mortal anyway."

A mortal? What did that mean? Was she some sort of a celebrity here and meant that in a mocking way? Nausea rose in his throat. Yeah, he probably had a concussion.

"Okay," he said. "As long as we're clear about that."

"I just wanted to ken if someone like ye—a man with a strong soul and a soft heart—has someone in yer life?"

A grunt started deep in Konnor's gut, but he stopped it. Was today "let's grill Konnor about his love life day"? First Andy, and now a complete stranger?

"I don't."

"Good," she exclaimed and clapped her hands. "I dinna see anyone in yer heart, but I just wanted to be sure."

"What is the point of this?"

"'Tis all for yer own good, ye'll see."

Getting hurt was for his own good? She was really testing his patience. As the owner of a personal protection agency, he had to deal with all kinds of clients. Sometimes his company was contracted by Hollywood celebrities and billionaires to protect them and their families, so he'd met his share of eccentric people, but he'd never had a conversation like this. Could the concussion be causing him to hallucinate?

"What are you talking about?" he said.

She giggled, and the sweet laughter reminded him of the ringing of small bells.

"I'm testing yer patience, aye? Ye're a good man. I wouldna have done this for a bad one. 'Tis like so..." She pointed at the huge pile of rubble and what looked like the remnants of a wall. "'Tis here was an ancient Pictish stronghold. 'Twas built upon a magical rock."

She looked pointedly at a large, flat rock that lay sunken in the dirt. It had what looked like an old, simple carving on it—a flowing river in a circle with something that looked like a road piercing it. Near the carving was the clear imprint of a hand. Just like the imprint of a shoe in cement before it got a chance to dry. Weird.

"They say there's a tunnel through time that opens for those who touch the rock. On the other side is the person who's destined for them."

Konnor raised one brow. "Wonderful," he murmured. "That's a looney story."

"There's a person for ye, too," Sìneag said.

"Oh, really?"

"On the other side of the tunnel of time, there's one person who'll make ye happy. Someone who can help ye soothe all yer wounds and stop running from all ye secrets. A woman ye can truly love. A woman who can love ye."

"Back in time? Do Highlanders have stories about time travel?"

An owner of one of the distilleries on their whiskey tour had been very enthusiastic about local folklore. She'd told them stories of kelpies, faeries, and silkies. But none about time travel.

"Aye, though nae many ken them. The woman I'm talking about is as hurt as ye are, and she needs someone who'll help her get back on her feet. Tell me this isna something you need, too?"

He shook his head. "What I need is to be left alone."

She smiled. "Ye humans amuse me. Ye make all kinds of excuses to cling to yer beliefs. Destiny will show ye, Konnor Mitchell. Remember, Marjorie will soothe yer soul."

He propped his hand against the ground. Was he hallucinating, or was the rock with the carvings glowing? No. Not hallucinating. There was a faint glow coming from the indentations of the carving.

"What the hell?" He looked up, but Sìneag wasn't there. He looked around. "Sìneag?"

The noise of the rain drumming against the ground and the leaves was the only sound, and the scent of lavender and cut grass was gone.

Where the hell did she go? "Sìneag?"

It seemed like the rock was vibrating. His pain and discomfort forgotten, Konnor stared at it. What was happening? The carvings were glowing clearly now—the waves blue, the straight line brown. And the handprint... It called to him to put his palm into it. What was the harm? Slowly, he moved his hand and placed it into the indentation in the rock. A buzz went through his fingers, like the distant rumble of an earthquake. It was as though his hand were made of metal and the rock was a magnet. Strangely, his head was full of one name.

Marjorie.

He fell forward, and the hard, wet surface disappeared, replaced with cold, fresh air. He saw nothing. Heard nothing. His ears were muffled, as though he'd been plunged into water.

He was falling and falling, and darkness consumed him.

CHAPTER 2

L ands near Glenkeld Castle, Loch Awe, summer 1308

MARJORIE PULLED BACK THE STRING OF HER BOW. THE TIP of her arrow was pointed at the stag grazing between the trees, his antlers a giant crown on his head.

The air was ripe with the scent of flowers, deer dung, and rotting tree trunks. Birds chirped, and the wind rustled through the leaves. Sunlight fell through the branches onto the grass and tree trunks, and the hair on the stag's body glistened where the sunrays fell on them.

Marjorie made herself breathe deeply to fight the violent drumming of her heart against her ribs. She imagined it wasn't the big, graceful animal with the crown of antlers beautiful enough to decorate a king's great hall. Instead, she imagined Alasdair MacDougall standing there with his back to her.

She often imagined the man when she trained with her sword, imagined piercing him with her weapons and bringing the most excruciating of deaths to him.

In her mind, he fought back every time. Now, just like the stag, he didn't. He stood there unaware of her presence. The arrow was in the perfect position to meet the target, but she couldn't let it fly.

Despite her years of sword, archery, and combat training, she'd never attacked and killed anyone. All she'd done was train. This stag would be her first truly large kill. She'd only hunted fowls and hares before.

Just do it already.

Marjorie let out a long, slow breath, making the last estimations of the flight of the arrow in her mind's eye. Everything was ready. The coarse string rubbed against her cheek as she pulled it back just a little.

Let go.

The stag raised his head and looked east.

Voices.

It took off.

"Oh, damnation!" Marjorie cursed and lowered her bow.

Tamhas and Muir, the clunky fools, must be looking for her. She may as well head back. She was alone outside the walls of Glenkeld Castle for the first time in twelve years. Her father and three brothers—Craig, Owen, and Domhnall—were north in the Highlands, fighting for King Robert the Bruce together with the rest of Cambel clan. Ian, her dear cousin who'd been fostered with her family for almost his whole life, had been killed in a battle with the damned MacDougalls soon after she'd been saved from Alasdair.

The warrior in her wished she were off fighting for her king with them, and finally using her years of combat training. Instead, she'd been left in charge of Glenkeld Castle, which both terrified and excited her, because together with the castle, she was responsible for protecting Colin, her son.

The sense of danger prickled against her skin as she quickly looked around. She better hurry to Tamhas and Muir. It had been pretty stupid of her to separate from them, but she'd wanted to test herself, to see if she was strong enough, if she was ready. The truth was, she'd been afraid of walking alone outside the castle walls ever since her clan brought her back from Dunollie. She was ashamed of her fear. Ashamed that she couldn't conquer it. Separating from her bodyguards for this small mission was a step towards putting an end to it.

She put the arrow back in her quiver and the bow on her shoulder. The voices grew closer, and she went in that direction.

"There's nae moat, and the walls are nae high. With ladders, we'll be in the castle in nae time."

She stopped. Those were not her bodyguards.

"Aye, and the top part of the wall is crumbled on the northern side. Chief will be pleased."

She hid behind a tree trunk, her stomach churning, her breath ragged. Crumbled wall on the northern side... Nae moat... That described Glenkeld Castle.

Cold crawled down her spine.

"Aye. How much longer to the horses? Canna wait to bring the news to Dunollie. Chief wants to march soon and get his grandson."

"Nae long."

Dunollie... His grandson...

The ground shifted under her feet. Her knees melted, and her blood turned to ice. The nightmare that had crippled her whole life was coming for her again.

MacDougalls.

Where were her bodyguards?

Her feet were as heavy as lead, frozen to the ground. With an enormous effort, and trying to calm her shaky breath, she turned and looked in the direction of the voices. The two men were walking east with their backs to her now. Their dark tunics swayed as they moved lazily through the trees like they already owned these lands.

She could kill them. She could send an arrow into one of

them, and if she were fast enough, she could kill the other one before he turned around. Her hands shaking violently, she took her bow and an arrow. She nocked the arrow in place, but it fell.

"Damnation," she whispered.

They were walking away.

She tried again. This time, she secured the arrow in place. She lifted the bow and pulled the string to her cheek. But her breath shuddered, and the arrow jumped up and down before her eyes.

They were leaving. If she wanted to stop the MacDougall spies, this was her last chance. She was almost out of time. She'd never actually hurt anyone, except for the occasional bruises and scratches during combat training.

If she shot now and the arrow missed, the men would be alerted and come after her. Then she'd really need to fight for her life. She couldn't let them take her again.

The past blurred her vision. She remembered lying helpless on a bed, unable to move, pain unlike any she'd ever known tearing her apart. Panic clogged her throat.

The men disappeared behind the trees, and she lost sight of them. She lowered her bow, breathing heavily, a strange mixture of relief and fear tearing her apart. Her mind went blank.

The memory of endless pain and despair flooded her. She could feel it again, her violated, torn flesh, the humiliation, the bottomless exhaustion and desperation. Her body acted before she could think.

She turned and ran.

Trees flashed before her eyes, and branches slapped her. She stumbled against roots and pushed against trunks. The air was a bog, slowing her, grabbing her. She turned to look behind her, but no one followed her. The only sounds were her ragged breathing, the chirping of the birds, and the wind rustling the leaves.

She came to a halt at the sharp edge of a ravine, rocks crumbling under her feet and falling down the slope. She panted and looked around. The MacDougall men were nowhere to be seen.

Thank God, Mary, and Jesu, it seemed like she was alone. Suddenly, she heard someone moan down in the ravine. Her hand jerked to her shoulder for her bow, but it wasn't there. She must have been so caught up in her terror she dropped it without realizing.

She heard the moan again, longer and louder now, and she narrowed her eyes, searching down below for the source of it. Maybe Tamhas or Muir had fallen, or maybe they'd been attacked by the MacDougall spies?

Someone moved. A broad-shouldered man in clothes the color of fading leaves crawled from the ruins of an ancient tower that most folk avoided. He sat up and held his head like he had a headache or had hit it hard. She didn't recognize him from the castle. Was he another MacDougall spy? She should just leave before he saw her.

The man raised his head, and for a moment, Marjorie thought he did look familiar. Not that she recognized his face, but there was something about him, like she knew him from somewhere.

"Hey!" he cried, wincing as he moved. "I'm pretty hurt, and I don't think I can climb up. Can you help?"

Marjorie hesitated. Leaving a man in trouble was cowardly. It had been cowardly to let those two spies go instead of rising up like the warrior she'd been training to be all these years. She just couldn't do it again. He was injured. How dangerous could he be?

"Can you call 911, or whatever you guys have here in Scotland?" he said.

She frowned. She'd heard an accent like his before. His soft Rs and broad consonants sounded like her new sister-in-law, Amy. Also, calling some numbers didn't make any sense.

"Ye must have injured yer head," she said. "Dinna move. I'm coming down."

"Don't. You may hurt yourself—"

But she began climbing down the slope, carefully balancing on the rocks and stones that crumbled and rolled from under her feet. Once or twice, she almost fell, but she held on to bushes and regained her balance by sheer luck.

When she was down, she studied the man from closer up. Oh, Jesu and Mary, she hadn't realized from high above how huge he was. She didn't think she'd ever seen anyone as muscular and tall—except mayhap Ian. Muscles corded under his wet clothes. He wore broad breeches with pockets, a tight, thin tunic, and a short coat the likes of which she'd never seen before. They were all completely wet. Had he swum in the brook? His brown hair was drenched and gathered in a pony-tail behind his head. His blue eyes were framed with long eyelashes, but there was pain behind them. Like he were carrying the misery of the whole world on his shoulders. Like pain was in his bloodstream.

And like no one could understand.

Her gut clenched as the thought reverberated within her like the echo of a voice in a cave.

"Are ye from around here?" she said.

"No. I was on my way to a farm nearby and had a bad fall."

"The Keir farm?" she said.

Her maid, Moire, had mentioned she had a cousin that was coming for a visit.

"Yes, the Keir farm," he said.

"Ye must be Moire's cousin. Sorry, I forgot yer name, although I'm sure she mentioned it."

"Konnor," he said. "But I'm not—"

A branch snapped somewhere above them, and Marjorie ducked and pulled him behind one of the large boulders. He crawled, wincing but not making a sound.

"What's wrong?" he said.

"There are MacDougalls nearby," she whispered.

"Are you in danger?" Something about his tone was so protective. It was as though one of her brothers asked the question. A warm sense of being safe settled in her chest.

"Mayhap," she said and peered from behind the boulder. "Can ye walk?"

"Unlikely. Can you not just call an ambulance?"

"A what?"

His warm eyes shone as he smiled. "I swear, you locals are weird. Totally into your Highland heritage, aren't you? The costumes, the arrows, the accent..."

"I dinna ken what ye mean, Konnor. 'Tis ye who appear strange to me. But I wilna leave a friend of my clan in trouble. Come, lean on my shoulder. We have a healer in the castle, and Moire will want to ken ye've arrived."

She squatted next to him and allowed him to wrap his arm around her shoulder. His scent reached her—something dark and foreign, like the fresh scent of rain, woodsmoke. She helped him stand, and the weight of him was heavy but pleasant against her skin. Her chest rose and fell faster, but it was only from the exercise, she told herself. Not because she was affected by this man in any way.

Because after what Alasdair had done to her, there was no way she could be affected by anyone.

CHAPTER 3

Konnor didn't know how long they limped through the woods. Between the agonizing pain in his ankle, and trying not to crush the beautiful Scotswoman with his weight, time crawled. Every second felt a year long.

When he'd woken up in the ravine, the rain had stopped. Strangely, there was no sign that a drop had fallen. How long had he been out? The last thing he remembered was the weirdest sensation of falling through the stone, but he was sure that was only a side effect of the concussion. Sìneag had said something about time travel. But the ruins were still ruins, and the ravine and the woods looked exactly the same. Sìneag was still nowhere to be seen.

Where on earth had this beauty come from? They were out in the middle of the wilderness right after a storm? And why was she completely dry, while his clothes were soaked through? This was all so weird.

"How far still?" Konnor said. "I must be heavy for you. Not every woman can support a hundred-and-eighty-pound male for miles."

She frowned, and there was a fleeting expression of confusion on her face. Then she glared up at him, a hardness in her

MARIAH STONE

moss-green eyes. Her long, braided hair smelled mysterious, like a fresh herb cocktail mixed with something sweet that he guessed was her own scent.

"Ye canna climb the slope, so we must take the longer route through the ravine."

"All right," he said. "All right." He considered asking if she could call someone with a car, but he decided against it. Judging by her clothes—leather pants, a simple linen tunic, and something like a leather coat—and the arrows in a quiver on her back, she didn't look like someone who carried a mobile phone around.

"Were you on a hunt?" He said it as a joke to lighten up the mood. He imagined she probably did archery as a hobby and had been practicing nearby. Or maybe there was a Renaissance fair or something.

"Aye."

"How did it go?"

"As ye see, I caught someone."

He chuckled. "Well, thanks for not shooting me."

"I dinna shoot the fallen."

A code of honor? Had she really been out hunting? "You have the arrows. Where's the bow?"

She shot him a sideways glance and raised her chin. "I dropped it."

"Why didn't you pick it up?"

She bent forward just a tad to correct the position of his arm over her shoulder and then sped up a little.

"None of yer concern."

Hmm. Mysterious all right.

"Is it like a hobby?" he asked. "I mean, archery? I don't know anyone who does it."

"A what?" she said. "*Hobby?* Dinna ken what that is, but I hunt to feed my people."

She was so serious. Was she in some sort of closed community, like the Amish, but in Scotland?

26

"Well, that's very noble of you," he said. "What's your name?"

"Marjorie."

Marjorie... A shiver went through him. That was the name Sìneag had said. Was this some kind of a joke? A setup?

She stopped behind a bush large enough to hide them both and carefully glanced through the branches. Ahead of them, the trees tapered off, and the small brook that flowed down the length of the ravine went into the loch. A castle stood on the shore, not a big one, though it was hard to see from this distance. Sheep grazed in the meadow before it, and the smell of dung reached Konnor's nose.

The surprising thing was that the castle wasn't a ruin. Actually, it looked quite new. Smoke rose from the chimneys in the towers and from somewhere behind the wall. Scotland was full of castles. He'd seen a couple of ruins during his trip with Andy. But this one... It could be Glenkeld, the closest castle he'd seen on the map. But that was marked as a ruin, so on second thought, this must be something else.

"Let us go," Marjorie said. "The way is clear."

Clear? Was she afraid of someone? Konnor scanned their surroundings, looking for any sudden movements, for armed men, for a shadow lurking behind the trees, for guards or snipers in the castle, for any patch of light reflected off a weapon.

Nothing.

"Are you in danger?" he said when she tugged him to continue walking.

"Aye," she said, and his gut tightened. "I think we mayhap be. I just saw MacDougall spies talking about a siege."

He blinked. Was he hallucinating again? "A siege? What siege?"

"The siege of Glenkeld, of course," she said.

Who would besiege a castle these days, unless they were role-playing? There were groups of people who liked medieval fairs and playing elf-and-dwarf battles and such... Maybe she was part of something like that?

All that reminded him of his childhood. As a boy, he'd read *The Lord of the Rings* and other fantasy and sci-fi novels. Feeling helpless against his stepfather, Jerry, Konnor had admired the characters who rose against evil and violence. Perhaps he'd been looking for strength for himself. But in real life, evil won. Jerry had mocked him for what he liked to read, and when Konnor didn't stop, his stepfather beat it out of him.

Konnor looked at the castle with astonishment as he and Marjorie approached. It was a simple construction, four walls connected by four towers on the corners. One of them was round and looked bigger and older than the others. The rest were smaller and square. Two smaller towers surrounded a massive wooden gate that stood closed.

"I thought Glenkeld was a ruin. Do you live here?"

"Aye. 'Tis my clan's seat. Ever since the bloody MacDougalls took Innis Chonnel after Alasdair MacDougall —" Her voice shook as she said the name, and she cut herself off. Something dark crossed her face, and he saw a bottomless pain dwelling in the depths of her eyes. He looked away. He knew that kind of pain all too well. But it wasn't his business. He wouldn't want anyone asking him about his. He shouldn't meddle in her affairs, and he'd be gone soon anyway.

Konnor looked back to the castle as they approached it. Now that they were a few feet away, he could see through the slit windows that someone was moving on the timber gallery built on top of the rampart. He'd learned that was what they were called when he and Andy had visited an old castle.

The gate opened slowly. A white-haired man in a heavy, quilted coat stood in the opening. A sword was sheathed on his belt. Konnor cocked his head, studying the man's costume. Something about the posture of the man said he wasn't kidding, and the Marine in Konnor tensed.

"Mistress, why are ye without Tamhas and Muir?" the man asked, one hand on his sword. "And who is this?"

"'Tis Konnor, Moire's cousin. He needs Isbeil. He's hurt his leg. Aren't Tamhas and Muir back?"

"Nae."

"Damn it. They're probably looking for me."

As they walked into the courtyard of the castle, four men tugged at the heavy gates to close them, and a weight settled on Konnor's chest when they closed with a *thud*. The inner courtyard was a perfect square with four towers in the corners, probably about a hundred and sixty feet in width and length.

There were several buildings in the courtyard. A large, rectangular stone building with a tall, thatched roof and small windows with no glass, a wooden building a man led a horse out of, and two small wooden houses with thatched roofs. The aromatic scents of soup and fermented hops reached him. Wow, this was a proper self-sustained community.

Most of the people in the courtyard were men wearing baggy leggings and long, belted tunics. They had bushy beards and shaggy hair and carried firewood, sacks on their shoulders, baskets with vegetables and bread. Their feet kicked up dust from the dirt-packed courtyard as they walked, and chickens and geese ran around cackling and squawking.

Had he walked into the past? How could this place even exist? Were they all so invested in their role-playing that they really wanted to live like it was the Middle Ages? If this community was what Sineag had meant by time travel, she'd certainly nailed it.

"I need to tell ye something, Malcolm." Marjorie looked around and leaned closer to the white-haired man. "I heard MacDougall spies in the woods. They sneaked around the castle and were talking about a siege."

Malcolm's face fell, and he was speechless for a moment. Was that panic showing on his face? "Colin..." His bright eyes flashed, and his nostrils flared. "Are ye sure, lass?" he said finally.

"Aye. Verra sure. They're coming. They ken the weakness of the northern wall. But they dinna ken I heard them."

"Good." He glanced at Konnor and then back at her. "Let me take over. Ye must be exhausted carrying a huge man like him."

Marjorie let go of Konnor, and Malcolm took her place supporting him. Disappointment ran through Konnor at the loss of her strong shoulder under his arm and the soft curve of her breast beside his chest. He searched her face, but she was looking at Malcolm.

"Right," she said, then she quickly glanced at Konnor and nodded. "Get better. Put him in the chamber next to mine, Malcolm. 'Tis the best one for a guest, especially a sick one."

"Aye, mistress," Malcolm said.

He turned with Konnor to enter the big, round tower.

"Wait!" Konnor said. "Can I use your phone? I need to call someone."

He needed to call the Keir farm and let them know he was running late. Maybe Andy was already there, and if not, he needed to ask them to go and find his friend so Andy didn't spend time out there looking for him. Marjorie and Malcolm studied him as though he'd just spoken Mandarin. They wore the same expression Sìneag had.

"A *phone*?" Marjorie said. "What's a *phone*?"

Konnor chuckled. They really were deep into role-playing. The medieval costume certainly suited Marjorie. The colors highlighted her soft, glowing skin, beautiful without a trace of makeup. She had slightly slanted eyes, full lips, and shiny, dark hair.

He might actually enjoy this, but he did want to call his mom and let his friend know he was okay. "Right. Funny. What's a phone? So you guys don't have one in a castle like this?"

"Nae."

"Damn. Where is the nearest one?"

"I dinna think I've ever heard of one," Marjorie said. "Sorry, Konnor. Mayhap ye hit yer head?"

She was mocking him, and Konnor was slowly losing his patience. "Come on, guys. Do you have a safeword or something for when you want to stop playing in the Middle Ages? If you do, I'd like to use it now. I really do need to use a phone. I have people who might worry about me."

Marjorie looked confused. "What nonsense are ye talking about?"

"Aye, lad," Malcolm said.

Konnor's fists clenched and unclenched. He hated being at the mercy of complete strangers. "I can't figure you guys out. Are you some kind of cult?"

Marjorie and Malcolm exchanged glances. "A cult?"

"Or neo-pagans?"

"We're Christians."

"Okay. Maybe very, very orthodox then, if you're refusing to use modern technology?"

"Malcolm, just take him away before he says something else and I decide to keep him locked up. 'Tis a good thing ye're Moire's cousin. If ye were a stranger, ye'd be locked in a cellar by now."

Konnor clenched his lips tightly together. Stubborn folks. He didn't understand why she was pretending as though she didn't know what he was talking about. But something told him not to push anymore. If he wanted her help, at least any medical help, he probably should let it go for now. Whoever this Moire was, once she announced she'd never seen him before, he'd be in trouble.

"Aye," Malcolm said, and the two of them limped through the dusty courtyard, into the tower, and up a narrow, round flight of stairs.

They passed through two massive wooden doors with thick

and wrought iron hardware, then went up another flight of stairs. Malcolm led him through a door into a small room with a single wooden bed and a fireplace. A slit window let in some light and fresh air. A chest stood by the wall and an unlit torch was placed in a sconce above it. That was it. No electrical outlets. No lamps. No glass on the window.

Malcolm helped Konnor to the bed and let him sit. He leaned over him with a threating expression on his face, and although Konnor wasn't afraid of the man, uneasiness settled in his stomach. Malcolm's bushy white eyebrows knit together, and his blue eyes flashed. "Look, lad, I'm the constable of this castle, so ye better watch yerself. I dinna ken what ye're playing at, but if ye hurt our mistress, or even look at her funny, I will cut off yer ballocks and serve ye them for dinner. Understood?"

Konnor returned the antagonistic stare. "I don't have any intention of hurting anyone. Especially not your mistress."

Every word Konnor spoke was the truth. He could never hurt a woman, especially not the most beautiful and intriguing woman he'd ever met.

CHAPTER 4

Marjorie walked out of the tower towards the northern wall. Aye, there was damage all right. The rampart was missing several merlons that had crumbled and fallen over the last several years. Rocks from the wall had been chipped away one by one with time.

Scotland had been torn apart in the war with England, and Scottish clans were split between those who supported their king and those who were allied with England. Clan Cambel was a loyal supporter of the Bruce, while the MacDougalls had pledged their allegiance to Edward II, king of England. Recently, the Bruce had made great progress. He'd won back a lot of territory in the Highlands and was now fighting in the east in Badenoch, where the Comyn clan, contenders to the Scottish throne, had the majority of their lands. After all the battles her clan had fought for the Bruce, there wasn't coin or manpower to repair Glenkeld.

She had to do something. She just didn't know what.

Marjorie cursed under her breath and looked down at the field below the castle where sheep grazed peacefully. The loch spread like a long and broad dagger from southwest to northeast.

To the south of the castle, on the border with a grove of trees, was the clan cemetery. Ian was buried there—or rather, an empty linen burial cloth. She remembered watching the funeral from the window of her chamber, the whole clan surrounding the grave like mournful statues. Ian's father, Duncan, had stood bent over like a hook. The MacDougalls had not even given back Ian's body.

The loch's shoreline bordered the fields, woods, and hills that grew higher and higher the more east she looked. To the east was the ravine where she'd found the strange and handsome Konnor. There was something about him she couldn't put her finger on. His manner of speaking—although foreign and strange—was comfortable and pleasant.

He was agreeable to look at, she admitted. He had broad shoulders and massive biceps under his strange tunic. The feel of his weight on her hadn't bothered her, which was strange, because ever since Dunollie, she didn't like men being too close to her. But she wasn't threated by him. She couldn't explain why.

"Ma!" the sweetest voice in the world cried, and Colin emerged from the entrance into the tower.

His dark, chin-length hair shone in the sun as he hurried towards her. He wore a tunic that reached almost to his knees and a wooden sword belted around his middle. He'd been growing so fast recently his breeches were getting too small. He was tall, like all Cambels.

Every time she looked at him, she noticed his Cambel features: green eyes, dark hair, high cheekbones, a broad mouth, and thick, straight eyebrows. He had long eyelashes and a straight nose that she used to love to kiss before he'd started avoiding her signs of affection. He was just growing up, she told herself. He already started training with wooden swords, could ride a pony, shoot arrows, and lay snares.

He was growing up to be a warrior.

Someday, he'd need to protect himself. People would call him a bastart, and there wouldn't be many good matches for him. But that would be many, many years in the future.

Now, she was the one who needed to protect him, sooner than she'd have liked. Marjorie brought him to her and hugged him, pressing his thin body to her own. He wriggled out of her embrace, and she kissed the top of his head before he could separate from her completely. He smelled of sunshine, summer dust, and baked bread. Her sweet, adventurous boy must have spent the morning in the kitchen, eating bread as soon as it was ready. The baker couldn't resist him.

"Did ye have a good hunt?" he said. "I wish ye'd taken me."

"Sweet, ye ken ye're nae allowed to leave the castle in the absence of yer granda and uncles. Aye?"

"Aye, I ken." He hung his head and looked longingly across the field. "But what could happen to me, Ma?"

What could happen? Apparently, now that the MacDougalls knew of his existence—many things could happen to him. They wanted him, no doubt, because he was Alasdair's only child. John MacDougall had other grandchildren, so Marjorie could only assume Colin was important to him because he was Alasdair's. How had he found out, she wondered? She'd realized it was only a matter of time, but she was still despondent. Servants talked. It was very possible that he'd been aware for years but had decided to act now because he knew their defenses were weak and most of the Cambel men were away.

But there was no way in hell she'd give her son to the cruel clan. Colin was a Cambel. He was hers, and hers alone.

"Anything can happen, son." She sank to her knees and looked into his green eyes. He'd tried to sneak out of Glenkeld once after being bored to death from being kept inside the castle walls for months. Mayhap she should conceal the information about the impending siege from him, but she couldn't.

He should know everything, that way he'd be more responsible and stop trying to sneak out. "I'll be honest with ye, sweet."

He frowned. "Aye."

"Our enemy clan, the MacDougalls, are going to attack us soon."

His frown deepened, and he looked beyond the castle walls. The loch was bright blue against the green hills on both sides, and white clouds reflected against its surface. The look of stern ferociousness on his face reminded her of Alasdair, and the thought was like a hundred knives stabbing her in the gut.

But even though his very existence was a reminder of the most horrific time in Marjorie's life, she loved her boy. Enduring it all had brought her boy into her life, so she couldn't wish it all away.

"So ye mustn't go outside, Colin. 'Tis very dangerous."

"But ye went outside, Ma," he said. "Ye didna wait for Granda and my uncles."

She inhaled. "I can protect myself. Ye're a lad."

"But ye're a woman, Ma. I can protect ye."

She hugged him and gave him a big kiss on the cheek, and he giggled. He was still her lad, even if he desperately tried to be a grown man.

"'Tis me who'll protect ye, son," she whispered. "Dinna fash. Just wait a wee bit longer, aye? Yer grandfather and yer uncles will be back soon, and then ye can go hunting with them, shoot yer arrows in the field, and see yer friends in the village. Promise ye'll be good and wilna run away?"

He sighed and smiled, but devils played in his eyes. "I promise."

"And what is a Cambel's word worth?"

"Everything."

"Good lad." She tousled his hair. "We'll train with swords later today, aye?"

Two figures walked from behind the small gathering of trees at the bottom of the cliff. Marjorie strained her eyes to look closer.

Tamhas and Muir.

"Go play, Colin. I need to talk to Tamhas and Muir."

She hurried to the courtyard. She'd paced the length of the wall three times when the gates were finally opened. The men walked forward, their faces full of worry and their eyebrows knit together.

"Where have ye been, mistress?" Tamhas said.

"I saw a deer trail and followed it."

"Why didna ye wait for us?"

Marjorie crossed her arms over her chest. "Ye were already far ahead, and I didna want to spook the deer."

"'Twas reckless, mistress," Muir said, scratching his graying beard. "Forgive me for saying so, but ye ken ye're nae supposed to go around alone."

Marjorie chewed on her lower lip. He was right, of course, and she knew he worried about her like he would about his own daughter. But if she was in charge of the castle, she had to be braver.

"Did ye see two men?" she asked. "The MacDougalls?"

"Nae, mistress," Tamhas said. "But Muir's right. What if they'd seen ye? Yer father and brothers would cut my head off and throw it to the pigs if we lost ye."

Marjorie cocked her head. "Just because we grew up together doesna give ye the right to berate me, Tamhas. I'm the mistress now. Besides, nothing happened to me. And now we ken they plan to attack, so we can prepare. Send a messenger to my father and brothers."

"That may be just what they want," Malcolm said.

Marjorie turned her head as Malcolm stepped closer to their circle, his arms folded over the heavily quilted *leine croich* —a long, pleated coat—stretched across his chest. She knew she could always rely on him. He was like a second father to her, like another uncle she wasn't related to by blood. Malcolm had served her da, Dougal Cambel, ever since she could remember. They shared some sort of oath, though she wasn't sure of the details. All she knew was that Malcolm would rather die than let any harm come to any of Dougal's children.

"John MacDougall may want yer clan to leave the Bruce to protect ye and Colin," he said. "That will weaken the Bruce and may change the course of the war."

King Robert the Bruce had been winning ever since he'd taken Inverlochy last November, and the English were no doubt looking for ways to take back the advantage. The MacDougalls were among the Scottish clans that had sided with the English. Clan Cambel was an important part of the Bruce's army, so keeping Glenkeld intact mattered not only for the clan, but also for the whole war. If Marjorie's father and brothers heard about their home being attacked—especially if she were taken into enemy hands again—they'd come to fight to get her back. That would mean about three hundred men leaving the main army, a third of the Bruce's forces.

The men exchanged heavy glances.

"Let me take over. I wouldna want to put ye under that kind of pressure, my lady," Malcolm said. "Having to coordinate the castle's defenses isna a task—"

He didn't need to say it. Marjorie's hands shook at the thought of being responsible for the worst outcome for her clan, her son, and the war. She had years of training from her father and brothers and was technically the most knowledgeable one left in the castle. But she had absolutely no war or battle experience. She hadn't even been able to shoot the bloody MacDougall spies, for God's sake. She was a coward. How could she ever protect the approximately fifty people inside these walls, including her son?

"I wilna let them take Glenkeld," she said with more firmness than she felt inside. "The castle must stand."

The look the men exchanged varied from dubious to respectful. Tamhas and Muir nodded.

She clenched her jaw. "We will train more. We ken the castle's weaknesses. We canna repair all the damage in time, but I will think of something."

CHAPTER 5

Konnor stared at the woman with a basket in her hands who stood in the doorway next to Marjorie. She looked at least a hundred years old. She wore a brown dress, her head was covered in a white kerchief, and her face was leathery and wrinkled, but her eyes seemed bright.

Was this the "healer" who was supposed to help him with his leg? Konnor had hoped that even though it seemed the whole colony was playing some sort of medieval game, they'd at least practice some modern medicine. They might not vaccinate and all that, but general health care was no joke. Unfortunately, it looked like they relied on herbal remedies and witchcraft.

He locked his gaze on Marjorie. She stood there, determined and sublime, like a queen in disguise. With her dark, shiny hair falling in cascades over her period clothing, and those cat eyes, she was like a badass queen from some sort of movie remake of a classic fairy tale. The more Konnor looked at her, the more dazzled he was. He remembered the feel of her body against his and how she'd smelled when she'd helped him walk here. He wanted her that close again.

"Is that him?" the old woman asked Marjorie. "Is he supposed to be Moire's cousin?"

"Aye," Marjorie said.

"Are ye English, lad?" the woman said.

"No," Konnor said.

"Good. The Sassenachs are nae welcome here."

She limped towards Konnor and sat on the edge of the bed he lay on. Marjorie followed her and stood nearby with her arms crossed over her chest.

"What ails ye, lad?" the old woman asked.

"Look, ma'am, you don't need to bother. Can someone perhaps take me to the hospital?"

From there, he could call the farm. The woman narrowed her eyes and looked him over with a different sort of curiosity.

"Havna heard anyone speak like ye in my life. Where do ye come from, lad?"

"From the States. Specifically, LA."

"Dinna ken what any of that means. Do ye, Marjorie?"

Marjorie shook her head, her gaze boring into him. He felt like he were under an X-ray machine.

Why would she still not admit to knowing something about the modern world? Was isolation so important to them? Wasn't this taking the role-playing a little too far? In either case, he would be better off lying low until he got help and could get out of here.

"Right," Konnor said. "It's far away."

"But ye're Moire's cousin, I hear?"

Konnor sighed. "Look, ma'am—"

"My name is Isbeil. Nae ma'am."

"Yes. Of course. Look, I'm not Moire's cousin. Marjorie, you mistook me for him—" Marjorie's face went blank, and her arms fell to her sides. "I guess I didn't correct you because you were the only one who could help me get out of the ravine. Just help me get to the Keir farm or to Dalmally, and then I'll be out of your hair."

Marjorie was livid, her eyebrows two furious arches. She took a step towards Konnor. Telling them the truth had been a mistake, but he just couldn't take any more of this circus.

"Ye lied to me?" Marjorie thundered. "Who are ye then, if nae Moire's cousin?"

Christ, she was beautiful when she was angry. "Just a guy."

Isbeil shook her head. "He speaks strange things I dinna understand. But he's convinced they're true."

"That makes him a madman," Marjorie said.

"Or someone who's here by chance," Isbeil said. "I dinna see any signs of madness."

"I'm not crazy," Konnor said.

"Aye. Ye're nae crazy." Isbeil clasped her hands and removed the linen that covered the basket. An aromatic mixture of herbs tickled Konnor's nostrils.

"Let me see yer ankle," Isbeil said.

Konnor moved his leg to give her better access. His ankle was swollen, and red-and-blue bruises shone through the skin. He also had a cut that was still bleeding a little.

"The cut isna deep," she said, "but there's dirt in it, and it needs to be washed. I'll put honey on it to keep rot-wound away. As for yer ankle..."

Isbeil took his foot and rolled it in a circle. Sharp pain shot through his leg, and he clenched his teeth.

"I can feel yer joint is unstable," she said. "'Tis a sprain, stranger, but 'tisna serious. Ye shouldna walk on it for a day or two. I can give ye willow bark for yer pain. And I'll put splints and bandage them. After two days, ye can start walking on it, but carefully. Mostly, what ye need is rest. Aye?"

The pain wasn't unbearable. He'd had worse.

"Okay, a sprain. Don't worry then. Just give me a crutch or something and send me on my way."

She shrugged. "I wouldna advise ye to try to leave, lad. Rest is what ye need."

"I'll rest in a hotel or something."

"It wilna take long. Marjorie, will ye give me that large bowl with water?"

Marjorie brought it over to the bed.

"Can ye wash his wound while I prepare the splint?"

"Aye," Marjorie said and sat on the bed.

She glanced at him, and there was curiosity and anger in her eyes, but also compassion. Isbeil walked to the chest, placed some jars and pouches with powder on the lid and started mixing things. Marjorie wet a clean linen cloth and looked him in the eye. Their gazes locked, and instantly, his mouth went dry.

Christ, she's pretty.

"This will hurt, Konnor," she said softly.

"It's fine. I'm not a stranger to pain."

Her eyes widened, and long, dark eyelashes trembled. He'd been wounded twice before while in service, but he'd been beaten countless times by his stepfather while he was a child. Pain was not foreign to him.

"Neither am I," she said as she put the cloth against the cut.

He wanted to ask her what she meant by that, and ask what had happened to her, but she put the cloth against his wound and pressed out the water, letting it wash dirt out. There was something soothing about her touch, and despite the pain, he lay back on the pillows and watched her face as she worked.

"'Tis clean, Isbeil," she said way too soon and stood with the bowl in her hands. Isbeil came to inspect the wound and gave a satisfied grunt. She sat on the edge of the bed and looked at him.

"I'm going to put a healing poultice on it and dress it. Then I'll put on the splint."

Konnor gave a curt nod. "I appreciate you treating me."

She didn't respond and spread the aromatic mixture on his cut and then bandaged it. Surprisingly, the mixture was cool and soothing, and his leg felt better. Then she took out two small planks from the basket and a linen bandage that looked clean. While Isbeil was setting the splints, Konnor looked at Marjorie's pretty face. Their eyes were locked across the room, and he didn't want to look away.

Finally, after what felt like hours, Isbeil said she was done.

He nodded and shifted to get up from the bed. "Thanks. Now I'm out of here."

As he looked at Marjorie, he wished he had swallowed his words. Her hands were propped on her sides, and she glared at him.

"Ye're out of here?" she asked, "Why are ye in such a hurry? Who are ye, Konnor? Is that even yer real name? Are ye a MacDougall?"

Her slanted cat eyes flashed, and there was a pink tinge to her cheeks. Her hair was in slight disarray. She was beautiful. Konnor was torn between smiling and being concerned for his safety. She wouldn't order Malcolm to behead him like an angry queen, would she?

"I'm not a MacDougall. And my name *is* Konnor. Konnor Mitchell."

"How can I believe ye? What if ye're a MacDougall spy?"

A MacDougall spy? This medieval game was going a little too far.

"I don't freaking know how you can believe me, okay? My passport is in the backpack that's back where the damn fallen tower is. I'm sorry I didn't say I wasn't who you thought I was. I thought you wouldn't help me if I told you the truth. And I was right."

Marjorie pursed her lips and didn't say anything for a moment, confirming that his assumption had been correct. Isbeil arched one eyebrow and started putting her sacks, jars, and boxes back into the basket.

"Look," Konnor said. "Like I told you, I don't want to inconvenience you, and I'm thankful for your help, but you can stop playing your fantasy games and just send me on my way. I'll be fine."

"He wilna be fine," Isbeil said. "He needs to rest, or his ankle will get worse."

Marjorie shrugged one shoulder. "'Tisna my concern. He's a liar. Who kens what else he's lying about?"

Isbeil put the last sack into the basket and looked at Marjorie. "I dinna think this one is a threat, dearie."

"Explain yourself, Konnor," Marjorie said. "The truth. Who ye are, and how did ye end up in that ravine?"

"I'm American. Please don't tell me you don't know what that means."

Marjorie shook her head and shrugged.

A low growl escaped Konnor's throat. "Come on, Marjorie, I think you're smart enough to accept the reality beyond these walls."

"I dinna ken what ye're talking about."

Her stubbornness was impressive. He wished she'd just drop the pretense.

"You know very well what I'm talking about, even if you don't want to admit it. I own a security firm in Los Angeles. I'm a Marine who served in Iraq. I've been hiking through the Highlands with my buddy. A woman asked me for help. She'd fallen down a ravine and seemed to be hurt. I went down to help her and fell. Next thing I knew, she disappeared. Then I saw Marjorie. That's the God's truth of what happened."

Konnor locked his gaze with Marjorie's and forgot anyone else was in the room. She shot daggers at him, and heat rushed through his blood.

Come on, Marjorie, believe me. Be the reasonable woman I know you are and give me a sign you're on my side.

She looked away and shook her head like she was disappointed.

"Was this all by the old Pictish stronghold?" Isbeil said.

"Aye," Marjorie said.

"There are legends and rumors about that place," Isbeil said. "I've heard strange things happen around it."

"Like what?" Marjorie said.

"Like ancient Pictish magic that can open a tunnel through the river of time."

Konnor frowned. That sounded exactly like what Sìneag had told him.

"'Tis an old story," Isbeil continued. "I heard it from my grandmother when I was a wee lass. She was a wise woman, mayhap even a witch. She was afraid the Holy Church would burn her for witchcraft, so she didna tell the story much. She said some faeries bring good health, some bring good luck. Others play with people's destinies and send them through the tunnel. Some say they do it so that people can find the one person they're really destined for."

Faeries? *Come on.* Although if he believed in fairies, Sìneag could probably pass for one. But he wasn't a little boy, and he didn't believe in magic.

Marjorie walked towards the window. "Out of all yer Highland tales, Isbeil, 'tis the strangest one."

Konnor wasn't sure he agreed. The story may be weird, but it was this place that was really strange.

"So ye believe him, Isbeil?" Marjorie said.

The old woman nodded.

"Well, ye havna been wrong yet in my life. But what of the outlandish things he speaks of, the security firm, the Los Angeles? What's all that? It sounds like he's from another world altogether."

"Mayhap he is," Isbeil said. "I tell ye, my grandmother warned me about that place. To never go near it. Ye dinna want to tempt faeries."

"I was just there," Marjorie said. "I didna notice anything strange."

"Didna notice anything strange?" Isbeil chuckled and

looked pointedly at Konnor. "I think ye brought the strange thing back to the castle."

Marjorie blinked and then rolled her eyes.

"Honestly, Isbeil, sometimes ye talk as if I'm still a child."

"'Tis because sometimes ye behave like one," Isbeil said.

Marjorie sighed thoughtfully. "Look, Konnor, ye're nae going anywhere. Ye canna walk anyway. Until I'm sure ye're nae a MacDougall or another clan spying for the Sassenachs, ye're staying here."

Konnor couldn't believe his ears. Now he was a prisoner in a medieval cult.

"You can't just keep me here."

"I dinna believe in fairy tales," she continued. "So I dinna believe yer stories about Los whatever and firms and hiking. Any of that." She turned around and walked to the door. "Ye've wasted enough of my time. Until ye tell me something I can believe, ye're staying here."

CHAPTER 6

L ater that night, Marjorie lay next to Colin as she put him to bed. She kissed his forehead.

"Would ye like me to tell ye a story, sweet?" she said.

"Aye," he said and nestled his head on her shoulder. "Granda told me stories of his travels. But ye havna been anywhere, have ye, Ma?"

Marjorie swallowed and looked around the small bedchamber. The tallow candle flickered as an evening breeze came through the slit window, making the light dance along the stone walls.

She wondered if the ghosts of her ancestors lived in that darkness and watched over her: her grandfather Colin, her cousin Ian, Diarmid the Boar—the legendary warrior who, according to legend, started the Cambel clan—her own mother, a woman she'd never known, and her stepmother, the woman who'd loved her as her own.

Fire crackled in the fireplace, illuminating the wooden shields and swords and the bow on the walls of Colin's bedchamber. There was one steel sword that glistened on the wall and reflected the firelight. It used to belong to Marjorie's grandfather, Sir Colin, who died in the battle to save her from the MacDougalls. The whole clan, including Marjorie's uncle Neil, who was the chief of the clan, decided it should belong to Marjorie's son, and it hung, large and beautiful, and almost as tall as its current owner, waiting for the day that Colin would be grown enough to wield it.

"*Ye havna been anywhere, have ye, Ma?*" Her son hurt her with the question, although he didn't realize it. She'd always wanted to travel like her father and her uncle Neil. She'd always wanted to see England, France, and mayhap even reach the Holy City. She'd heard so many stories of the Crusades.

But she couldn't. Today was the first time she'd been alone outside the castle walls in twelve years.

"I havna, son," she said, swallowing the hurt behind a forced smile. "But I'd like to."

"Mayhap, we can go together one day."

"Oh, I'd love that, sweet." To go together into the big, dangerous world and know there was nothing that could hurt her son or her because she was strong enough to protect them... That was what she wanted. Mayhap, one day she would have that.

She looked at her grandfather's sword and remembered how she'd seen it twelve years ago lying in the dirt next to him. He'd been unmoving and pale. She often told Colin stories of his great-grandfather to keep the memory of the man she dearly missed alive. Ian had also fought to save her in Dunollie. He'd died later as a result of the feud between the MacDougalls and the Cambels.

She wanted to tell Colin the story of how Ian had saved her, how they'd lost Innis Chonnel to the MacDougalls. But she didn't want Colin to know she'd suffered so much, so she decided to come up with a different name for Ian.

"Since I canna tell ye of my own travels, let me tell ye about a great red-haired hero called Seaghán. He was tall and big and brave, and as strong as a great oak tree. His hair flared like flames, and he fought with the bravery of a hundred men."

Her eyes watered as she remembered Ian training with swords in the courtyard with her brother Owen. She was eighteen years old the last time she saw Ian in the courtyard of Glenkeld. He'd been fostered with her family as long as she could remember, and he was like a brother to her.

"He had a sister and three brothers, and all of them loved one another. Even at his young age, people looked at him with respect, and his enemies cowered in fear. While they were growing up, a son of the king fostered with them. They all grew up together and knew one another well. Soon, it became apparent that the prince was as evil as his father. Unfortunately, the prince wanted Seaghán's sister. He did things when they were children..." Her throat clenched as she remembered Alasdair torturing a frog and twisting a duckling's neck. "He did things that made her fear him. She started avoiding him, and that made him want to chase her even more. He'd take her by the arm too strongly, or pull her hair so hard she cried. But whenever Seaghán saw that, he'd protect her and make the prince stop."

"Evil bastart," Colin muttered sleepily. His eyes were still open, but he was starting to drift off.

"Oh, aye. One day, the evil king wanted to take their home." She skipped the part when Owen, her younger half brother, lost MacDougall gold intended for King John Balliol, which started the feud between the two clans. She skipped the part when Alasdair kidnapped her and then her clan came to her rescue. "Seaghán lived in the castle together with his family. 'Twas big and beautiful, with walls as tall as mountains and as thick as boulders. 'Twas built on a small island in the middle of a loch."

She was talking about Innis Chonnel Castle. It had been the previous clan seat where her grandfather Colin had lived and where Craig had taken her after the clan saved her. A few months after she was freed from Dunollie, she'd still been recovering mentally and had lived mostly in a fog. She'd locked herself in her bedchamber and had been terrified to come out. Nightmares had tortured her, while in her heart, she was hollow and cold. She'd wondered if she'd ever feel again and had been coming to terms with the fact that she carried something of Alasdair inside of her.

"The evil king came with *birlinns* and hundreds of warriors. Everyone in Seaghán's clan thought the castle was invincible. But it wasna. The enemy warriors climbed the walls like spiders. Fire arrows landed on the thatched roofs and wooden constructions."

She remembered screams, and the smell of smoke and death. And all that reminded her too much of Dunollie. The memories pulled her back in time...

Panic and fear tore at Marjorie from all sides. She screamed, hearing her own voice as though from a distance. Someone came into her room, and strong hands took her in a safe grasp.

"Marjorie."

Brown eyes and blazing-red hair came into focus in front of her.

"Marjorie, 'tis Ian. I've come to take ye. We're leaving Innis Chonnel."

She stopped screaming.

"Good lass. Can ye walk?"

"Aye."

"Good. Then let's go."

She walked behind him on shaking legs, bile rising in her stomach. They climbed down the narrow stone stairs. One, two, three flights. Just before they walked into the courtyard, Ian stopped and turned to her. "I want ye to listen to me. The MacDougalls have come to take the castle."

She jerked in reaction to the name, her gut clenching like a tight fist. Horror rode through her in a black, icy-cold wave.

"Dinna fash, they wilna take ye," Ian said. "I'd rather die than let them take ye."

Marjorie bit her lip, fighting to stop the panic from her memory taking her over now.

"The evil king was winning," she continued her story to Colin. "His men infiltrated the castle and swarmed the court-yard like wasps. Seaghán wanted to get his sister on the boat, evacuating the women and children of their clan. But just as he got her out of the castle and close to the boat, a band of the king's warriors reached him."

She squeezed her son's hand and buried her nose in his hair, inhaling the clean, herbal scent of him.

"One had a great sword, the other a spear, the third an ax. They came at him all at once, from three sides just as his sister got on the boat. The boatsman pushed the boat off the shore and began rowing away. Seaghán's sister watched in horror as he fought the three men. He killed the one with the sword, but while he fought the axman, the man with the spear wounded his shoulder. The last thing his sister saw before the boat arrived at the opposite shore and she had to run together with the other women and children, was that Seaghán had been gravely wounded near his heart and had stopped moving."

She wiped the tears from one cheek, and Colin reached and wiped them from the other.

"Did he die?" he said.

Marjorie nodded. "The clan had to retreat after that, leaving their seat to their enemy, and their hero's body as well. He died saving his sister."

Not just his sister, but his nephew, too. And she'd never forget that.

She glanced at the shadows. *Thank you for watching over him, Ian.*

She kissed Colin's forehead and tucked him in. "Good

night, my sweet, let yer dreams be restful and safe. The heroes of yer clan are watching over ye."

She blew out the candle and walked to the door, leaving only the dim light of the glowing ambers in the fireplace to illuminate the room.

"Ma?" Colin called after her.

"Aye, son?" She turned around.

"Seaghán is Uncle Ian, isna he? And ye are his sister?"

She let out a shaky breath. He was too smart for his age.

"Aye, sweet."

"I would have liked to meet him."

"I would have liked ye to meet him, too."

She wished him good night for the last time and walked out of his room. She leaned against the door after she closed it and simply breathed for a moment. She was safe. She was all right. Thanks to Ian. Thanks to all the men of her clan. Men she could trust.

While Colin would never have a father as a male role model, and she'd never trust a man with her heart, her son did have plenty of great warriors to learn from, like Marjorie's father and brothers. That was enough.

CHAPTER 7

After a night in the castle, Konnor's confidence that this was some sort of reclusive community was fading. He looked out the window and saw the guards on the walls. They appeared way too serious and way too armed to be playing around. If this were a role-playing game, how long would these people keep up the pretense? If this were a closed community, wouldn't they still have to have some connection to the outside world?

If they really expected a siege—and judging by their somber expressions, one was coming—that meant there was another group of people who lived the same way.

They couldn't be completely isolated. Growing and keeping food required gardens, crops, and animals. Yes, there were animals in the courtyard, but he hadn't seen gardens or fields around the castle. They must buy that stuff from a grocery store.

Something was off. Everything in the room looked like it had been made by hand: the blanket, the bed, the chests, and the torches. There had to be a logical explanation to all of this. There was one possible explanation, but Konnor completely refused to believe it. It was there, nevertheless.

Both Sìneag and Isbeil had talked about ancient Pictish magic opening a tunnel through the river of time.

There was no way time travel and magic were real. He could just imagine Andy and his other buddies back home laughing their asses off if they heard he was even considering it. He didn't know what was wrong with this place or how to explain all of it, but there was tension in his gut and tilting under his feet, as though he were on a lurching ship during a storm. Maybe he was just paying for all the whiskey he'd dulled his senses with yesterday.

His ankle didn't hurt as much today, and it felt like the swelling was going down. He was grateful for Isbeil's treatment, despite the lack of modern medicine.

He wasn't going to sit in one place, so he asked a girl who brought him porridge and buttermilk if she could find him a crutch he could borrow. She'd said she'd ask and left the room.

He was going to find a way to escape, hopefully before any siege started. The Marine in him couldn't help wondering what weapons would be used. Surely whoever these MacDougalls were, they wouldn't use guns against swords and arrows? He couldn't just run away and leave the people here at the mercy of a well-armed force, could he?

Konnor shifted, put both his feet on the floor, and laced up the shoes.

"Are ye planning something?" Marjorie asked from the doorway.

He turned his head and forgot how to breathe. Her hair was tied up now, and she wore a simple, almost manly tunic that hung to her knees. The baggy clothes highlighted her femininity even more. Her thin waist and the gentle curves of her hips was hugged by a belt. She was strong and willowy, like a taut bowstring. There was a crutch in her hands—a straight, thick stick with a small piece of wood across the top of it to fit under his arm.

Konnor cocked his head. "Thanks. I want to look around."

"Ye're nae leaving the castle, aye? I thought I was clear yesterday."

"You were." He chuckled, enjoying the fire in her voice. "But I can't sit back and wait for the walls to fall. You talked about a siege. Can I help?"

"Ye?" She looked him up and down.

"I'm a Marine. Served in Iraq."

"Iraq? Again yer strange words." She sighed. "Why am I wasting my time with ye when I have my warriors to train?"

She took one long stride into the room and stood right before him. She handed him the crutch. He took it and slowly looked up her body to her face. She was like a Highland queen from ancient legends, with her big green eyes against her pale skin. Her cheeks were rosy from the exercise, and her lips were round and red. He itched to trace his knuckles against the side of her face. She didn't wear makeup—and she didn't need any. Long, thick eyelashes framed her eyes, and her lips were so kissable.

"You're so beautiful," he said without thinking.

She froze, and her eyes widened in shock. Her cheeks blazed instantly, as red as a sunset over the ocean. She stepped back, and... Was it fear that crossed her face? One hand clutched at her neck, and she stared at him in horror.

What the hell did I say?

She blinked, and her hand went to the sword on her belt. "If ye touch me, or any woman here, I swear to God, ye will need a crutch forever, because ye'll be missing a leg. Or something else that ye're thinking with right now."

Seeing her reaction was like running into a cold, hard wall. He'd seen that very look on his mother's face. The look of a hurt, baited animal. There was fear and helplessness in her eyes that he'd felt as a young boy, too.

His mother had dated Jerry for a few months, and eight-year-old Konnor had accepted the man who bought him toys and made a great sloppy joe. Konnor had been ready to protect his mother, just like his father had asked him to before he died in the hospital two years before that, but there hadn't seemed to be anything to protect her from with Jerry.

One night, she'd come home with bright, shiny eyes and a ring on her finger.

"Sweetheart," she said to him as she tucked him in that night. "Jerry asked me to marry him, but I said I wouldn't say yes unless you agree, too."

"What does that mean?" Konnor asked. "If you marry him, how will our life change?"

"Well..." She took his hand in both of hers and kissed it. "For one, we'd move into his house. He has a big pool and a giant backyard, and he's promised to buy you a car that you can drive there and even a big tractor."

She meant a battery-operated car and the toy tractor he'd been begging her to buy. Konnor's chest lightened with excitement. "Really?"

"Yeah." She smiled that excited, slightly exaggerated mom-smile of hers. "Really. It also means we can go on vacations, and I can quit my job and stay at home to help you with your homework more and make you really great dinners every night."

Konnor didn't think there was anything wrong with microwave dinners and his mom coming home and telling him excitedly of her day working as a manager of their local supermarket. She liked organizing things and talking to people every day. After his dad died, it seemed like that helped her get through everything.

But Konnor wanted to make her happy, and so he said, "Yeah, Mom. You should say yes to him."

A couple of weeks later, Konnor and his mom moved into Jerry's house. Soon after, Konnor woke up one night from loud yelling and screaming coming from downstairs. He walked out of his new room, still empty of the posters and pictures he wanted to put up, and stepped barefoot on the softest carpet, his heart beating fast and furious.

He froze on the stairwell, clutching at the polished wooden railing with both his hands.

"Don't you dare question my authority," came Jerry's booming voice. Standing on the first-floor landing, Konnor could only see their feet in the living room of the ground floor. The lights reflected off the hardwood floor next to Jerry's huge black-socked feet. "Especially not in front of your son. He should learn to listen to me. He should do as I say. I'm his new father."

"You're not his father, Jerry. He loves his dad—"

Slap.

The sound of Jerry hitting his mother rang out loudly through the opened doors. She fell on the beige couch—and her face came into Konnor's view, full of surprise and shock. That wasn't the look he'd seen on Marjorie's face, though. The hopeless, helpless look that Marjorie and his mother shared had come later. Konnor stood still, in shock, unable to understand what had just happened, not knowing how to react.

"Jerry—" His mother held a hand to her cheek.

Jerry didn't let her finish. He sank to his knees in front of her and took her hands in both of his. "I'm so sorry, hon. I didn't mean to. I had a couple of scotches, and when I drink, I can't control my emotions. It's just that Konnor makes me angry when he's so cold towards me."

Konnor wasn't exactly cold. Yeah, there was this distance between them, but Konnor couldn't just replace his dad with Jerry. He didn't want to do things like kick around a soccer ball with him, because that was something he and his dad had done together.

His mom had forgiven Jerry. They kissed, and Konnor returned to his room, still unable to sleep.

"Take care of your mom, son." His father's last words to him

kept spinning in his head. But he hadn't taken care of her. He'd just let Jerry hit her. His father would never have done that.

It had taken a month for him to start seeing Marjorie's expression on his mother's face. A fleeting panic, a tension and withdrawal, as though expecting a hit. His mom had never been the same. Even after Jerry died, she never fully recovered, and that's why Konnor had to go back to LA as planned.

Damn it! Marjorie had been hurt. Something bad had happened to her. Something bad that he was too familiar with. He itched to find the guy who had dared to put that look in her eyes and beat the living shit out of him. But the best way to deal with victims of violence wasn't to press. It was to make sure they knew they were safe.

"I'm sorry." He put his hands up. "You have *nothing* to fear from me. I only meant it as a compliment."

She swallowed and breathed deeply. Her eyes were like dark-malachite gemstones.

"Dinna ever look at me like that again," she said.

Konnor's jaw ticked. He hated that she could even assume he was anything like Jerry. "All right." A cold shiver went through him. "Is someone bothering you in the castle?"

Her eyes widened in surprise. "Here? Nae! 'Tis my home. 'Tis my clan. They'll all die before they let harm come to me or another woman here. As I will for them."

He liked that, the Highland code of honor. He'd been ready to die for the men in his unit, was still ready to die for Andy. So maybe he and Marjorie weren't that different.

"Okay, okay. But if you suspect anything or anyone, you tell me, okay?"

"I dinna need any protection from ye," she said, although there wasn't any of the previous spirit in her tone. "My brothers and father have trained me to be a warrior. I'm capable of defending myself. In fact, I am the one who supervises the training of the men while my father and brothers are not here."

Konnor blinked. A warrior? She did look athletic and wore her sword confidently, as though it had always belonged to her.

Wow.

He couldn't help being more attracted to her with each passing moment, despite her threats. He ran his hand through his hair. "Great. I'm sure you're more than capable of defending yourself. You look like you know what you're doing."

"Aye."

Konnor used the crutch to pull himself to a standing position. "I'm going to look around," he said.

Marjorie threw him a hard look and shook her head. "I still dinna ken if I believe ye or nae. If ye're with the MacDougalls and are here to spy for them—"

"I'm not with the MacDougalls. I'm not with anyone. Just my buddy Andy."

She sighed. "I may regret this, but ye have my permission to leave yer room. Every man in the castle has been warned about ye. One wrong move, and they are allowed to render ye harmless by whatever means necessary." She looked at his ankle. "Ye canna get far on one leg anyway."

If they'd met in another time and place, he would've asked her out on a date. Banter with her and enjoy a little playful flirtation. And if the chemistry between them was there, which he was sure it was, he might even get to take her on a very long and delicious climb towards a mind-blowing orgasm. He'd like to show her that not all men caused women pain. That if she would let him, he would only ever bring her pleasure.

The thought surprised him. He didn't date. He didn't want a woman in his life.

Maybe just for one night.

But he couldn't sleep with and then abandon someone like Marjorie. It was best he didn't think about her that away.

"Deal," he said and cleared his throat, trying to chase the images of her naked body out of his head.

"Ah, yer strange words again." She turned and went to the

door, leaving the scent of wildflowers and leather in the air. "I must continue training the warriors. Forgive me if I dinna give ye a tour."

She left, and Konnor stood there for a moment, inhaling her scent again. Why was he so attracted to her? She was exquisite, strong and fragile at the same time, but she'd made it clear she wasn't interested.

He shook his head. Best just stop thinking of her.

Using the crutch, he slowly made his way towards the door. The crutch was a little short for him, but it was better than nothing. It would just take some getting used to. The way down the round stairs was challenging, that was for sure. The crutch slipped several times on the smooth stone, but by some miracle, and after several close calls, he made his way down. He stepped out of the tower and into the dirt-packed courtyard.

The chaotic sound of metal against metal rang out through the yard. Thirty or so people fought with swords against each other in pairs. They were all dressed like medieval warriors with long, belted tunics or quilted coats, breeches or pants, pointy leather shoes. All were men, save one.

Marjorie.

Konnor's breath caught in his throat at the sight of her. She was graceful and strong. She cut and stabbed with precision and elegance. When her partner thrust his sword at her, his giant muscles bulging, she twisted out of his reach like a spinning top and slashed her sword at him, stopping right before it reached the man's side.

She stole Konnor's ability to breathe. Not only was she gorgeous, but she was also strong, and kind, and brave. She was like Joan of Arc on the front lines, fighting for others. He'd never seen anyone quite like her. Something boiled inside Konnor's chest, trembling and vibrating.

And that was bad.

He should get out of here, get far away from her as soon as

he could. He didn't need more mess in his life than he had already. There was no woman in his future because he would never be a good husband or father after what he'd seen growing up. All he could offer a woman was good sex and a brooding face. He was done hurting women emotionally.

CHAPTER 8

I n a downward stroke, Marjorie pummeled Muir's raised
sword like a blacksmith. Her shoulders and arms were on
fire from the exercise. Sweat covered her whole body.
And through it all, she felt Konnor's gaze on her skin like the
caress of a cool breeze.

"You're so beautiful." His words rang in her head again and
again. She was flattered. No one had told her anything like
that since she'd come back from Dunollie. She didn't think
he'd meant to offend her. But even the reminder that she was a
woman and he was a man who might want her triggered
memories of that week with Alasdair.

Aye, she'd reacted too harshly. All he'd done was compliment her and look at her like a man looked at a woman he
wanted. She'd seen it between husbands and wives, between
lovers, between her brother Craig and his new wife, Amy,
when she and Colin had gone to Inverlochy about two
sennights ago.

Konnor's look hadn't been malicious. It would ignite desire
in a regular, undamaged woman. Especially from a man like
Konnor.

Malcolm brought his blade down and from the side.

Marjorie barely managed to deflect his sword.

"Stay in the fight." Owen's words rang out in her head. Her half brother had told her that over and over again in the first year of her training after Colin was born. *"Stay in the fight. Dinna slip back into that dark, dangerous place ye've just crawled out of."*

Owen was four years younger than her. He was a rebel and a rake and made their father frustrated enough to pull out his hair, but Owen had always been there for her. He and Isbeil were the two people who'd gotten her out of the bottomless pit of desperation she'd been trapped in.

He'd distracted her with tall tales and even made her laugh once in a while. During her whole pregnancy, she'd refused to believe there was a part of that monster inside of her. She hadn't wanted anything to do with the baby, and she'd even considered asking Isbeil to give the bairn to a good family in one of the Cambel villages.

But she hadn't. The moment the baby was placed on her chest, she'd known there was not a drop of Alasdair in him. He was pure and beautiful and hers. Her son. Hers alone. He was a Cambel through and through. And that had been the start of her healing. In a way, her son had saved her.

She stepped forward, stopping just short of smashing the pommel of her sword into Malcolm's face.

"Aye. Good, lass," Malcolm said, breathing heavily, his wrinkled forehead glistening with sweat. "In a real battle, that unexpected move might be why ye win."

Marjorie panted, too. She leaned forwards and put her hands on her knees.

Real battle... A chill ran through her.

"I'll ken what a real battle is sooner rather than later," she said.

Aye, she'd know whether she wanted to or not.

Marjorie glanced at the entrance of the tower where Konnor had stood watching her, but he was gone now. Her stomach dropped in disappointment. She was very conflicted about him. On the one hand, she was being careful. He was a stranger who'd lied to her to get into the castle. A stranger who was talking about things she'd never heard of, demanding her to call some numbers. He wanted a *phone*. What the hell was all that about?

A spy wouldn't draw attention to himself like that. A spy would blend in and be unnoticeable. So chances were Konnor wasn't a MacDougall spy. He really must be a man in trouble, and mayhap he was more injured than he thought he was.

At the same time, he was handsome. So handsome, that for the first time since Dunollie, Marjorie had noticed a man. For the first time in twelve years, someone had stirred feelings in her, feelings she'd never thought she would have. Excitement bubbled in her stomach playfully and clouded her head like a strong ale.

Nae. She didn't need this. Whoever Konnor was, he was a distraction. She should take this sudden attraction to him as a sign she was mending. One wee step at a time, she was healing. But nothing more than that. Even if she was getting better, she would still never take a lover or a husband. Her decision in that regard wouldn't change. She would never act on her feelings towards a man like Konnor. He was handsome, powerful, and made her heart beat faster.

"Mistress, while ye're taking yer rest, may I have a word?" a male voice said from the side.

She turned, and saw Tamhas standing there with his dark hair tied in a partial ponytail wet from sweat.

"Thanks for the practice, Malcolm," she said and turned back toward Tamhas. "Aye, of course."

Tamhas had taken her kidnapping personally since they were the same age and had grown up together. He'd been one of the guards on duty in the castle the day she disappeared. When she'd begun training as a way to release her anger and the darkness that had gathered within her, he'd been against it.

"*A lass shouldna bother herself with swords and archery. Especially when she has a bairn to think of. Ye should take care.*"

But Marjorie had started learning combat anyway, so Tamhas had helped her and sparred with her. After years of daily exercise, he was more skilled than Marjorie because he was more experienced in a real battle.

Marjorie went to the round well made of rough stone in the center of the courtyard. Using the rope, she pulled up the bucket of water, her biceps burning from strain. She took a big, wooden ladle and drank from it thirstily. The water was cool and refreshing against her lips. She drew more water and handed the ladle to Tamhas, who muttered a thanks and downed it like it were *uisge*.

"So," Marjorie said, leaning against the wall of the well with her hip. "What is it?"

"'Tis about the new man, Konnor." He dipped his hands into the bucket, drew some water, and splashed it on his face with a small grunt.

Marjorie's heart lurched at the mention of Konnor's name. "Have ye met him?" she asked.

"Nae. But I've heard about him from Malcolm. And I've seen him wobbling around."

She shifted her weight. "And?"

Tamhas wiped his mouth and shook his head once. "I dinna like him. Malcolm is also suspicious of him."

Marjorie chuckled. "What do ye want me to do about it?"

He stared straight at her. "I want ye to send him on his way."

She drew in some air. She'd considered it, but she just couldn't bring herself to do that to an injured person. Besides, there was still a chance he could be a spy for the MacDougalls. And she was intrigued by him. Something about him made her want to keep him— No, she shouldn't even think like that, let alone say it out loud to Tamhas.

"He's still hurt. I canna do that," she said.

"He's already hopping about. He can manage."

She crossed her arms over her chest and looked at him again. "'Tis unlike ye, Tamhas. Ye're usually more soft-hearted than that. What ails ye?"

Tamhas sighed, the jaw muscles under his dark stubble working. "I dinna like how he looks at ye," he said quietly. There was a threating tone she'd never heard from him before. Something about it was blood chilling.

"How does he look at me?"

"In a way that makes me want to break his neck."

What did that mean? Did he look at her like he wanted her? That was what Marjorie had seen, too, right? Or was there more than just desire? Was there something else in his eyes? Did he look at her like Alasdair had?

She didn't notice that, but mayhap Tamhas saw more than her. The thought made her blood chill. Mayhap he was right. Mayhap it was a good idea to let Konnor go. No one knew him, and no one had any idea if he could be a threat—to her, to Colin, or to anyone else in the castle.

"Mayhap ye're right," she said. "He should leave. I kent I could trust ye."

Tamhas's eyes burned. Something in his gaze made her uncomfortable, like she wanted him to leave. It was too much. Too much love, too much support, too much devotion. He was her childhood friend, and she'd known him her whole life. He was like another brother to her. She knew he used to have a crush on her when they were teens. He was a man now with wants and needs, and she wondered why he'd never married.

She didn't want to think of Tamhas like that.

He gave her a nod, and a lock of his black hair fell on his forehead. "I'll tell him."

He turned to leave, but she called after him. "Tell him to leave on the morrow. He can rest one more night."

Tamhas gave another nod and walked to the tower. Strangely, the thought of Konnor leaving made her very sad.

CHAPTER 9

Later that evening, Konnor made his way to the dining hall. It was a separate stone building that looked like a church without a bell tower. It had tall walls of rough rock and mortar with narrow, long glassless windows that were split horizontally by the shadow cast from the curtain walls, one part dark and one bright orange from the evening sun.

Konnor's stomach rumbled when he wobbled inside using his crutch. Orange-golden sunrays fell from the slits in the windows and onto the long tables where men sat huddled over their bowls and cups. The large room smelled like fresh bread, cooked meat, vegetables, and beer. Konnor couldn't quite distinguish the wooden shields with painted emblems that decorated the walls. A large fireplace was lit, and a fire played there cheerfully. The floor was covered with rugs made of reeds.

There were around forty people in the hall occupying half of the long tables available. Braziers made of straight, riveted pieces of iron stood between the tables, and the fires in them cast devious shadows on the rough walls. A servant woman in a long, woolen dress and white kerchief on her head walked along the tables with a basket of bread and distributed loaves on the tables.

The longer he was here, the more often the probability of time travel came into his mind. A tiny part of him wondered if Sìneag was right after all.

But the rest of him, the logical grown-up in him wasn't convinced. He had seen death and witnessed the closest person in the world to him get hurt in the worst possible way. He didn't believe in miracles and magic. There must be another explanation, and if Marjorie refused to tell him, he'd find someone who would.

Heavy, estimating gazes followed him. Warriors who'd been engaged in friendly conversations with one another turned cautious and even antagonistic. Great. But he hadn't come to make friends. He needed information.

He glanced at the main table. There was a big wooden throne with intricate carvings there. And there was Marjorie, the Highland queen. She wore a beautiful blue medieval dress with draped sleeves. Her hair was gathered in a braided hairdo, and her lips glistened red as she bit into a chunk of bread and chewed on it. He wished he were that piece of bread she held and touched with her lips. Her eyes locked with his, and she stilled, stern lines forming around her lips.

He looked away and searched for a free spot. He saw two familiar faces, the warriors he'd seen Marjorie talking to, and he went to sit at their table.

"Is this seat taken?" he asked as he stood at the head of the table.

The table full of men glanced at him. The Highlander with long white hair gathered in a ponytail frowned at him. Malcolm.

"Nae," he said and shifted on the bench without breaking eye contact. "Take a seat."

Across the table sat a tall, lean man who looked about thirty years old. He had long, dark hair that he'd gathered in a partial ponytail and had stubble on the lower part of his chin.

"Tamhas," the man said, but his face practically said he wanted to murder Konnor the first chance he got.

Why did Konnor feel like he was walking into a trap? Every instinct set his body to alert. His muscles tightened, and his knees bent a little. He relaxed his grip on his crutch in case he needed to use it as a weapon.

The man next to Tamhas was a little younger than Malcolm, short and stout with a graying beard and hair. He had intelligent eyes and a big, meaty nose. Konnor immediately liked him.

"Muir." The man nodded with a smirk in his eyes.

"Konnor Mitchell," Konnor said.

"I've been looking all over the castle for ye," Tamhas said.

Konnor's jaw ticked. "Oh yeah? What did you want?"

Tamhas took an empty cup and poured some beer from a jar into it. He moved the cup towards Konnor. "Sit. Drink. I'll tell ye."

Konnor glanced at the other two men sitting across the table. They were watching the exchange with frowns.

Cocking his head, Konnor sat at the bench and drank the beer. It was warm and tasted like weak Guinness.

"Is there something stronger?" He wiped his upper lip with his sleeve.

"Aye." Malcolm reached to his belt and unhooked a leather wineskin. "Uisge."

He poured the liquid into four cups. The men took their cups and drank without clinking. The liquid went down his throat like fire, and Konnor realized it was moonshine, not whiskey.

"Hmm. Why do you guys drink moonshine instead of a proper scotch?"

The men exchanged puzzled glances.

"Who talks like that?" Muir chuckled. "What's a proper scotch? Scotch what?"

"I think he may be a wee bit slow," Malcolm said.

Konnor's hands tightened around the cup. "Come on, guys. Let's stop the pretense. We all know you have this whole eclectic community thing going on. But I'd hoped we could speak man-to-man. Drop the bullshit."

Malcolm's face fell. "Bullshit? 'Tis ye who should drop it." He removed a dagger and stabbed it into the tabletop, his fist clenched around the handle.

Tamhas leaned forward. "Everything is strange about ye. The way ye speak. Yer clothes. Even yer goddamn hair. I canna place ye anywhere. Are ye a nobleman? A Sassenach? Do ye belong to a clan? Chances are, if I canna understand yer background, ye're a threat to our mistress. And that is just something I canna have."

Konnor ground his teeth. "I'm a regular guy from the States. What's wrong with you? These are regular cargo pants." He pointed at his legs. "This is an army jacket. This is a T-shirt."

They scowled at him as he pointed to his clothes.

"I've never seen anything like those in my life," said Malcolm. "And what is that thin material? Wool? Linen?"

"Dinna ken," Tamhas said. "And dinna want to ken."

Konnor wasn't a stranger to animosity. There were all kinds of guys in the Marines, and he wasn't afraid of any of them. He didn't particularly like these guys, though he understood why they were being like this. They thought they were protecting Marjorie. He'd hire every one of them as a bodyguard at his firm. Their dedication to her was impressive.

"My business is protecting the mistress," Tamhas said, "And right now, ye're more a threat than a friend, simply because I dinna believe ye and dinna trust ye."

Tamhas threw a glance at the main table and the mistress

herself. What was that Konnor saw in his eyes? Longing. Admiration. Love.

Was the guy in love with her?

Unexplainable jealousy slashed him across his gut. That wasn't Konnor's business. He didn't belong here. There was absolutely nothing between him and Marjorie—and there wouldn't be. But he wanted to punch the guy for looking at her like that.

"Are you her bodyguard?" Konnor asked.

"Aye," Tamhas said. "Muir and I are."

Konnor looked him over from the perspective of a soldier and someone who owned a security firm. The man was tall, though probably a bit shorter than Konnor. Under his slightly dirty linen tunic were broad shoulders and lean muscles. He looked like a professional athlete. He had intelligent eyes, like someone who could think for himself and estimate threats. Though Konnor would need to see him in action, the dedication to Marjorie was certainly there.

Konnor leaned forward. "So what about this siege that's coming? Who are the MacDougalls, really?"

"One of the most powerful clans in the eastern Highlands," Tamhas said, looking a little bewildered.

Maybe Konnor could get the truth this way. "And what kind of weapons will they bring for the siege? A catapult or something?"

Tamhas leaned back and crossed his arms on his chest. "They could if they wanted to. They certainly have the wealth to order a war engineer and have one built."

Konnor drummed his fingers against the table. "Will they bring guns?"

"Guns?" Malcolm said like he heard the word for the first time.

Gimme a break.

"So just swords and shields?" Konnor said, the hope they'd show any sign of reason and open up was disappearing quickly.

"Nae, spears and bows, too," Malcolm said. "Mayhap even crossbows."

Spears and bows... Crossbows... They weren't backing down.

Konnor leaned forward and looked at them conspiratorially. "But they're plastic, right? Like props in a movie?"

"What the feck is plastic?" Tamhas said. "And a movie?"

Konnor sighed. At least he'd tried. He should just accept his failure with them. In the end, all he wanted was to get out of there.

He looked at the loaf of bread and chunk of cheese. He reached for it, but Tamhas took Malcolm's dagger and thrust it between Konnor's hand and the food.

Konnor could disarm him with two easy movements and stick that dagger right into the guy's eye. He looked at Tamhas's snarl. "Now, now. That's dangerous. You should take care when you play with grown-up toys, or you might cut yourself."

"Shut up. Ye're here because of mistress's kind heart. But even she is out of patience now. She wants ye out of here on the morrow."

Konnor looked at Marjorie, who had turned and was talking to a servant girl. Her long, dark hair had spilled over her shoulders. Her eyes sparkled, her hand held her cup gracefully, and something in his chest squeezed at the thought of leaving her.

"She said that?" he asked.

"Aye. With her own words."

What changed, Konnor wondered? She'd been afraid to let him go because he might be a spy, and now she wanted him gone. Was that because of his compliment?

So he'd leave tomorrow. Good. He was grateful to Marjorie and Isbeil for treating him and for feeding him, for taking care of him, and despite the strangeness of this place, a part of him didn't want to go. A part of him didn't want to leave Marjorie.

Though even if he stayed, nothing would be possible between them, no matter how attractive she was. His life had taught him well that romantic love only led to pain. He'd experienced that for himself. Although he tried to avoid relationships, he had liked a woman enough to give the whole girlfriend-boyfriend thing a try. It was five years ago. She was sweet, kind, and beautiful. A nurse. Spoke Spanish. Surfed. Volunteered at a homeless shelter. Great sex. The whole package.

They'd dated for about three months. She'd said she didn't really know Konnor and started asking him about his childhood. Wanted to meet his mom. Suggested they go on a weekend trip to Santa Catalina Island.

If he hadn't even told Andy about what he'd endured from Jerry, how could he tell her?

It only took a couple of weeks after that for them to break up. Well, for her to break up with him because he was "*an emotionally unavailable fuck.*"

"Good," he said. "Then she's finally came back to her senses."

Tamhas removed the dagger, and Konnor tore a piece of bread from the loaf. But as he chewed it and looked again at Marjorie, he couldn't help but wonder how he would ever forget her.

CHAPTER 10

T he sound of footsteps in the hallway woke Konnor later that night. Using an old soldier's trick, he opened his eyes without moving another muscle. He was still in his room in the castle. It was dark, the middle of the night, and the torch on the wall was out. He was alone, as far as he could tell.

He heard another scrape of a shoe against the stone floor from somewhere outside his room. He automatically slid his hand under his pillow for a weapon, only to find nothing there. He cursed inwardly. Of course, he didn't have a gun, or even a knife. The castle was full of swords and spears and arrows, but he didn't have anything.

He sat up and reached for the crutch. He'd gotten the hang of it during the day, making his way up and down the stairs and along the uneven stone floors and the courtyard. Without putting his shoes on, he stood up and made his way towards the exit. He put the end of the wooden crutch against the floor as quietly as he could. Once he came to the door, he listened. Someone yelped, and then there were muffled grunts and curses.

Hell.

Marjorie's room was next to his. He opened the door to a slit. The landing was lit up by a torch.

Empty.

The sounds came from the circular flight of stairs leading to the next floor. Metal clanked softly, barely audible. Steps.

That didn't sound good at all.

Konnor took the crutch in his hands like a weapon and moved onto the landing without a sound, ignoring the pain in his ankle. A muffled cry reached him from upstairs.

What was there? Someone's room? Konnor made his way towards the stairs, making sure he stepped without a sound. Halfway up the stairs, he heard a voice.

"Dinna make a sound, or I'll cut yer throat," a man whispered loudly.

Konnor peeked around the round wall at the next landing, his ankle tearing him apart from pain. Empty. But one of the doors was open.

He moved towards it and looked inside. There were three men in the room. Two held a boy in his bed, trying to tie him up. One stood by the door with his back to Konnor.

Konnor didn't hesitate. He took five steps and hit the back of the man's head with the crutch. The intruder fell to the floor like a rock. The two others looked up at Konnor, as did the boy. He was probably ten years old, eyes big and white against the darkness of the room, and he thrashed and kicked in the hands of the jerks.

Fire lit Konnor's blood. He wouldn't let them hurt the child.

One of the men left the side of the bed and drew his sword. The blade glistened in the moonlight. He thrust the sword, but Konnor ducked, stepped aside, and hit his side with the crutch. The guy crumpled but rose to his feet again.

The boy thrashed harder, and the man by his side grunted in pain. The boy's scream pierced the air. A hard slap followed, and he was silent for a moment. He screamed again, but the man gagged him.

"Finish him," the guy growled. "He's just a cripple with a stick!"

A cripple with a stick?

Konnor swung the crutch and struck the man on the side of his head. His sword fell to the floor with a loud *bang*, and Konnor leaned down to take it, but his opponent was smarter than he'd thought. The man thrust both elbows into the back of Konnor's head. Pain exploded in his head. He fell forward and landed against a wall, knocking wooden swords and shields that hung there.

There was one real sword that glistened in the light of the fireplace. Konnor grabbed it, spun around, and slashed at the man. The blade sliced through flesh, and blood sprayed on Konnor as the man yelled in pain and fell.

Without knowing if he was holding it right, Konnor thrust the sword towards the third guy but hit only air. The man holding the boy let him go. The guy drew his own sword and came towards Konnor making a series of downward strikes. Konnor defended himself from the thrusts with his sword and moved back step by step.

Clunk. Clunk. Clunk.

The room was filled with the ring of metal against metal.

From the corner of his eye, Konnor saw Marjorie appear in the room, a sword in her hand, and fear for her twisted in his gut. He had to act. The man he faced wasn't bigger than him, but he was much more experienced. Konnor took the initiative and went on the offensive, but the man easily deflected his strikes.

Somewhere in the storm of sharp swords, blood, the unconscious man lying on the ground, and the men's attempt to hurt Marjorie, a thought entered his mind.

This is real.

He knew it like he knew he might die by the sword wielded

by this intruder. This castle wasn't a small medieval community. It wasn't a cult. And it wasn't a dream. Whatever explanation there was for all this, this was a different world—or era —altogether.

Suddenly, time travel didn't seem like such an impossible explanation.

Konnor's back was against the wall. The man raised his sword high above his head. Just as Konnor stared death in the face, Marjorie appeared behind the man and pressed the edge of a sword to his neck. The man froze, his eyes wide.

"Aye, ye pig," Marjorie said. "If yer life is dear to ye, throw yer claymore on the floor far away from ye and step away from *him*."

The man's lip curved downward in an angry snarl. He threw the sword, and it landed on the floor with a loud *clank*. Konnor put the tip of his own weapon to the man's throat.

"Put your hands behind your head," Konnor said. "And lie on the floor facedown."

The guy did as he was told. When he lay on the ground, Marjorie's and Konnor's gazes met. He now noticed she was in a nightgown. The shape of her body was visible under the thin white material in the moonlight.

She rushed to the boy, who was now standing. With the sword trembling in her hands, she cut the ties on his wrists and then scooped him in a hug.

"Oh, Colin, my lad," she said, her voice a shaky whisper. The boy buried his face at her chest.

"I'm all right, Ma," he said.

Ma? Mother...

Konnor remained still and speechless, eyeing the boy. Konnor had seen him in the castle with his wooden sword here and there, chatting with the warriors and the servants, playing with a dog, standing on the walls watching the fields around the castle. He'd even seen him talk to Marjorie. But he hadn't realized he was her son. He'd thought he was...just a boy.

But now he could see the similarities. Their faces were the same shape, and they had the same unruly dark-brown hair. He was skinny but had strong shoulders and arms. His chin protruded stubbornly as he stared at Konnor with careful apprehension.

Konnor blinked, coming back to his senses. Marjorie had been abused. And Marjorie had a son.

"Thank ye, Konnor," she whispered, tears glistening in her eyes. "I thought I'd woken up to a nightmare. If it wasna for ye..."

The sound of footsteps thundered up the stairs and across the landing, and Malcolm and five more men barged in, swords at the ready.

"Mistress, Colin, are ye all right?" Malcolm shouted, looking around the room.

"Aye," Marjorie said.

"Who are they?" Malcolm said.

"I woke up to shouts and banging from Colin's room. They came for him, and Konnor saved him."

Malcolm took three giant steps towards the third man and sank to his knees. He took out a dagger and pressed it against the guy's ear.

"Who are ye?" he said.

"I think ye well ken who we are," the man answered and spat at Malcolm's shoe.

"MacDougalls, of course," Marjorie said, her voice shaking. "Who else?"

Malcolm stood and kicked the man in the stomach.

"Came to take our mistress's son? Well, that isna bloody happening, is it?" he growled. "Take them away." He turned to Marjorie. "Dinna fash yerself, lass, I will question them. We need to ken how they got in. We will look around the castle for more men."

Marjorie looked at Colin. "Go to bed, sweet. I'll stay until we ken there isna anyone else here."

"I can stay with you," Konnor said. "Just until we know it's safe."

Marjorie glanced at him, looking lost and shaken, and nodded. Colin got in his bed, and she covered him with a blanket. As Cambel men carried and dragged the MacDougalls out, Marjorie sat on the bed by Colin's side and kept stroking him. Konnor stood by the door and watched her and her son, something turning in his chest over and over. Something he didn't want to think about.

After a while, the boy closed his eyes and fell asleep.

Malcolm stuck his head into the room. "'Tis all clear, mistress. There's no one else here. Go to sleep."

She stood up and kissed Colin on the head.

"Will ye put a man to guard him, Malcolm? I'll sleep better."

"Aye. Of course, mistress. I'll guard him myself."

"Thank ye."

Marjorie and Konnor went down the stairs to the landing. She stopped before her door, hugged herself, and began to shake.

"Are you all right?" he said.

She didn't reply, standing like a tree shaking in a strong wind. "I thought I'd woken up twelve years ago and was about to relieve the worst days of my life."

CHAPTER 11

As she spoke, darkness crept towards Marjorie from the corners of the landing and from the corners of her mind. Cold seeped through the nightgown, and she walked into her room and climbed on her bed. She covered herself with a blanket and shivered. Even twelve years later, she still felt the pressure of fingers digging into her wrists, the weight of one of the men on her legs, the filthy palm on her mouth.

The possibility of her son going through the same thing made sickness rise in her and her head spin.

Konnor walked in the room after her and closed the door.

"What happened?" he asked, pulling her out of the black hole of memories.

No, she couldn't go there yet. The memory was still too close, too frightening. She couldn't fall apart now. The whole castle needed her. Silly her, thinking she was mending.

"I'm cold," Marjorie said.

She wrapped the blanket closer around herself, got up, and went to the fireplace. The coals were still hot and glowing, and warmth spread through her as she sank to her knees and stretched her arms out. She reached out to the pile of firewood and put a couple of logs on the coals.

"How did ye hear them?" Marjorie asked without looking back at Konnor. "Even I didn't until 'twas too late."

"Military training," Konnor said. "I'm a Marine. And I have a security firm."

She looked over her shoulder at him. He winced as he lowered himself to sit on the edge of her bed. She was suddenly aware he was shirtless. A handsome, shirtless man. He sat with his injured foot on his other knee. She could see his broad shoulders in the semidarkness of the room, and the muscles of his arms played as he massaged his leg around the splint. This was the first time a man—a half-naked man—had been in her room, and yet she felt as safe with Konnor as she did with her brothers.

"A security firm?" she said. "So 'tis how ye ken sword-fighting?"

She suddenly realized that Konnor had protected her son with her grandfather's sword. If that wasn't a sign of Sir Colin watching over his great-grandson, she didn't know what was.

Konnor shook his head. "I held a sword for the first time in my life tonight."

"Then how could ye be security for someone?"

He pursed his lips, his jaw muscles working. A thoughtful expression clouded his handsome face.

"Can I ask you a question?" He paused for a moment. "What year is it?"

Marjorie chuckled. "What year is it? 'Tis the year of our Lord, 1308."

He exhaled slowly, his lips forming the letter O. Strange reaction.

"Why?" Marjorie said. "Did ye forget?"

She turned back to the fireplace. The firewood was only charring from the heat of the coals, and she put some kindling under them. She leaned forward and carefully blew on the coals until the kindling flared up.

Marjorie turned back to Konnor. He stretched his leg out and watched her with a thoughtful frown, as though he couldn't decide on something important.

"I didn't forget," he finally said. "So you really don't know what the USA is?"

"Nae."

"Hmmm. Who rules Scotland?"

"King Robert the Bruce, although we're fighting with King Edward of England, who's allied himself with several Scottish clans, including the MacDougalls. 'Tis why my brothers, my father, and the rest of my clan are nae here."

Konnor rubbed his forehead.

"And the word 'democracy,' does it mean anything to you?"

"'Tis something Greeks tried once, nae?"

Konnor nodded and hung his head as though doomed. He put his hands on his forehead and ran his fingers through his hair. This didn't look right.

"Konnor, what is it?" Marjorie said. "Why does the year matter, the king, the democracy?"

He sucked in a breath, looked at her, and then exhaled.

"It matters because you say it's 1308. And last time I checked, it was 2020. I was born in 1987. In my time, there are no more kings other than symbolic ones. And democracy is how the world operates. For the most part, anyway."

Marjorie winced, trying to work through what he'd just said. His words made no sense, yet he seemed so convinced. He looked desperate. Confused. A little scared even. He spoke like a madman but behaved like someone in trouble. Mayhap, he was aware of his madness?

"Say something," Konnor said. "You must think I'm crazy."

Marjorie scoffed. "'Tis exactly what I think. I'm a woman of logic and reason, nae of superstitions and magic. Do ye mean to imply Isbeil was right about the tunnel through time?"

Konnor pulled himself up, using the bed to support himself. He put the crutch under his armpit and made a movement towards her but winced. He sat back on the bed and started to retie the bandage on his ankle.

"I don't freaking know, Marjorie, okay? As insane as this sounds, I think it's the only explanation. The alternative is I'm dreaming all of this. But the blood on the floor, the swords, and the pain in my leg all seems too real." He tied a knot and looked at her. "You feel too real."

The fire shone brightly in the fireplace now, giving her room a pleasant, golden glow. Marjorie threw on more firewood, parts of her mind fighting with each other. She was a Highlander, and she'd grown up on tales of kelpies, faeries, and magic. But she was also Christian, and a reasonable person who knew those were just old stories. Still, even the logical part of her saw that Konnor wasn't just speaking of strange things. He was dressed differently. Those green, broad breeches with pockets, the shoes with thick soles she'd never seen the likes of before. His jacket and short tunic were made of fine material she didn't even know the name of. He had English letters on his undertunic saying "Born to Be Wild." His haircut, his strange accent and manner of speaking. The words he'd used: ambulance, hospital, phone. If he was from the future, things must be different there.

"Look, I don't expect you to believe me, okay?" Konnor said. "But tomorrow, I will go back to those ruins with the rock and try to get back to my time. I hope you know now I'm not a threat to you."

The thought of him leaving made her chest tighten.

"Aye," she said. "I dinna think ye're a MacDougall anymore. Ye saved me from those men. I'll be forever grateful."

She swallowed, her stomach sinking. "Go get some sleep. I'm all right."

His face brightened, and Marjorie wished it weren't because he was leaving her.

"Good night," he said and limped towards the door, the crutch knocking against the floor.

She glanced at the drying blood on the floor. He'd defeated two men while injured. Not only was he a great warrior, but he was also brave and resourceful. If he indeed came from the future, which she didn't fully believe yet, mayhap he knew some tricks or something that would help her defend the castle.

"Though I do wish ye'd stay longer," Marjorie said to his bare back.

He stopped and turned to her. "What?"

Marjorie rose and tugged the edges of the blanket tighter around her.

"The MacDougalls are going to attack, Konnor. I havna been in a war. I havna killed anyone. My castle is crumbling, and I'm afraid we dinna have enough men to defend ourselves." She swallowed, her eyes burning. "If the MacDougalls take Colin... Or me again..." She choked on the words, lacking the air and the ability to say them out loud.

Konnor's face darkened like a stormy sky. "Again?"

He stepped towards her and led her to the bed. They sat down, his gaze not leaving her. It was time. He needed to know what this battle would mean. What it would mean to her if he helped.

"'Twas twelve years ago. Our clans used to be allies, and the MacDougall was our overlord. The chief's son—" She paused and swallowed the knot in her throat. "Alasdair," she spat his name like a curse. "He asked for my hand. But there was something about him I'd never liked. He'd never been kind to anyone. I asked my father if he'd allow me to say nae, and he did. So I refused Alasdair."

She exhaled, gathering the strength to tell Konnor the worst. She looked at her hands, unable to meet his gaze. A familiar sense of shame burned her cheeks. Silly. As though it were her fault what he'd done to her. And yet she believed it was. If she'd been stronger...

"One day, I went to gather flowers outside the castle. Only my maid came with me. Horsemen came out of nowhere, and one of them snatched me up on his horse. No matter how much I struggled, he held me."

Tears blurred her vision, but she saw Konnor's hand curled into fist on the bed.

"Alasdair held me prisoner," she said, her voice tight from the tears that couldn't be stopped anymore. "Every day, he came and beat me and took me like I were his property."

She wiped her eyes with her hands, but the tears kept coming. She still couldn't look at Konnor.

"My clan finally found out who was responsible. They came for me, and my brother Craig killed Alasdair. In the skirmish, my grandfather died."

She finally looked up at him. Konnor's nostrils flared, his own eyes were bloodshot and watery, his mouth pinched in a grimace. His chest rose and fell quickly, his breathing loud. Something about his anger brought relief.

"You were..." he rasped. "And Colin is his?"

"Aye."

"And you're afraid if they come, they'll take Colin?"

She nodded.

He shook his head. "No, they won't, Marjorie. I'll stay and help you." He reached out but then hesitated, looking into her eyes. It was as though he was asking her permission to touch her. Something relaxed in her stomach. She placed her hands into his. His palms were big and warm and callused. They felt like home.

"No one will touch a hair on your—or your son's—head as long as I have a say in it."

His blue eyes stared at her with determination, flames dancing on his face in a golden hue. She felt safe and protected, and for the first time in her life, she wanted to kiss a man.

CHAPTER 12

Konnor tossed and turned after he returned to his room. Now he knew without a shadow of a doubt that Marjorie and his mother were victims of the same darkness.

Konnor couldn't leave her after what he'd found out. If those pricks the MacDougalls had kidnapped and raped Marjorie, he couldn't just go back to the twenty-first century and leave her in danger. It couldn't have been easy for her to give birth to a child out of wedlock in this century. What a strong woman. Was she choosing to be alone because of her trauma? If so, he could relate. That was exactly the choice he'd made.

She didn't believe him about time travel. Heck, he didn't quite believe it himself, but the more he thought about it, the more it made sense. He needed to talk to Isbeil again and ask her for more details about those Highland legends and tunnels through time. He had to make sure he could go back through that stone to his own time.

His gut clenched with worry for his mother, left alone without his financial or emotional support.

He remembered the day his father died. Konnor had been

six years old. His dad had been wounded in action while deployed as a Marine and sent to Walter Reed Medical Center in Maryland, outside of Washington DC. Konnor remembered how he'd entered the hospital room and froze, scared to see his strong father as white as the pillow and breathing raggedly.

"Help your mother," his father said. "Protect her. You're the only one she's got."

Two years later, Konnor thought of those last words the evening after Jerry hit his mother. Mom placed dinner on the table, and the atmosphere was thick and silent, like everyone was afraid to breathe.

A plate with roasted chicken lay, golden and delicious, in the middle of the table. Mom covered the bruise on her face with the locks of her blond bob. She wore pink jeans and a long-sleeved sweater despite the warm weather, perhaps to hide the blue marks in the form of fingers that decorated her forearm.

Jerry and Konnor sat at the table waiting for her to put mashed potatoes on their plates. Jerry glared at him with bloodshot eyes, whirling the glass of whiskey in his hand.

"How was school, Konnor?" he asked.

"Protect her. You're the only one she's got." His father's words rang in his head. Guilt chewed at his stomach. Konnor hadn't done anything to protect his mom the night before, but he could do something today. Jerry should know he couldn't just beat her.

"It was fine," he said, his gut trembling with both fear and anger. "Mom, are you okay?"

She glanced at him with wide eyes and flashed a forced smile, keeping her head low. "Of course. Never better. Peas?"

"Mom, I heard. Last night, I heard everything."

His mom's eyes widened in horror. She dropped the plate and it fell with a loud *bang*, peas rolling all over the floor. Jerry's square-jawed face reddened, his mustache shaking. He stood and grabbed her by the upper arm and drew his arm back to hit her.

"Stop it!" Konnor cried, and darted forward to hang on Jerry's arm. Jerry shoved him back. Konnor staggered and fell, hitting his head on the edge of the chair. He whimpered, his head exploding with pain.

"Jerry!" his mom exclaimed and pushed Jerry away from him.

"Don't you dare push me, you bitch," Jerry cried and slapped her. He grabbed her by her hair and brought her face to his. "You try that one more time..." He was livid and drunk and spitting the consonants.

"Don't touch him," Mom growled.

Slap. Slap. Konnor watched with horror as her head shot to the left and to the right when Jerry's hand came to her face.

"I will touch him in any way I see fit if he disrespects me like that in my own house." As if to demonstrate, he grabbed the collar of Konnor's T-shirt and lifted him up. Konnor stared into his bloodshot, drunken gray eyes and began wriggling.

Bam. Came a blow, right to his cheekbone. *Bam.* In his stomach, blinding him with pain.

"Stop it!" Mom screamed and turned Jerry to her. He let Konnor go, and he crumpled on the floor. She stood between Konnor and Jerry. "Go to your room, Konnor," she whispered. "Lock your door."

And, like a coward, he did. He didn't stay. He didn't distract Jerry. He ran and he let her take his beating.

But now that he was a grown man, he'd take every hit for her. He'd protect her and take care of her until the day he died.

A knock on the door pulled him out of his memories. Morning light spilled through the slit window into his room. He sat up in the bed, and his ankle ached in response. Marjorie appeared at the door, and she slid her gaze down his naked torso before she pointedly returned to his eyes. A slight blush covered her cheeks. He'd be flattered if he weren't worried about making her feel uncomfortable.

"Konnor, I want to hold a council about the castle's defenses with my men. Will ye join us?"

Join her? Did she trust him so much already? He had no experience with castles and swords and bows. But if she needed his help, he'd give it to her in any way he could.

"Yes, of course." He lowered his legs to the floor, picked up one shoe, and put it on his good leg.

"I'll wait on the landing while ye dress," Marjorie said.

"Sure."

While Konnor was putting on his clothes, he realized his leg felt much better, and he didn't need a crutch anymore. When he was dressed, he went in search of Marjorie. He found her looking fresh and beautiful, with her dark hair in a single braid that fell over her shoulder. She wore pants and a short tunic, dressed like a man again, but the belt hugged her thin waist. There was a sheath on her back, and the strap of it went between her breasts. Konnor pointedly looked at her face and didn't allow his gaze to move an inch down, but even her full lips were torture.

They made their way down the tower, then across and into the next one. After climbing two flights of stairs, they walked through the entrance that connected the tower and the fortification wall. Malcolm, Tamhas, and two more armed men stood there waiting.

Tamhas narrowed his eyes as he studied Konnor.

"We need to decide what to do with the wall." Marjorie pointed down at their feet.

The wall was about ten feet thick, with merlons and crenels that had slits for archers at regular intervals. Where they stood, the merlons were gone, and the floor and outer part of the wall had crumbled. It would be dangerous for the defenders to stand here. The wall was lower and would be easy to climb. Konnor looked down and noticed another problem.

The rubble and rocks that had fallen hadn't been cleared away. They formed a nice hill to make it even easier for the attackers to get into the castle.

"The MacDougalls came through here." Marjorie pointed at the area.

"Aye," Malcolm added. "The bastarts climbed unnoticed in the darkness, killed three watchmen, and sneaked in. 'Twas that easy."

"When do you think they'll attack?" Konnor said.

He sank to his knees, wincing from the pain in his ankle, and touched the cold, rough stone. The crumbled part had disintegrated to an almost sandlike substance. Konnor brushed it with his hand, and the small shingles were sharp against his skin.

"I dinna ken," Marjorie said. "The spies didna mention when."

"I think soon," Malcolm said. "They are probably waiting for them and Colin. Once they realize their men are nae coming back with the boy, the chief will ken we have them and that we ken of the attack. He might come sooner rather than later."

Konnor nodded in agreement. They needed to repair the damage to the castle wall and fast. But if they only had days, there was no way they could get enough rocks and mortar in time for it to dry.

"We need to find a mason and order the repair, aye?" Marjorie said.

Malcolm nodded in agreement, but Tamhas frowned.

"You likely have days, Marjorie," Konnor said. "I doubt it can be done so quickly."

"Well, nae, but surely the mason will at least ken how to repair it to some extent within days."

That would not work. Konnor's back was covered in cold sweat at the thought of what could happen to Marjorie, Colin, and her people if the MacDougalls got in. Adrenalin shot through his blood.

"No, you're wrong." Konnor said. Marjorie jerked her head back as though he'd slapped her. "What you need to do is take matters in your own hands."

He fingered the dry mortar in a slit between the rocks, then stood up.

"What you need to do is make it difficult for the enemy to enter here. Rather than hiring a mason to start fixing the wall, ask a blacksmith to make you iron spikes to make it hard for them to climb over the wall, like big arrow tips. Or you can have men make them out of wood, but have the blacksmith attach them securely to the wall." Konnor imagined bird spikes that were used as anti-intruder protection on fences and walls. "Make it so the enemy can't climb here."

Marjorie looked at him wide-eyed. "But 'tis nae but a quick fix."

"You don't have time for a proper repair. You also need to remove the rubble below." Konnor pointed down the wall, and everyone looked at what he was talking about. "They'll have less of a ramp and more of a climb."

"That will take men," Marjorie said. "And they need to train to prepare for the fight."

"What they need is to be smart," Konnor said. Marjorie opened her mouth and frowned again, clearly unhappy he'd contradicted her. "Next, you should build rows of wooden stakes at the base of the walls so they cannot use siege ladders."

Marjorie shook her head, her eyes flashing. "Ye have nae idea what ye're suggesting. That will take all the men. Every single one. They need to polish their fighting skills for when the enemy gets in."

"What I'm suggesting will prevent the enemy from getting in."

Malcolm nodded. "He's right, lass. I think he has good ideas."

"He canna contradict the mistress like that, she kens better," Muir said.

"I'm not done," Konnor said. "In Iraq, we used drones for early detection, but you can put watchmen out in the woods in all directions, preferably from where the MacDougalls are likely to show up. Give them a signal, something your men can recognize. Something that can give you advance warning."

"But that would mean risking the lives of more men! I already lost three last night. I canna lose another." She shook with anger. Her cheeks reddened, and her eyes were shooting lightning bolts. Like a Celtic goddess of war, she was ready to fight him.

"But—" Konnor started.

"Nae, 'tis quite enough. When I asked for yer help, I didna mean for ye to suggest strategy that would undermine mine. Ye dinna ken our ways, and ye dinna ken this castle. Leave. I dinna need yer help nae more. My men and I will decide, nae ye."

Her rejection stung, but worse was the fear for her. The mistakes she was about to make would get her into the exact nightmare she was trying to escape from.

"Listen to me—" Konnor said.

"Leave," Tamhas insisted. "Ye heard the mistress."

"Marjorie—"

"Go," she said and turned away, her shoulders rising and falling quickly with her rapid breathing.

Konnor stared at her back, his nostrils flared, his fists clenching. *"Go to your room, Konnor. Lock the door."* The helplessness of the little boy he'd once been dragged at his arms, enveloping him in a tight, sticky cocoon. He couldn't protect his mother from danger all those years ago. And Marjorie, this beautiful, beautiful Highland queen, needed more protection than anyone after what she'd been through. And he wouldn't let any harm come to her son.

He wouldn't abandon her, wouldn't let her anger chase him away. "You want me gone?" he said, and she turned to him, her green eyes ablaze. "Well, too freaking bad. I'm not leaving. Deal with it."

Ignoring her widened eyes and the sinking feeling of helplessness in his gut, he walked towards the tower. He had to do something. He couldn't leave, and he couldn't sit and watch her dig her own grave. He'd find a cart and start removing the rubble at the base of the walls himself.

CHAPTER 13

Konnor picked up a rock and tossed it onto a pile of stones in the garden cart. It landed with a loud *bang*. He'd been working for a while through the pain tearing his ankle apart.

The northern castle wall loomed over him into a blue sky. The two guards standing on the wall threw curious glances at him from time to time. Despite the sun, the wind bit the skin of his bare back, wet from sweat.

He didn't get women. First, Marjorie wanted his help. Now, she wanted him gone. What exactly had changed? All he'd done was give his advice, just like she'd wanted. Ignoring the pain from the callused, raw skin on his palms, he leaned down and grabbed another rock, his nostrils flaring, his blood still fuming at Marjorie's dismissal.

He threw it onto the pile and straightened, breathing in deeply to calm himself. The air was rich with the scents of fishy, lake water that came from the loch, flowers, and dung. Sheep were grazing peacefully nearby, and Konnor tracked the herd with his eyes and then looked into the woods he and Marjorie had come out of. The stream he and Marjorie had followed on their way to the castle two days ago would take him back to the ruin with the magical rock. He could leave and get back to his time and to civilization. Then he could forget all this BS.

Yes, he'd get back home. He'd make sure his mom was okay, visit her twice a week like he'd always done. Do some repairs on the house, take out the garbage, run errands for her, and keep her company. She'd cook and show him the new paintings she'd completed. She'd picked up painting after Jerry's death at the suggestion of her therapist, and it had been really good for her.

Her art used to be dark, a combination of black colors and reds, but with time, they became lighter and started varying in themes: a sunny Californian beach, the landscape of the Rocky Mountains in a snowstorm, flowers, and such.

Before his trip to Scotland, he'd brought her groceries and she'd showed him the painting portraying a lonely ship in a turbulent sea. Something about the dark waves, the black sky, and that sole white triangle of a sail had shot right into his heart. Did she feel lonely like that?

Or did he?

"Mom, this is really good," he'd said with what felt like a stone in his throat. "I'm no expert, but you should show this to someone. How many do you have now in your shed?"

She'd waved her hand at him and chuckled. Her blue eyes had dimmed as she'd looked at it. She'd tucked her blond lock behind her ear. "I've no idea. Hundreds, maybe? Ten years' worth of pain and seventeen years' worth of therapy, hon."

Therapy, yeah. Thank God for therapy. With the years, she'd even started dressing with more colors. Blank, gray sweaters and pants were replaced with flowy, light tops, long, colorful skirts. She'd started dyeing her hair regularly and tried new haircuts. She'd even hosted a weekly book club at her home where, from what she'd told him, she and her friends mostly drank wine and chatted.

"You're good, Mom," Konnor had insisted. "They belong in a gallery."

"Ah, stop it." She'd stood up, holding her lower back with one hand and the painting with the other. The earrings one of her friends had made with sea glass clanked. "All my artwork is like entries in my personal journal. Who'd want to buy my therapy? By the way, I thought of you when I was doing this one."

Konnor's chest had tightened. Had she perceived his loneliness? She was his mom, so he shouldn't be surprised. Yeah, he was lonely. A part of him did want a relationship, a real connection. But that was impossible. He'd only hurt the woman with his inability to open up.

He'd taken out two thousand dollars and laid the bills on the coffee table. "This should be enough until I'm back."

She'd stared at the money. "This is too much, Konnor."

"Just in case. I won't be here, so who knows. I'll feel better if you have a bit more than you need."

Yeah, he'd be back, and she'd show him another painting. He'd continue managing his business. He'd need to hire more guys, because he was getting more and more inquiries from Hollywood.

He'd remember Marjorie. He'd torture himself thinking about how he'd left her in the midst of danger when he'd promised to protect her. Glenkeld didn't stand a chance in the condition it was in. The image of her, wounded and bleeding, invaded his mind. Her dark-brown hair spilled on the ground, her eyes darkening with death. Pain gripped his throat, and he stopped to take a breather.

But what could he do? She didn't want his help. He was alone, hurling these damned rocks. And besides, Marjorie was right. He didn't know this world. He did need to listen to her, not just boss her around.

Konnor had seen people die in a battle before—his friends

and Marine buddies who'd gone too early. Every time he thought of them, sharp pain pierced his chest.

He couldn't save everyone, but he could swallow his pride, go back to the castle, and find a way to work *together* with Marjorie to protect her.

Yes, he'd only met her a few days ago. He didn't really know her. But he felt for her much more than he wanted to admit. The Highland queen could bring him to his knees. What had happened to her connected them beyond words, even though she didn't know it. He just couldn't walk away.

Did he believe in destiny? Not really. Not until now, anyway. But after he'd found out about the common threads in their pasts, Isbeil's words about finding the person you're really destined for by traveling through the stone didn't sound as absurd as it should.

Fact was, Konnor couldn't live with himself if he up and left Marjorie in peril now. He just couldn't. He had to try to make this right.

And the way to make this right lay with him opening up to her and working together with her. And that could cost him so much more than she could ever imagine.

That could cost him his heart.

MARJORIE RAN THE BLADE OF HER CLAYMORE ACROSS THE whetstone, and it let out a satisfying *whoosh*. The blade didn't really need sharpening, but after Konnor left the council, she'd needed an excuse to do something physical to distract herself.

Going out riding would have been good, but she was not going to set foot outside the castle, not while MacDougalls could be out there, waiting for her to make one mistake.

She was so mad with Konnor. What an infuriating man. She'd only asked for his advice and help as a soldier. She hadn't expected him to lay out a whole strategy in front of her and her men and completely undermine what she had in mind.

The truth was, it was her pride that hurt. She was inexperienced, but she was in charge of the castle and her whole clan. She needed to appear like she knew what she was doing. And he'd pointed out she didn't.

She ran the blade over the stone again, her hands warm in the blacksmith's gloves.

"I think it's already sharp enough," Konnor said.

Marjorie's heart gave a lurch and galloped against her rib cage. She looked up. He stood in the doorway to the smithy. Marjorie straightened and brushed her forehead with the back of her gloved hand. Her cheeks burned, but that must be from the exercise, surely not because he was looking at her like that with his handsome eyes. How could a man have such long eyelashes? And what was that pleasant warmth spreading in her stomach at the sight of him?

"Did ye need something?"

"Yes. I need to keep my word."

"Oh?"

"I promised to help you, to do anything to protect you. In my life, I've seen enough people harmed, and I couldn't do anything about that. But I can do something to try help save you."

Marjorie's heart jumped again. Those words melted something within her. Was he being truthful? Could she trust him? He was a stranger, after all, no matter how dashing and charming.

"Why? Why is it so important for ye to stay and save me? I'm no one to ye. It seemed just yesterday all ye wanted was to go back to...wherever it is that you came from."

"You helped me," he said. "I'm a soldier and a bodyguard. I won't be able to live with myself if I don't try to protect you."

She studied him. A grimace of inner turmoil flickered across his face. "Nae, there's something more."

He walked into the smithy and stood by her side, his eyes on the sword. In the semidarkness of the workshop, the outside world disappeared. All she could hear was the sound of her heart drumming in her ears.

His hand lay casually next to hers. "Yes. There is. I know the pain you went through."

Her breath fled her chest.

"Ye were—"

"Not me." He met her gaze, and she choked from the pain in his eyes. "Someone very close to me, though."

She looked down, and her vision blurred. "I dinna need anyone to point out I'm weak," she whispered. "That I'm nae suited for the role of protector of the castle. That I need to show some courage."

Konnor reached out and gently lifted her chin, making her look at him. "That's not at all how I meant it. I think... I think you're the strongest woman I know."

Her throat convulsed painfully as she tried to swallow the tears. She shook her head. "How? I've trained to be a warrior for years, and yet I havna been in a real battle. Yesterday, if it wasna for ye, I'd have lost my son to the MacDougalls. I proved I couldnae defend him in my own home."

He removed his hand, and she quickly wiped her eyes and then ran the other side of the sword across the stone. She put the blade against the light and inspected the edge. It ran smooth and was blemish-free, like the first ice on the loch. Perfect. Sharp.

"Trust me, I dinna need an outlander to remind me how little chance we have under my leadership."

"Look, Marjorie"—he gently took her hands in his and lowered the sword—"you are the best chance the castle has because you care about it like no one else. Because no one else has been through what you've been through, and no one will put their heart and body on the line like you will."

Something released in her chest, and she breathed easier.

"And what you lack in knowledge and experience," Konnor continued, "that's what teamwork is for. You have Malcolm, who looks like he's seen his fair share of battles. And you have Tamhas. You have your warriors. And you have me."

She sank into the blue sea of his eyes, and everything around her blurred but him.

"If you let me stay and help."

Jesu, his voice enveloped and caressed her, bringing her soothing relief. His face was so close, she could see every bristle on his square jaw. How would it feel if she touched him? Sharp and raw? Or smooth? She'd like either. His eyes were dark blue, like the loch before rain. Oh, she could sink in them, let them take her into their depths.

"Aye," she said. "If ye wilna speak to me like that again."

He nodded, and a playful chuckle slipped past his lips. "I didn't mean to offend you or to imply you're incompetent. I should have asked what you had in mind first. I need to learn how you do things...here. So I'll listen to what you have to say and suggest we work together. Good enough?"

Marjorie smiled. Hope blossomed inside her. "I'm nae master of diplomacy, either."

Their eyes locked, and Marjorie flew high up into a warm cloud of sunlight.

"And I was thinking, maybe you could teach me to fight with a sword," Konnor said.

The idea of fighting with him, seeing his big arms swinging a sword, weakened her knees. "Aye, I can do that. And I'd like to hear more of what ye suggested about removing the rubble and building the stakes as a means of defense."

"Good," he said. "I've already started."

"But what of yer leg? Can ye train with it?"

He shrugged. "I think so." He gently took the sword out of her hands. "We can start with you showing me how to sharpen this."

She became aware of his scent filling her nostrils, that foreign, fresh scent of the sea and heather. And magic.

Her mouth was dry, so she licked her lips. She removed her gloves and gave them to him, and he laid the sword on the anvil so he could put them on.

"Take the sword, pick the part ye want to sharpen. Place yer hands so that they border that part."

He did, but he picked only a small section of the sword.

"Nae." She put her hands on his and guided them farther apart. Her arm touched his, and a small lightning bolt of excitement jolted through her. Her breath quickened. Without removing her hands, she helped him place the flat side of the sword against the stone.

"Now slide it forward, nae too strong and nae too gentle, like so." She made a movement, and her side connected with his. She buzzed from the touch, the feeling unfamiliar and beautiful. She wanted more. She couldn't let go yet.

They repeated the movement again, and Marjorie's skin melted against his. She felt him looking at her and glanced up from the blade. He was so close and was watching her with anguish in his eyes. And heat.

Just lean forward, and ye'll find his lips. How will they feel? Hard or soft? How will they taste?

Someone coughed, and Marjorie jumped back and away from Konnor. Colin stood in the doorway, eyeing Konnor as though the man had just killed someone.

"Ma," Colin said, scowling at her and Konnor, "Malcolm sent me to tell ye the blacksmith approves of the plan. He can begin forging the spikes."

Marjorie bit her lip. Her poor boy hadn't been himself since yesterday. He was anxious and worried, and she was trying to occupy him with different tasks around the castle to distract him.

She'd taken some of Konnor's suggestions after she'd thought about them. Once she'd cooled off, she'd realized

Konnor was right about many things. She needed to tell the blacksmith the edges needed to be sharp enough to prevent the men from holding on to them. "Good. Verra good. I'm coming."

Disappointed she'd need to separate from Konnor, she took her claymore from Konnor's hands. "I'll see ye later. For the training."

Without waiting for his answer, she marched towards Colin, kissed him on the head, and walked out of the smithy into the fresh air. But even that didn't cool the fire in her veins.

Konnor had awoken something in her—something she'd thought she'd never get to experience in her life. And it was surprising, and wonderful, and scary. She didn't know what exactly it was, but it reached to her very soul.

Nae. Best to nae touch him or get closer.

She had a feeling getting close to Konnor would put her in danger of being heartbroken like never before, but she wasn't sure she'd be able to resist.

CHAPTER 14

Konnor studied Colin's wooden sword and shifted his weight uncomfortably. What did one say to an eleven-year-old boy?

"So ye're the man my mother found in the woods?" Colin said. "And the one who saved me."

The words "saved me" sounded more accusatory than grateful.

Konnor cleared his throat. "Yeah. I suppose I am."

"Why did ye come here?"

"I...got hurt." Konnor gestured at his ankle. "Your mom helped me."

Colin tapped his foot, still scowling at Konnor. "So why dinna ye leave?"

"Because I want to help. To protect your mother from the bad guys."

Like I wish someone had protected my mom back then. Like I wish I had.

"She dinna need yer protection. She has me. And she has Tamhas. If anyone will marry my mother, it will be him."

Colin looked Konnor over with his estimating, smart eyes, and without another word, he left the smithy.

Konnor stared at the empty, sunlit doorway. What was the saying? A bull in a china shop? That was exactly how he felt with kids.

He had no idea what a healthy family looked like. Yeah, it was good he'd decided to never marry. What could he offer as a husband and father after what he'd seen in his childhood?

He remembered his own father vaguely. What did Konnor really know about him? His dad's last words to Konnor were the brightest memory he had. Most of the time, his father had been deployed, and then he'd died, and it was Konnor and his mom against Jerry.

The taste of ash in his mouth, he limped into the court-yard. *Clunk. Clunk. Clunk.* Swords clashed against each other as a dozen or so men sparred on the sunlit, dirt-packed courtyard. The walls of the castle loomed in a granite square.

He saw Colin run towards Tamhas, who stopped training with another man and tousled the boy's hair. Colin, his shoulders sagging, looked up at Tamhas. The two talked, and the man threw his head back, laughing with the boy.

Tamhas bent down, put his sword on the ground, and picked up a sparring stick. He took up a position, bending his knees and holding the sword at his right shoulder. With a chuckle, he nodded to Colin, who took the same position with his wooden sword. The two sparred, Tamhas crying out commands and encouragements to Colin. A perfect picture of a father-son relationship.

Konnor swallowed the bitterness in his mouth. Tamhas should be with Marjorie. He knew her history and clearly cared about her and Colin. He could protect them. He knew the rules of this medieval world.

What was Konnor even doing here? He was in over his head, pretending, lying to himself that he could protect a mother and her son against an army. She clearly had people who could do it much better than him.

The sense of helplessness he knew and hated took over his

body. The helplessness he'd been fighting against his whole life. The helplessness he'd thought had disappeared when Jerry died.

No. Konnor wouldn't let himself be like that. He was a Marine. He fought terrorists and pirates and took bullets and fought for his country. The whole reason he'd joined the military was to protect others like he wished he could've shielded himself and his mother. Could he keep a woman and her son safe?

He didn't know. But seeing Colin brought out the roaring, sucking darkness within him that he had locked away. Every day that he'd served in the Marines had put lock after lock and bolt after bolt over it.

All he knew was he'd rather die than let harm come to Marjorie or Colin. And that meant he needed to put his self-doubt aside and get to work.

CHAPTER 15

The next morning, Konnor's ankle felt even better as he went down to the great hall for porridge. Isbeil had looked at it last night and said it was healing better than she'd expected. Because his cargo pants were dusty and dirty, and his T-shirt reeked of sweat, he asked for some fresh clothes before he went for a swim in the loch, hoping it would be a good enough replacement for a shower.

Dressed in breeches and a long, belted linen tunic that reached to his knees, he felt like he'd put on a costume for a historical movie set, except there were no cameras and no director. He kept his comfortable hiking shoes on. He was the only one who didn't wear pointy medieval shoes. Thank God for small favors.

Two pairs of men sparred with swords in one corner of the courtyard. A rhythmic *tong-tong-tong* came from the smithy, which was in another corner of the courtyard. A donkey pulled a cart full of rocks through the open gates, its large, wooden wheels squeaking lamentably. In another corner, men were constructing what looked like a sawbuck: a simple wooden construction with planks hammered in the form of an *X* at each end and joined by a large log at the intersections. They'd use it to hold wood while it was cut into pieces.

As he approached the great hall, Marjorie came through the doors. He shouldn't be surprised she could make such a simple act of walking look sexy, but she did. Her hips moved under her tunic in a graceful, catlike motion. Unlike female servants he'd seen walking about, Marjorie wore men's clothes: a tunic and breeches similar to those that hugged his muscled legs. But on Marjorie, they hung like harem pants. Unlike any women he'd seen, she also had a sword on her belt. Her hair was up in a braid that lay over her shoulder and chest. Dark locks framed her face and waved in the wind.

When their eyes met, her red lips parted, and a small expression of joy flashed across her face. She came to stop a step or so in front of him, and her herbal, berry scent reached him. Was she blushing? The thought spread warmth in his chest. He itched to brush her flushed cheek with his knuckles. In the dim light of a cloudy day, her skin glowed like polished stone against her dark hair. If Snow White existed, she'd look like Marjorie. She was the most beautiful woman he'd ever seen.

They stared at each other for a moment or so, and he felt a stupid grin spread on his face.

"Hey," he said.

"Good day to ye, Konnor." She nodded a little and bit her lip, as though to stop a smile from blossoming on her face. She looked him over. "Are ye feeling better?"

He lifted his ankle and moved his foot. There was pain, but he'd had much worse than that. He chuckled. "I'll live."

"Good. Do ye think ye can manage a sword-fighting lesson today?"

"Sure."

She beamed. "Then please break yer fast and then come join me here when ye're ready." She walked away from him towards the sparring men.

"I'll see you in a bit."

She looked back. "Ye keep saying that, but ye must tell me what ye mean by this one of these days."

Konnor didn't think he'd ever wolfed down a meal this fast. He shoved spoonfuls of tasteless porridge into his mouth. The hall was quite empty, but the men who were eating threw curious glances at him. A servant girl he hadn't seen in the castle before stopped to chat with him, but he managed to get out of her curious questions with one-word answers. He just wanted to be done with food and go to wherever Marjorie was.

He went out into the cloudy day and made his way straight to Marjorie. She stood talking to Tamhas with two long, round sticks in her hands that she put against the ground like ski poles.

Tamhas loomed over her, a wry smile on his face that Konnor knew right away was the smile of a man who was attracted to the woman he was talking to. He didn't like that one bit. A stab of jealousy in his gut made him want to punch the man in the face. But he had no right to do that. She wasn't his. He'd be gone soon anyway. She'd be better off with a man from her time.

As Konnor walked, her sweet voice reached his ears, resonating straight in his chest like the vibration of a tuning fork. She caught his gaze, and everything in his life began making sense again.

Tamhas stared at him with open animosity. "Konnor," he said when Konnor came to stand by Marjorie's side. "Ye're nae gone yet."

"I have no intention of leaving until I'm sure Marjorie and Colin are safe," he said.

"There are other people who can make sure of that," he said.

"All right." Marjorie raised her hands with the sticks. "All right. Are ye ready to train, Konnor?"

"Ready is my middle name, Snow White," he said.

Tamhas walked to stand next to the wall with his arms folded over his chest and scowled at Konnor.

Marjorie handed him one of the sticks. "Who is Snow White, and why did ye call me that?"

"Because you remind me of Snow White."

Konnor weighed the stick in his right hand, then in his left.

She came to stand next to him. "Bend yer knees like so, and always keep them bent. This will give ye flexibility."

How hard could this be? He thought of *Star Wars* and every historical action movie he'd seen. Copying the heroes from those movies, he held the stick vertically with both hands by his right shoulder and bent his knees a little, the standard fighting position from judo. Marjorie watched him with an amused look on her face.

She moved his hands to hold the handle of the stick higher than his shoulder. Her touch sent a sweet wave of tingling through his arms. Their eyes locked, and he forgot how to breathe as he sank into the pale jade of her irises.

"And who's Snow White?" She stepped back from him, though her eyes were still on him.

Konnor remembered the original Brothers Grimm fairy tale. His mom had told him she'd discussed it in her book club. "She's a princess from a fairy tale. She was chased away from her castle and taken in by seven dwarfs, who protected her and sheltered her from the evil that chased her."

She swallowed. "Oh, aye?"

"But the evil found her."

She blinked. "And then what?"

"She bit into a poisoned apple and fell into a deep sleep. Thinking she was dead, the dwarfs put her in a crystal coffin."

Her face was unreadable. "Huh."

"And then a prince came." Konnor lowered the sword, his arms suddenly refusing to cooperate, and rasped, "And the prince found her in the crystal coffin."

She didn't say anything, but her cheeks flushed.

"And he woke her up."

She sighed and shook her head once. "What about the evil?"

"The prince dealt with the evil for her."

Marjorie arched one brow. "Right. Well, I dinna see why I remind ye of this Snow White. Take yer position, Konnor. Time to spar."

He chuckled and did as she asked.

"And by the way"—she grasped the stick with both her hands and took the position—"I dinna think a prince can wake someone who's been poisoned by evil. And the prince shouldn't fight Snow White's battles."

Konnor tilted his head, studying her, fascinated. She bent her knees, assuming a fighting stance, and looked at him from under her brows. "Aim to cut my neck off. Attack."

Her voice sounded like it were made of steel. Christ, how pretty she looked, this warrior queen, with her back straight, and her arms holding the stick at her shoulder. Konnor bounced on his heels up and down, still careful not to put too much weight on the ankle.

He'd be careful not to hurt her, of course. The thought of accidentally hitting her or pushing her lay uncomfortably at the back of his mind. Though he'd sparred many times with female partners in his judo classes and served with female soldiers in the military, the thought of harming Marjorie in any way was disturbing.

He moved forward, bringing the stick down, mindful not to use all his strength, and aimed for her neck, as she'd directed. But she deflected his stick with surprising strength and a loud *knock*. She made a circular movement he didn't see coming until it was too late, and his stick lay on the ground.

Whoa. He'd seen her spar with other warriors, and she was incredible. But it was one thing to see it, and quite another to experience that this gorgeous female could kick his ass.

"Pick it up." Her lips curved in a wry, satisfied smile. "Attack. Don't hold back. As ye see, I can take it."

Konnor leaned down and picked up his stick. She was no fragile flower. She was a Snow White who could fight her own battles against evil.

"I see I need to watch my ass," he said and took the position.

"Come on," she said, stepping back several steps to give him space to attack her.

With a lightness in the center of his diaphragm, like the joy of a game, something he hadn't felt often, he moved towards her. Hesitation pulled at his arms as he brought the stick down on her, but she met his blow with a strong, precise counter-strike. He slashed at her with his stick again, and she deflected. He hit for the third time, and she protected herself with the ease of a master.

She was good.

"Come on, Konnor!" she shouted with fervor and a huge grin that lit up her face. "Harder."

He couldn't stop the grin on his own face. She bit her lip. "I dinna think I've seen ye smile before," she said. "We should train more often."

He found himself thinking that as long as he could put a smile like that on her face, he was ready to do anything.

He came at her, attacking with a different feeling now. He knew she could take it, and he knew she was a master. What a woman. She'd been through a lot, and yet she'd risen above and gained more strength and power than before. The experience hadn't broken her. It had molded her like fire could shape steel.

He reached a state he'd often gotten to in judo training—when he let his mind take a back seat and his body took over. They danced in the courtyard, exchanging blows, fluid and connected. She let him attack, and she deflected and then attacked him, too, giving him a run for his money.

The sticks clunked together, and Marjorie rained blows down on him. Left, right, left, right. His ankle ached, the muscles in his shoulders strained from the exercise. He missed a block or two and groaned as her stick landed on his ribs and his hip. She certainly didn't go easy on him.

He backed up, retreating to protect himself from her attack, and his foot caught on something. His bad ankle gave in with a sharp snap of pain. He tripped, and Marjorie leaned towards him, as though trying to hold on to him so he wouldn't fall. He caught her sleeve, and they both tumbled down.

He landed on his back, her warm and soft weight pleasant on top of him. The smell of her, flowery and musky from the exercise, combined with her breasts pressed against him and her legs spread, made him harden. She felt it. Her eyes widened, her lips parted, and her eyebrows snapped together.

What the devil was he doing, getting hard like that? He didn't give a damn about anyone's reaction but hers. He must have frightened her, probably triggered memories or something. But she didn't look afraid. Her lips were so close, he could just lean forward an inch and kiss her.

She actually looked like she was...

Excited?

Realization widened her eyes, and fear flickered through them. She pushed herself off him, red-cheeked, her eyes watering.

Tamhas was at her side in a moment.

"Mistress?" he said, standing between her and Konnor. She hugged herself.

Konnor slowly stood. "I didn't mean anything."

"I dinna feel so good," she said. "Mayhap 'tis best ye continue yer training with Tamhas."

She turned and walked away, retreating to her tower. Konnor helplessly watched her hunched form, feeling like shit. Tamhas looked at him, an angry snarl forming on his upper lip.

"Did ye hurt her?" he barked.

"No," Konnor said, watching the entrance to the tower where she'd just disappeared.

"What happened?" Tamhas said.

What happened was he'd exposed her to something she was still not ready for. He should really stay away from her. The last thing she needed was a guy getting horny around her like that.

"I must have bruised her, after all," Konnor murmured.

Tamhas stepped towards Konnor and stabbed his index finger at him. "Ye wilna touch her again."

"Trust me, buddy," Konnor said, picking up the stick. "I have no intention to."

He turned to Tamhas and nodded at Marjorie's stick on the ground. "Are we doing this thing or what?"

Scowling at Konnor, Tamhas picked up the stick. "I wilna go easy on ye."

"I don't want you to." Konnor stood in a fighting stance, actually looking forward to blowing off some steam and trying to beat the shit out of this guy. Finally, sparring man-to-man.

As Tamhas came at him, thrusting the stick vigorously, Konnor thought she deserved to be loved and cherished. Someone needed to help her heal. That man wasn't him. He wasn't going to be here long and would head back to his real life as soon as he knew she was safe.

And until then, he'd make sure he kept his distance.

CHAPTER 16

Marjorie panted, leaning on the hard, cold rock of the wall.

Air. She needed air. There wasn't enough of it, even up on the castle wall with the whole sky above her like an endless ceiling and the ground far below.

What had just happened? A man had gotten excited because of her. That was something natural for a normal woman. But she wasn't normal. She was damaged. She was hurt. She was still broken.

She—the warrior who'd trained for years—had gotten scared.

It had been wonderful to spar with Konnor. He was a good partner, though obviously inexperienced in swordsmanship. But laughing with him, smiling with him, and just breathing the same air with him had made her feel alive. When the unmistakable, hard bulge between Konnor's legs pressed into her lower belly, it had taken her breath away.

Not because she was disgusted or afraid.

Because she'd gotten excited. Something warm and pleasant had flashed in her core, a place she'd only known as a source of pain and torture before.

And that was terrifying. It was new and wonderful and completely unexpected. Was that the feeling all regular women had with a man? Was that a glimpse of healing for her?

And if so, why was it so frightening? Why did the hope mix with dread in her soul and tighten her lungs as though they'd shrunk to the size of a ball of yarn?

She knew why. She couldn't trust another man after what Alasdair had done to her. She was dirty. Stained. Used like a worthless piece of cloth.

Tears welled and fell down her cheeks, leaving burning traces. She leaned with her back against the wall and slid down until she sat on the cold, dirty floor. She hid her face in her palms.

She wanted to be normal. She wanted to be a regular woman who could fall in love and be mindlessly happy. But how could she if deep inside she was still that tormented and abused lass, helpless and desperate.

Konnor was right. In a way, she was in a crystal coffin after being poisoned by evil, trapped somewhere between death and sleep. Could a prince really wake her up? Could Konnor?

"Lass?" Isbeil's voice said, and Marjorie raised her head. The woman stood at the entrance to the tower, leaning against the hard stone with one hand. Her dark eyes pierced Marjorie —the perceptive eyes of a healer, and the caring eyes of a friend. She was the closest thing Marjorie had to a mother, even though her stepmother—Domhnall, Owen, and Lena's mother—who had died a few years ago, had been nothing but supportive and loving.

Isbeil and Owen were the two people who'd helped her heal after she'd gotten back from Dunollie Castle.

"Isbeil..." she whispered and felt her face grimace as another wave of wailing hit.

"All right, all right. Ye calm down," Isbeil soothed. "I am coming. Ye ken how I dinna like the height." She began to slowly make her way towards Marjorie without lifting her feet from the floor, instead shuffling them against it. She still held on to the wall. "A man isna meant to be so high above the ground," she mumbled. "Why couldnae ye have chosen to cry somewhere in yer room, lass? I'm coming. I'm coming. Dinna ye fash."

Marjorie watched the short woman approach, her wrinkled face stony in concentration. The simple brown dress swiped the floor as she wobbled on her short legs towards Marjorie.

Ah! How could Marjorie sit and cry and feel sorry for herself when the old woman was going above and beyond for her? Hastily wiping her tears away, she stood and hurried to Isbeil. She supported the old woman under her elbow. Isbeil was holding her fist to her chest.

"Are ye all right, Isbeil?" Marjorie said.

The old crone looked up at her, her weathered, wrinkled face suddenly lit up in a wide grin of empty spaces and remaining yellow teeth.

"Aye, lassie," she said and clapped Marjorie's hand that supported her. "I am. And so are ye. See, when ye're too busy caring for others, somehow ye forget to indulge in yer own sorrow."

Marjorie scoffed. "I should have ken ye'd just trick me."

"I didna trick ye. I dinna like this height one bit. What happened?" Isbeil covered her hand with her dry and warm one. "Is it that time traveler?"

Marjorie's face fell. "Time traveler? Ye dinna believe him, do ye?"

Isbeil cocked her head to one side and raised her chin to look behind the merlon. "I went to the ruins, lass, to look for the rock he mentioned." She looked sharply at Marjorie. "'Tis there. Flat, large, and with a handprint. A handprint in a rock as though it used to be clay and someone laid a hand in it."

Marjorie let go of Isbeil's hand. "That doesna mean he traveled in time."

Isbeil sighed and pressed her fists against her hips. "Nae

that alone. But I felt it—the faerie magic. Aye, that place is saturated with it. 'Tis like the scent of lavender. And when I touched the rock... It shifted the air as though a great many invisible butterflies were flapping their wings around the rock. And although I didna see the faerie herself, I kent she was there, mayhap watching me from behind a tree."

A chill went through Marjorie. Was the old healer finally mad? Marjorie didn't know how old Isbeil was, but she'd been wrinkled and aged for as long as Marjorie could remember. As small children, Marjorie, Craig, Owen, Domhnall, and Lena had huddled together by the brazier in the great hall, listening to Isbeil telling her Highland stories. Her small black eyes reflected the orange flames, her mouth dark against the leatherlike skin. The children had been afraid to go near the loch for at least a year, afraid that a kelpie would come out of the water and take them.

"Are ye thinking the auld Isbeil's lost her mind?" Isbeil said with a sad smile.

Marjorie didn't reply. Isbeil was family. Her whole life, Marjorie knew she could trust the woman like she could trust herself. And although she didn't believe in the legends and stories of faeries and ancient heroes, she'd been raised on them, drinking them in like her mother's milk, alongside the stories from the Bible.

Something within her knew that if Isbeil told her Konnor was a time traveler, he was, no matter how mad it sounded. Together with the strangeness of Konnor's speech, his clothes, the words he used, his manners, even his hair, it all suddenly came into a complete picture, and she knew.

"Nae, Isbeil," she said. "I believe ye."

He had traveled in time. He told the truth. And somehow, the wild mixture of hope and dread in her soul tilted to the side of hope. And Konnor entered the very secure and guarded circle of people she could trust within her soul.

Only that fact meant that sooner rather than later, Konnor

would need to return to his time and disappear from Marjorie's life forever.

CHAPTER 17

Marjorie's pulse jumped as someone came into the great hall. She glanced over her cup of ale, hoping to see a certain head of brown hair and a pair of broad shoulders that made her mouth go dry. Instead, it was Alpin, one of the warriors.

Damn it.

She hadn't seen Konnor since their sword training. Where was he? It was evening mealtime, and almost everyone was here, filling the room with the hum of voices. Her great chair was hard and smooth under her fingers, and the warm air was stuffy from the number of people.

Everyone looked exhausted, but unlike yesterday and the days before, the atmosphere was cheerful. As though after a hard day of work, they'd seen some progress. Eyes were brighter, shoulders straighter, chins higher. There was even the occasional laughter here and there.

It was more than Marjorie could have asked from them, given that many of them could die defending the castle very soon.

A man came in. No crutch.

Konnor.

He was tall and so handsome her stomach squeezed, and her knees went weak. He glanced at her, nodded curtly, and went to sit at one of the tables with other warriors. Without talking to anyone, he rounded his shoulders over a bowl of stew and ate. Marjorie gestured to Muir, who always kept an eye on her.

"Aye, mistress?"

"Please tell Konnor to come eat with me."

His eyes hardened, but he didn't protest. "Aye."

Marjorie's heart fluttered like a bird in her chest as Muir came to Konnor and leaned to speak into his ear. Konnor glanced at Marjorie, his mouth set in a line, but he nodded and stood up with his bowl and hobbled to her.

Muir watched him approach, and he wasn't the only one. It felt like every pair of eyes in the hall were on Konnor and her.

Konnor took the seat next to Marjorie's and looked at her expectantly, his impossibly blue eyes hard.

"You wanted me?" he said.

Oh, she did. She craved his presence near her like the warmth of a fire in the freezing, dark depths of winter. The intensity of it both scared and excited her. She'd never wanted to be near someone like she wanted to be near him. In the few days she'd known him, she'd become more attached to him than she'd ever been to anyone. How could she have grown to care so much for someone in only a few days? And what did this all mean?

Despite everything, she couldn't distance herself from him.

"Aye." She cleared her throat. "Drink?"

He nodded, and she poured some uisge from a jug into a nearby empty cup. He cocked his head as a way of thanking her and downed the contents of the cup. Then he grimaced.

"Hmm." He looked at the cup dubiously. "Again with the moonshine."

Marjorie hid a smile. "I talked to Isbeil. She went to the

ancient fortress to see the rock for herself. She found it and believes yer story about falling through time."

Konnor raised one eyebrow and leaned back. "Oh, yes? And what about you?"

Marjorie straightened her shoulders. "I do, too. She's never been wrong in her life. She knows those things, magic and such."

"So you didn't believe me before?"

"Nae. Nae completely."

"But you believe her?"

"Aye."

She wanted to add that she was sorry but stopped herself. She didn't owe him an apology for suspecting he might be a threat. But she loved the glimpse of trust that had emerged between them after he'd saved her from the MacDougalls, and she wanted to keep it.

He sighed and poured more uisge into his cup, a small smile on his lips. "Look, I don't blame you. I wouldn't have believed someone talking about time travel, either."

Relief eased the tension in her chest. "But now I want to ken everything about yer world. Tell me about the future." Eager to hear his stories, she shifted to the edge of her seat and tangled her hands together on the table.

He chuckled. "What do you want to know?"

"Everything. The words ye mentioned, the hospital, phone, ambulance... How do people live? What do they eat? Drink? How do they dress?"

He leaned closer to her, and she shifted towards him, too.

"I do have something very important to say," he said and raised the cup. "You Scotsmen make a much better whiskey than this in my time."

He threw the cup back and groaned.

"Whiskey?"

"Well, it's not like this moonshine in the future, I can tell you that for sure. The stuff is exquisite. I suppose history needs a couple of hundred years before you guys can catch up."

"Good. Ye like a Scots drink." She waved her hand. "What else?"

"There are huge machines"—he drew even nearer and his scent reached her—"called airplanes that fly in the air. They transport people across the ocean in a matter of hours."

Marjorie's head spun. Machines? Oceans? Airplanes? What were all those things?

"Are ye telling me people can fly?" she said.

"With the help of technology. Yes."

Goose bumps covered Marjorie's skin. She imagined something like a dragon from stories and people sitting on its back. Aye, that would be a fast way to travel.

"What else?" she said, moving an inch towards him.

"A hospital is where sick people get treated. They have cured many diseases you guys have now, and people live much longer in the future. Older people get their hips replaced with artificial ones made of metal. Dying in childbirth is not as big a threat as it is in your time. Thankfully. Organs that don't work can get replaced."

The noises in the great hall quieted. She stopped seeing anyone else in the room. Only Konnor existed sitting before her, and those images he created in her head. Marjorie listened with an open mouth, her imagination running wild. It all sounded like skilled witchcraft being widely accepted and practiced. Colin would love to see it all.

"Do people in the future develop magic skills?"

Konnor laughed softly and shook his head. Marjorie smiled with him. He had the most beautiful smile. His teeth were so white, and dimples that were invisible on his usually stern face formed on his cheeks.

"I'm sorry, I'm not laughing at you," he said. "It's just so adorable you said magic."

She wasn't offended. She hadn't thought he was laughing at

her. He reached out and brushed his knuckles against her cheek. The touch sent a current of pleasant tingles through her.

"It does sound like witchcraft," he said. "But it's not. It's science. Technology. The world has developed so much since all this."

He looked around, and Marjorie cleared her throat, suddenly aware she was sitting way too close to him. Their heads were practically touching.

She moved farther away from him, sorry the magic spell had to be broken.

"What about houses? Horses? Or do people fly everywhere in yer time?"

"No. Instead of horses, we have cars. They're like your carriages. Like carts with roofs and a steering wheel. They drive fast, sixty to a hundred miles per hour, and they make it easy to move from place to place."

Marjorie burst out a small laugh. "But is that nae witch-craft? A cart that moves on its own?"

He laughed, too, and she echoed him.

"You need to see it for yourself," he said.

Marjorie's smile fell. She would really love to see all this magic. Was that even possible?

"I'd be a very fortunate person to ever get the chance."

"Well. I'm fortunate to be able to see your time. When I get back..."

Suddenly, the good mood was wiped off his face, too.

"What then?" she said.

"No one will believe me if I tell them." He chuckled.

She swallowed, her leg shaking under the table. "Do ye have a wife? Children?"

His mouth flattened in a mournful smile, and he looked down. "No."

"Oh."

Something within her rejoiced that he didn't, but there was a tension in his voice that told her there was more to this.

"Why nae? Ye're a good man... Strong and capable..."

And handsome and stubborn and so sweet.

He looked at her, and she could see his shields were lifted, and longing and endless pain gazed from within his eyes.

"I wouldn't want to inflict my darkness on any woman or child."

She inhaled sharply, studying him, trying to understand what darkness he spoke of. He looked away, and when he met her eyes again, the shields slammed down.

"Doesn't matter," he said. "But it might interest you to hear women have equal rights with men. They work, earn money, they can choose whether to have children or not. There's excellent birth control."

Marjorie's cheeks burned. "Ye mean, women may nae get with child after..."

He looked at her, his eyes dark. "Exactly."

"Ye make it sound so fine, the life in the future."

"It's a damn convenient life, but we have problems, too."

Marjorie traced an indent in the table. She really wanted to see all that for herself. It was impossible, of course.

"Ye've given me much to dream about at night, Konnor," she said.

He locked his eyes with hers, and her mouth went as dry as sand. "Trust me, you've given me plenty to dream about, too."

She let out a small laugh. He was as relaxed as she'd ever seen him. And she hadn't felt at ease like this in a very long time. It was as though they were on their own small island, and no one else existed.

"Tell me," she said softly. "When ye said ye dinna want to inflict yer darkness on a woman, what did ye mean?"

His face fell, and the invisible cocoon around them threatened to break.

"I—"

But she couldn't back down now. "Please, Konnor, I see this weight on yer shoulders. I've told ye the worst thing that has happened to me, the thing I'm ashamed of, the thing that broke me. Almost." She shifted her hand closer to his but didn't touch it. "I want to ken yer darkness, too."

He frowned, anguish on his face. She found the courage, reached out, and covered his hand with hers.

"Will ye tell me?"

His mouth curved crookedly downward. He kept looking at her, obviously torn.

"I'd love to, Marjorie, but I can't. You'll never look at me with that wonder in your eyes again."

She shook her head. "I dinna care. I want the truth. Ugly. Monstrous. Soul-shattering. Tell me the worst."

He inhaled sharply and nodded. He took the jug with uisge and two cups, then rose to his feet.

"Come, take a walk with me."

CHAPTER 18

T hey climbed the stairs of the castle wall, Konnor trying not to watch Marjorie's round behind swinging from side to side before him. Once on the wall, she asked the two sentinels to move to the other tower, telling them she and Konnor would take the watch.

The sun was setting behind the mountains on the other side of the loch. It decorated the still surface of water in a golden, pink, and purple glow, leaving the mountains as black forms. The air chilled Konnor's skin, the wind bringing the aroma of lake water. He breathed in the scent of grass and trees and flowers. It would always remind him of Marjorie. The Highlander warrior queen from the past.

He stood at the parapet and leaned against the merlon, the stones cool under his palms. His ankle ached slightly now, but it felt much better. Still, he avoided putting weight on it. He'd need all the strength he had for the battle.

He looked at Marjorie, who stood by his side, her lush hair cascading down her shoulders and back, the slightest breeze playing with her locks. She turned and met his gaze, a small smile on her lips. The wind brought a single strand of hair across her face, and Konnor itched to reach out and move it away.

Instead, he poured the moonshine into their cups. For homemade liquor, this was excellent. But he missed the good scotch he knew from the twenty-first century.

"Cheers." Konnor clunked his cup with hers and the contents slipped down his throat, leaving a pleasant burning trace.

Was he really going to tell her? He had decided downstairs in the great hall that he would, but even though she'd said she wanted to know his darkest secret, he doubted she'd accept it.

When she found out that he carried the darkness she was so afraid of, he wouldn't be able to stand the look of horror and disgust on her face.

Still, he wanted to tell her. The need itched and pained like a wound in his soul. She'd trusted him with her deepest trauma, and he wanted to do the same. He wanted to give her everything, to be everything for her. To take her pain away. To make her feel safe. To help her see how truly powerful and magnificent she was, this medieval Highlander woman with the most beautiful eyes he'd ever seen.

"Tell me, Konnor," she said.

He took in a lungful of sweet air. "When I was six years old, my dad died, leaving my mom and me alone."

Deep sadness saturated Marjorie's expression. "I am sorry. I ken what 'tis like."

They looked at each other for a long moment, something connecting them deeper than ever before. "Your mother?" he said.

"Aye. My mother died before I could remember her. My father remarried soon, a sweet woman called Christina, the mother of Owen, Domhnall, and Lena."

So she had a stepparent as well... Konnor had never in his life talked about this with anyone, not seriously, not with the possibility of connecting with people about this. At school, he'd been this brooding kid who'd rather solve a problem through violence and acting out than by talking. He'd been a troubled kid and surely on his way to incarceration. That had been his way of dealing with the violent situation at home, the one he couldn't change.

It was only when his mom made him join the soccer team at the age of twelve that he'd learned to channel that violence into a sport. He'd even became a team captain, though only for his soccer skills, not for his ability to make friends.

Konnor fiddled with the cup in his hands. "So you have a good relationship with her?"

"Aye. She was my second mother."

His lips tightened. "Was?"

"She died."

"I'm sorry to hear that."

"Thank ye."

"But I'm glad to hear you had good relationship with her. God knows, you've had enough trauma to deal with in your life. I wasn't that lucky. My mom remarried two years after my dad died. A guy named Jerry. We moved in with him pretty quickly, and about a week after that, he started to—"

His throat contracted. He'd never said the words out loud, not even with his mother. They avoided talking about Jerry altogether, but he'd been there, between them, invisible and omnipresent.

He swallowed what felt like a boulder stuck in his throat. "He beat her," he spat out.

With an effort, he looked at Marjorie. Her eyelashes trembled, and two tight lines formed around her mouth.

"I was eight years old," Konnor said. "And I watched him do that, not able to do a damn thing about it."

"Did he beat ye, too?" she said with an emotionless voice, though her eyes were wet and glistened with the mixture of anger, compassion, and bottomless pain.

"Yeah. But she often ended up taking the hits intended for me."

A tear rolled down her cheek. "Konnor..." she said in a broken voice.

How could his name sound so much like a prayer? How could it resonate in his chest like a painful crack of thunder?

His eyes prickled with burning tears, and he shook them off. But too late. The emotion, her compassion, the fact that he was talking about the biggest trauma in his own life for the first time weakened the chains on the door he'd locked the monsters behind.

They spilled out in a roaring, raging, clawing wave of memories that scraped his insides and hollowed him out.

"That's why I must go back to her."

"Oh." She bit her lip, a mournful expression on her face. Didn't she want him to go?

"I couldn't protect her then, Marjorie," he said as though he felt the need to justify himself. "I must protect her now," he rasped.

"Aye. Of course, ye must take care of yer mother."

She was an angel for saying that, but he still felt like he needed to explain, to make her understand. "I tried to shield her from him. Once. The first time."

Tears burned his eyes, and he pinched the bridge of his nose, willing for them to stay back.

She laid her hand on his shoulder blade, warm and heavy and soothing. "Ye were an eight-year-old lad..." she said. "What could ye have done?"

"Something. I should have called the police."

She didn't reply, and he looked back at her. Right. The puzzled expression. She didn't know who the police were. "They're a law enforcement agency. They make sure there's order and that people follow the law."

"Oh. Aye. Ye should have those. The chief punishes those who break the law, steal, or murder."

"Mom told me not to," he said. "She told me it's just a phase. That Jerry wasn't well, and he'd get better. When I grew up, I realized we needed the money. She'd sold our house when we moved in with him, and she quit her job. She'd given him all the savings we had."

"Could her da or her brothers help?"

"There was no one." He sighed, pushed himself off the merlon, and ran both his palms through his hair. "Just her sister, Tabitha, but I don't think she ever knew. Not until Jerry died and my mom started therapy."

"Therapy?"

He looked at her. "Healing of the soul," he said softly. "That's what my mom calls it."

Marjorie nodded and took a small sip of her uisge. "Aye. 'Tis necessary. I wouldna have done it without my brother Owen and Isbeil. They were the two who helped my soul to heal. And Colin, of course."

"How was it for you to be pregnant with your attacker's child? That couldn't have been easy."

Marjorie pursed her lips, and they reddened against her alabaster skin. "Aye." She lowered her head, and her cheeks blushed. "I hated that bairn every day. The thoughts I had of it in my womb— I'm ashamed of them. Thoughts of ill will. Wishing it the worst... Wishing it the unspeakable."

Konnor's skin chilled. He couldn't imagine Marjorie wishing ill on anyone, let alone her own son.

"But once that wee bairn was in my arms, and I looked into his eyes for the first time, all that disappeared like a bad dream. I saw that there was nothing in him but goodness. I saw that he was a gift of our Lord Jesu Christ. And that he had nothing in common with his evil father, and he never would, as long as I had a say in it. I had to pick myself up and start to live. I had a reason to do so, thanks to my son."

The sweetest smile spread across her lips.

"He's the reason I'm a warrior and nae a ghost hiding from the world in my tower."

Konnor's chest tightened in a sweet ache. What would it be like to love a child like this? He'd never know. Was he even capable of love like that?

"He's a great kid," Konnor said.

Marjorie's eyes widened. "Kid? A goat's bairn?"

Konnor chuckled. "We call children kids where I come from."

Marjorie laughed softly and wiped the remnant of a tear. "Aye, well, he is a wonderful goat's bairn."

Konnor sighed with a big smile.

"But, Konnor, if ye were afraid to tell me that ye and yer mother were beaten and abused by yer stepfather, ye didna need to worry."

He clenched his jaw and swallowed hard. "That's not the darkness I was talking about."

The lightness of the moment would make what he was about to say easier. He met her eyes. Konnor gulped the last of the moonshine. The anguish in his chest numbed a little. She looked at him with compassion, with care. She stood so close he could smell her scent, the one he'd recognize in a crowd. She cared about him. She wanted to know his darkness.

Oh damn.

Was this the last time she would want to stand near him? Would want to talk to him? But there was no way back. He had to tell her the truth. His breath caught, and his gut tightened like he was about to jump into an abyss.

Marjorie, don't hate me.

"I killed him, Marjorie."

Marjorie's face went blank. He'd expected her to gasp in shock or cry or widen her eyes in horror.

No, she was completely frozen. Still like that loch. Silence hung between them. Only crickets chirped, and the leaves rustled gently in the trees. The slight buzz of voices came from down in the great hall.

Fear went through him in cold quivers. There. He'd blown it. It shouldn't matter. There'd never been a chance at a life together for them anyway. But damn it, he felt something for this bewitching woman. Damn it to hell.

"Do you hate me?" Konnor said.

"Hate ye?" Her voice came out with a rasp. "Nae. Of course nae. Craig killed Alasdair. If he didna, and if I'd had strength to, I'd have wanted to do it myself."

He sighed. Relief flooded his veins. But maybe it was only because she didn't realize what it meant.

"I endured his beatings for ten years. One evening, when I was eighteen, I realized I didn't have to anymore. I could fight back. Something snapped in me. A wild anger that I'd harbored for so long took over. I saw red. All I could see was red. I shoved him against the wall and beat him and beat him until my hands were slippery from his blood."

Marjorie's face was as still as a stone mask.

"I looked at my bloody hands, at his face beaten to a pulp, and I hated myself." He closed his eyes, willing to swallow the next words, regretting that he'd said this much out loud. "I became *him*."

Silence fell between them, thick and palpable, like an invisible wall. Planets could've been born and died in the seconds that passed by.

And then she broke it with one word. "Never."

"He was not the first man I'd hit. I was violent after my mom married him, even as a kid Colin's age. If I hadn't gotten into soccer—it's a team sport—I would've kept on getting into fights and stealing stuff. Then I enlisted into the Marines. I'd always wanted to because my dad was a Marine."

He swallowed a painful knot. "As a Marine, I didn't hesitate to kill people, Marjorie."

"Neither did my grandfather, my father, my uncle, and my

brothers." She swallowed. "Neither will I when the MacDougalls come. 'Tis the way of a warrior."

"But—"

"Have ye ever raised yer hand to a woman or a child?"

"No."

"Then ye dinna have a thing in common with him."

Konnor exhaled shakily. Her words seeped through him like a cool balm on a burn wound.

"Disgusted by my actions and afraid I'd finish him, I left the house," Konnor said, "He was alive when I left. I later found out that he made it to his car and tried to drive—probably to a hospital. But on his way there, another car hit him, and he died." His gut churned. "Had I not beaten him, or had I taken him to the hospital, he might be alive today."

The words and the guilt burned his gut like acid.

"I believe 'tis destiny that brought us together," she said. "We share this darkness, this experience with violence. Mayhap because of yer care for an abused woman, ye're the first man I've felt safe with besides my brothers."

She laid her hand on his chest, and Konnor's heart thumped against it. Did she think of him as a brother? His shoulders dropped with disappointment. He wanted her to think of him as a man. But she felt safe with him. That mattered more.

"Ye make me want to have a normal life." She stepped closer so that their hips and stomachs touched. Konnor sank into the depths of her slanted eyes. In the twilight, they were the color of a forest after the rain, and he lost his breath, mesmerized by their magic and mystery.

"Ye make me want to love someone," she whispered. "To kiss someone."

Konnor's blood buzzed. "Do you want to kiss me?"

She exhaled. "Aye. Verra much."

Konnor lifted his hand and cupped her warm, smooth jaw. "I've wanted to do this from the first moment I saw you."

Her eyes sparkled with excitement, anticipation, and desire.

Slowly, to give her the chance to jump back if she changed her mind, he leaned towards her without breaking eye contact. Then gently, he covered her lips with his.

They met him with such softness he thought he would lose his mind. She smelled like a field of wildflowers, of wind and of freedom. He touched her lips softly, then again and again. The silk of her warm mouth and her scent made his head spin and his blood boil.

She gave a barely audible sweet moan.

Damn it.

He wrapped his arms around her, bringing her closer, and pressing his lips against hers harder. She didn't run away. In fact, she wrapped her arms around his neck. He stroked her lips with his tongue, and she parted them.

With a groan, he dipped his tongue into the depths of her mouth to meet her tongue and lick it, play with it. She tasted like magic, like the uisge and her own sweetness.

She responded as he teased her. But then suddenly, she stepped away, leaving him empty-handed with coldness spreading in his core.

CHAPTER 19

Marjorie panted. Her heart beat like an army of Celtic drums. Her cheeks flamed with heat, and her breasts ached with longing. A slight warm breeze cooled her face, and she inhaled the air hungrily, hoping it would calm her down.

What was this witchcraft? Could a kiss cause this?

Aye, it could. And the worst was, she wanted more. Where was the fear she'd expected? There was only curiosity now, wonder, hunger.

"Too much?" Konnor said.

His eyes dark with the mixture of desire and worry, his body stiff with helplessness. He looked like he wanted to step towards her and take her into his arms, but he restrained himself.

"I…" She breathed out. "I dinna ken. Aye, too much, but also nae enough."

"Have you not been kissed before?" Konnor said.

"Nae like this." She turned and leaned her back against the merlon. "Before Dunollie, I had two kisses, and neither resembled anything like this. And then, Alasdair…"

His kisses had left blood. His touch left bruises. Konnor's brought healing and wonder and magic.

He stood by her side so that his shoulder connected with hers. Even through her tunic, she felt that he emanated heat like a furnace—or maybe it was her. The touch caused a wave of tingles to race through her arm. His lovely scent in her nose, his deep voice caressing her... She flattened her palm against the stone merlon to calm herself down.

"I didna mean to be so dramatic," she said. "But 'tis hard. I dinna ken what to think. I thought when a man touched me, all my body was capable of was pain."

Konnor turned to her and cupped her face with his big, rough palm. "You have no idea how much I want to kill the monster who did that to you." She leaned into his palm and closed her eyes, enjoying the warm touch of him. "Your body was made to sing under the touch of a man who loves and worships you."

She let those words wash over her for a long, sweet moment. A man who *loved* her... *Worshipped* her...

Nae, that wasn't possible for her after Alasdair. She'd forever be tainted. Impure. Spoiled by evil. No man would ever want to connect his life with hers—and she'd never want to imprison anyone in a marriage with an unworthy, cowardly wife.

Invisible shields rose around her heart, hiding it in an iron cocoon. Strange. She hadn't even noticed she had let them down with Konnor.

And even stranger was that she didn't want them up when he was around. Her body did sing under his touch.

"Konnor, ye're verra kind with me. But I dinna think any man would want to."

His gaze seized her with the depth of its blue darkness. "You have no idea how wrong you are."

She went still in response to the hunger in his voice. The whole wall threatened to lurch and crumble from the possibility of what he was implying... That happiness was real for her, that someone could love her.

Konnor?

The shields went up again, spreading coldness through her chest. She wanted to believe. She wanted to see a future where sweet kisses existed. Where nights wouldn't be full of loneliness and pain, but of warmth and singing and love. Where Konnor would be by her side every day. Where she'd feel brave, safe, and secure.

But Alasdair had taught her a lesson she'd never forget.

Besides, Konnor had made it very clear he needed to go back to take care of his mother. How would she feel if Colin one day disappeared without a word?

"'Tis late, Konnor." She peeled herself off the wall. "I better go to sleep. And ye, too. Let yer leg heal. On the morrow, we shall continue practice. I would like to train ye, but if ye'd rather spar with Tamhas, I will accept that."

He opened his mouth to say something but looked down and closed it. Then he gave her a soft, heartwarming smile.

"You're right, Marjorie. I'll only train with you. As long as you have me."

THE NEXT DAY, MARJORIE WATCHED KONNOR APPROACH her as he walked out of the tower. Her breath held, and her mouth went dry as she stared at the bulges of his biceps, the broad, hard pecs, and the hard stomach hugged by the thin linen tunic that the wind pressed against his skin.

He caught her gaze as he walked, and the somber gray day grew brighter around her, colors became vivid, and sounds around her trailed into the distance, replaced by the loud thumping of her heart.

She realized his stubble was growing darker and longer on his chin, and with his hair gathered at the back of his head, he looked like a man from her time in the tunic and breeches, even with his big shoes.

He looked like a powerful lord, with his strong physique, his straight, proud back, and his dark gaze, the gaze of a man who'd seen death and seen the world. The way he looked at her melted her bones and set her marrow simmering.

She wondered about his life in his time. What did his home look like? What did that bewitched iron carriage that he drove look like?

He'd soon leave her, she realized. He'd soon go back to his future world with all those magical things. He had someone who needed him. He didn't belong here. But why did she hate that thought so much?

He stood before her, and a slow grin spread on his lips. "Good morning, Marjorie," he said, and her knees wobbled.

"Good morning to ye, too, Konnor," she said and handed him the training stick. As he took it, their fingers touched, sending a pleasant jolt through her. "Ready?"

He held the stick with both hands, just like she'd taught him. "Ready to kick your butt."

She forced the corners of her mouth to stay down, though his words brought a strange sense of elation into her core, like the freedom of a gentle wind moving across the purple-green hills of the Highlands.

She took up her position as well. "This time," she said, "aim to surprise me."

He cocked his head in response, walked three steps towards her and brought his stick down in a sweeping motion, aiming for her head. With a sharp knock, she deflected it and he went from another side. The courtyard filled with a rhythmical, wooden clatter.

Their eyes locked. He stroked to the side, and she deflected, but he started an onrush of strikes. She glided back as he pushed forward. He wasn't bad for the second day of training, she found herself thinking. Unlike other beginners, Konnor's movements had both strength and grace to them. Where inexperienced lads locked their knees, his were bent, giving him the ability to move easily and react quickly. His shoulders were straight, and he kept his balance.

Mayhap, by the end of the day, she could start training him on actual swords and even give him a shield. The strength of his blows reverberated in her arms and shoulders, making her muscles ache dully.

Clunk, clunk, clunk, went the sticks.

Thump, thump, thump, went her heart.

He stepped forward, and she stepped back. They became one in this dance. She'd never had a sense like that in all her years of training, not with any of her sparring mates. What would it be like to be one with him, as a woman and a man, no swords and no wooden sticks, and no clothes?

Yesterday's kiss invaded her mind. She'd melted from his hot, soft lips against hers. His tongue had gently probed and teased and played. His strong arms had wrapped around her without imprisoning her. They'd protected.

Uplifted.

Worshipped...

A hard blow came at her shoulder.

"Ow!" she spat, and a wave of irritation at herself prickled through her.

He stopped and stood with his stick facing down. "You okay?"

That strange word from the future... *Okay.* He must be asking if she was all right. Her shoulder stung, but her pride hurt more. She was the master here, and yet she'd let her student distract her with his kiss. She clenched her jaw, her fist tightening around the stick.

In a lightning-fast strike, she pierced the air right in front of his heart. Her stick pushed at his ribs just as he lifted his arm to deflect her attack.

"Defend yerself!" She gritted through her teeth as she pivoted to give him another hard blow.

As her stick met his with a loud *knock*, she promised herself not to give him any slack and not to get distracted by him or the effect he had on her anymore. She was a warrior first. This wasna a dance, and he wasna courting her.

This was war, and she was training another warrior who'd help her protect her son and her castle. Nothing more than that. No matter how beautiful it had felt to be with him and how sweet the air was when he was nearby.

She'd better guard her heart against him, because he'd either die in the battle with MacDougalls or leave her and go back to his time. The thought of losing him made her ache.

CHAPTER 20

T he sun hung low over the hills on the other side of the loch when Konnor went for a swim. He'd been training with Marjorie pretty much the whole day. After he'd accidentally hit her, she'd given him a run for his money, and by the end, he'd been drenched in sweat. Later, they'd started training with swords, and seeing her with one was an experience. Precise movements, calculated strikes, and deceptive maneuvers, she used her brain and her body to fight —and the combination was striking.

After the swim, Konnor washed the tunic and the breeches he'd been given earlier, and now he walked from the loch back towards the castle with them under his armpit. He was shirt-less, walking in the new breeches that a servant had given him. Konnor enjoyed the clean feel of his body. His muscles sang pleasantly, like they did every time after good exercise. Especially after one with Marjorie. He'd take training like that with her every day.

The slight breeze was pleasant on his bare chest and back. He ignored the sharp pain that shot through him when he stepped on his injured leg. His ankle would be fine. He'd had worse injuries.

He breathed in a lungful of fresh, pure air. No plane contrails in the sky, no pollution, no plastic bags or water bottles swimming around in the loch. The castle stood three hundred yards away, and Konnor saw with satisfaction that the pile of rubble against the wall had been cleaned away, and the men were putting sharp stakes in the ground under the northern tower, just like he'd suggested. Up the wall, the mixture of iron and wooden spikes, and even kitchen knives were being hammered into the wall.

That made him feel so much better about their chances of surviving the siege. Though there was still no sign of the enemy.

The men at the base of the wall moved slowly, visibly tired after a whole day of heavy work. They stopped from time to time, leaning on the shovels and wiping sweat from their foreheads, no doubt anticipating dinner after an honest day of work, just like Konnor was. Yeah, dinner in Marjorie's company and a cup of cool ale was all he'd want right now.

He hadn't seen Marjorie for a short time—probably not even an hour had gone by, but he already missed her. A dull ache in his chest at the sight of the castle scraped at his heart. What was Marjorie doing now?

Damn it. He'd never thought about a woman as much as he thought of her. It felt like ever since he'd met her, he'd expanded somehow, changed. He'd opened up to her about Jerry, and what he'd done to him, and she'd accepted him, not gasped in horror. She'd even kissed him...

It felt like his chest was so full with her—with a whirlwind of light, and bliss, and gratitude. He was so full with these feelings that his heart was about to burst open like a ripe watermelon.

What did it mean?

He was screwed, that was what it meant.

He was in over his head, forgetting his promise not to get

attached, not to get emotionally involved. Fear chilled his bones and marrow. He was not falling for her, was he?

As he walked, he saw a small bunch of green hazelnuts surrounded by leaves with sharp ends lying on the ground. When his dad was alive, Konnor and he had kicked a soccer ball together in the backyard. That was how Konnor's fondness for soccer had started. After his dad died, Konnor didn't touch a soccer ball. He'd missed his dad so much, playing had been too painful. But while he waited for the school bus, he'd bounce pinecones or hazelnut bunches to occupy his time. Later, when Jerry started tearing Konnor's and his mom's lives apart, soccer hadn't been painful anymore.

Playing soccer became a salvation. An escape. A way to feel closer to his dad. Perhaps, that's why he'd been so good at it and had become team captain. Same with the Marines.

He stopped before a hazelnut cluster and kicked it, smiling to himself as he did. Even here, seven hundred years back in the past, he felt like his dad watched over him.

He kept kicking the hazelnut bunch and didn't notice how close he'd come to the castle. He was already in front of the gates when Marjorie and Colin walked out, and Konnor's heart gave a lurch at the sight of her. Their eyes locked and connected. She gave him a small wave, and he raised his hand to wave back.

She blinked as she looked him over and blushed. If he could, he'd show her how much he wanted to press her against him, skin to skin, to feel her naked and trembling against him. But he couldn't. Konnor swallowed and put the fresh tunic on. She looked away.

An image came to his mind—of her watching him coming back from a hunt, beaming with joy and love and happiness, Colin and perhaps another child or two with broad smiles. A normal, daily routine, people who cared about him, who depended on him.

A family.

A family? Who was he kidding? He had no idea what a normal, daily life was. He knew he didn't want to be like Jerry. He knew he didn't want to have a family like the one he'd grown up in. Even when his dad was alive, he'd been deployed more than he was ever home, and Konnor only had a couple of memories of him. So what could he offer a woman with an eleven-year-old son?

Absolutely nothing.

Even if he did try, he'd never be able to stay here. His mom needed him. His business was waiting for him. What kind of fantasy was he indulging in?

This heart-expanding bullshit and the elation in his chest was just an illusion.

He kicked the hazelnut bunch with his knee straight up and caught it. Marjorie and Colin stopped, waiting for him to approach. The boy stared at him with a suspicious frown.

Marjorie stood behind him. She'd changed into a simple dress the color of heather with white embroidery on the chest. Her hair was done in two buns, one on either side of her head and decorated with white ribbons woven into the hair. She looked like a noble medieval lady from a fairy tale. And despite the more feminine look than her usual breeches and a tunic, she had a dagger on the belt around her thin waist.

Breathtaking.

He only just stopped himself from dropping to one knee and swearing allegiance to her like a goddamn knight. He was losing his mind. She dressed like this for dinner, but she looked especially beautiful tonight.

"Is there a special occasion?" he said as he came close.

She seemed to blush even more. "Nae. I dinna normally dress in breeches, Konnor. This is how I dress every day. The work for today is done." She threw a cautious glance at Colin. "But 'tis good to feel normal, especially with the danger looming over us."

Colin crossed his arms over his chest and blinked several

times, watching somewhere behind Konnor's back. Konnor followed his gaze but saw nothing, only the rare woods and grassy hills along the shore of Loch Awe. The boy looked anxious, breathing quickly, his face pale.

He was probably more shaken than Konnor had realized from the attempted kidnapping. Konnor locked his eyes with Marjorie and nodded in understanding.

"Of course, we do need to feel normal."

"See. 'Tis all calm. Dinna be afraid, sweet," Marjorie said. "With me and Konnor and all these men, no one will take ye."

Colin raised his chin, though he was still pale. "I'm nae afraid, Ma."

Konnor nodded. The boy needed a distraction, and maybe even cheering up.

"Hey, buddy, do you want to learn a game?"

His eyes lit up. "A game?"

"It's called soccer."

"Soccer?"

"Yeah. It's a game where I come from."

His eyes burned with curiosity. "A game?"

Konnor glanced at Marjorie. Somehow, having her near made him feel less awkward with the boy. Plus, talking soccer was something he was comfortable with.

"'Tis all right," she said. "He isna allowed to go outside the castle normally, but ye're here, and I'm here, and my men are building the stakes nearby, so I think 'tis safe. Ye can show him."

Konnor chuckled. "All right. Look, Colin, soccer is normally a game for two teams of eleven people. But even two people can play. Even one sometimes. We do need a ball for it. But sometimes all a man needs is a hazelnut bunch."

Konnor looked at Marjorie. "Would you like to play?"

She giggled. "Me?"

"Sure. If you want."

"I'd like to learn games from the future." Her eyes sparkled.

Colin looked at him with wide eyes. "From the future?"

Marjorie bit her lip. "I shouldna have said anything, should I?" She sighed. "Colin, son, ye must keep this a secret, aye?"

Colin nodded. "I swear on my life, Ma."

Marjorie sank down to kneel in front of him. She took his hands in hers, and Konnor's gut twisted in memory. How many times had his mom sunk to her knees to be at the same eye level with him when she'd wanted to calm him down or say something important, to make him feel like she understood him. But usually it was to feed him one illusion after another. *"Jerry will change. It will be over soon. We just need to let him heal and come back to his senses. He'll stop, we just need to be patient. He's unwell."*

"Konnor is a time traveler," she said. "He was sent here by a Highland faerie."

"Sìneag," Konnor said without thinking.

Colin's eyebrows lifted into the thick bangs on his forehead. "A Highland faerie?"

"Yeah," Konnor mumbled. "I was born—or will be born—almost seven hundred years in the future."

"Seven hundred?" Colin repeated with an expression of awe.

Konnor wondered how his young brain would've reacted to meeting someone born in 2700. He'd have loved the idea of something like that when he was Colin's age.

"Yeah," Konnor repeated like an idiot.

The boy's gaze scanned him up and down, and he felt uncomfortable.

"Ma, are ye certain?" he said. "I ken that faeries dinna exist."

"Apparently, they do," she said. "What do ye think about that?"

"I think... I think I'd like to see the future. What are swords made of, Konnor? Are castles made of gold? Or glass? Does King Robert the Bruce win?"

Konnor chuckled. "Yeah, the Bruce does win the war. And some castles are made of glass, though they do look quite different. Some are taller than that tree." He pointed at the tallest tree in the nearby grove—a pine. "Gold is still very valuable."

"Tell him about the carriages that drive themselves," Marjorie said.

"Yeah. There are carriages that drive themselves, no horses needed."

Colin stared at him. "Are they driven by magic?"

"No. By engineering."

"What is engineering?"

Konnor chuckled. At least the boy didn't hate him. He seemed to be enjoying the conversation. "Well, science is about how things work. What makes an arrow shoot from a bow, or how to make a wheel turn better and allow a cart to move faster. Or how to design a boat or a sail so that it catches more wind."

Colin glanced at the loch. "How *do* ye catch more wind?"

"I don't know. But engineers in my time do."

"C-can I look at the future, too? Ma, can I?"

Marjorie pursed her lips. "I'm sorry, sweet, I'd like to see all those wonders, too, but we canna. Our life is here."

And Konnor's was in the twenty-first century. That was the sad reality.

Konnor clapped his hands together once. "All right. Who's ready to play a game from the future?"

"Me!" Colin cried.

Marjorie giggled, and her laughter was like a bell ringing. Konnor wished he could make her laugh like that every day. "And me."

Her laughter was infectious, and their combined excitement kindled joy in his chest, too. "Great. Marjorie, you'll be a goalkeeper. Stand here." He walked to a spot between two bushes with about four feet of space between them. "This will be the goal." He raised the bunch with four hazelnuts. "This will be a ball. Colin, we need to kick this into the goal. Marjorie, protect the gate and try to deflect the ball and not let it pass through. We'll count who manages to score the most goals, and that person wins. You can only use your feet and your head, though. You're not allowed to touch the ball with your hands. Got it?"

Colin nodded enthusiastically. "Aye."

Konnor put the hazelnut bunch on the ground, swung his leg back, and kicked it into the makeshift gate. Marjorie stepped into the direction of the bunch, but was too late, and it flew by her and into the gate.

Konnor raised his arms in the air and made a half-hearted triumphant run. "*Yeah!*"

Marjorie and Colin watched him with amusement.

"So it's one point for me," he said. "Colin, you try now."

Colin beamed. Marjorie threw him the bunch, he caught it and put on the ground. He kicked it but missed.

"It's okay," Konnor said and came closer. "Try again."

Colin aimed his shoe at the bunch and kicked again, but this time he only scratched the surface of the bunch, and it rolled diagonally. Damn it. The thing was too small for pointy shoes.

"It's too small. What we need is a ball," Konnor said and demonstrated the size with his hands. "A ball? Where can we get one?"

A lightbulb moment illuminated everything around Konnor. It was ridiculous that he was enjoying this so much. Perhaps he wasn't so bad with kids. Colin did look more cheerful and seemed to have forgotten about the kidnappers.

"We can make one." What could he use, though? He scratched his chin. "I think the easiest would be to take a small heap of hay and wrap a layer or two of a hemp rope around it, like a yarn ball, to hold it. Later, I can help you make a real ball. What do you think, buddy?"

Colin looked at Marjorie. "Ma, ye dinna mind if I make a soccer ball with Konnor?"

Marjorie's eyes connected with his, and there was so much gratitude and light in it that it took his breath away.

"I dinna mind, sweet."

CHAPTER 21

The hay ball worked great, and although Marjorie had to go and inspect today's work while there was still light, Konnor and Colin had a great time playing with the ball outside of the castle. Colin was clearly happy to be out of the walls for a while, and Konnor felt honored that Marjorie entrusted him with the boy's safety.

Once the sun set and the sky was painted in a dark indigo mixed with orange and red, Colin started getting tired. Konnor took Colin back into the castle, and they had a meal together in the great hall, where Konnor told Colin more about the future: the cars, the boats, and the planes.

Unfortunately, he'd soon return to his time, and the boy would need to stay here. Talking of the twenty-first century, he thought again of his mother, and worry for her jabbed him in the gut. She was all right, he told himself. She was fine. She still had money. And she had people to look after her if something went wrong.

The best thing was to keep busy and prepare for the attack by improving his sword-fighting skills and helping with the castle fortifications.

Next morning, after a breakfast of porridge, Konnor went

outside the castle walls to see if he could help plant the stakes in the ground. About ten men worked there, including Muir and Tamhas.

Malcolm was showing a man how to cut the sharp edge of the stake. White saw shavings fell from under the blade of the ax, filling the air with the scent of fresh wood.

Konnor stopped next to Malcolm. "Do you need an extra pair of hands?"

Malcolm looked him over, estimating. "Aye, lad. Always." He nodded at Tamhas and Muir, who were digging holes in the ground at the base of the northern wall. "Ye can plant the stakes that are ready in the holes. Muir can help." He pointed at the heap of long, wooden stakes lying nearby.

"Sure," he said.

Muir approached him and greeted Konnor with a short nod. They took the stake together. It was damn heavy, and Konnor's arms strained with its weight. Both men put the stake on their shoulders and carried it to the trench where other stakes had been planted.

Tamhas had just finished digging a hole and glanced at Konnor with a frown. His nostrils flared once.

"On my count," Konnor said. "One, two, three."

He put the end of the stake into the hole, and both Konnor and Muir held it at a forty-five-degree angle while Tamhas put shovels of dirt over the planted end.

"I saw ye playing something with Colin and the mistress," Tamhas growled as he shoved the dirt. "Dinna ye dare get too close to her."

"Tamhas, lad, calm down," Muir said.

"Dinna patronize me, Muir," he barked across his shoulder. "I wilna stand and watch this stranger hurt our mistress and Colin."

"The last thing I want is to hurt her," Konnor snarled through his teeth, his biceps aching from the weight of the stake. "Or her son."

"Well. That remains to be seen." Tamhas stabbed the ground with the shovel, then moved dirt into the hole.

"Work faster," Muir said. "This stake is nae a feather. Have ye done this before, Konnor? How did ye ken how to improve the fortifications?"

Konnor cleared his throat. Although Colin and Isbeil knew about him being from another time, he was pretty sure it wasn't a great idea to tell everyone. Didn't they burn witches and such in the Middle Ages?

"No. Just common sense. I have fought for my country, though, so I know military tactics."

"And what country is that?" Tamhas said.

Damn. He shouldn't have said that. "I doubt you know it. It's far away."

Tamhas threw another batch of dirt. "Ye dinna think I ken other kingdoms? I'm a Cambel, too, from my mother's side. I was fostered with Marjorie and her brothers and educated by the monks just as Craig, Owen, and Domhnall. I can read and write."

The log was pressing on Konnor's chest, making it hard for him to breathe. He shifted it to move the weight a little. "I never said you couldn't, man. It's in the west. No one knows it."

"What is in the west, actually?" Muir grunted. The weight was getting to him, too.

"Ireland," Tamhas said. "Are ye a gallowglass?"

What the hell was a gallowglass? He hoped it was some sort of warrior.

"Sure," he said. "I am."

"Aye. Makes sense. They're brutal. Dinna the MacLeods provide Ireland with gallowglasses?"

"I say he's full of shite," Tamhas said.

"Ah stop it," Muir said. "The lad saved Colin when the MacDougalls came into his bedroom. And he was injured. I have enough sense in me to ken he is an asset. Did ye learn to fight like that in Ireland?"

Konnor cleared his throat. "No. A master of judo came to teach the Chinese art of combat. This is where I learned it from."

Muir slowly nodded, contemplating the information. "Simple fists, elbows, and knees nae suffice?"

"Actually, they do," Konnor said. "Only used differently."

Tamhas threw the last patch of dirt and placed a pitch pole under the stake to prop it up at the correct angle. Konnor and Muir removed their arms from it, and relief surged through Konnor as blood flowed down into his hands.

"Next stake," Muir said and walked to the pile.

Konnor turned to join him when Tamhas caught him by the shoulder. His eyes glistened with a contained threat. "Ye stay away from her, ye son of a bitch."

A bolt of anger slashed through Konnor's gut. "Don't provoke me, man."

Maybe Tamhas saw something in Konnor's eyes, because his expression turned challenging.

"Dinna provoke ye?" he said. "And what happens if I do?"

He pushed Konnor's shoulder. Red crept into Konnor's vision. *Calm down*, he said to himself. *This isn't high school. You know how to handle this. Remember what you did to Jerry...*

But it raged within him, the need to punch Tamhas in the face. He remembered his stepfather. His bloody, swollen face, the completely shut eye, the broken nose. All because of Konnor's hands.

No. He needed to be stronger than the young man who lost control. Stronger than Jerry.

"Go to hell," Konnor said and turned around to follow Muir, but Tamhas turned him around.

"I dinna care if Robert the Bruce himself trained ye. Ye stay away from Marjorie, outlander. I see how she looks at ye, and how the lad is excited. Ye'll die in the battle or will be gone soon anyways. And I'll be left to gather the pieces of her heart. She fell apart once and could barely pick herself up. Dinna repeat the experience for her, do ye hear me?"

Tamhas removed his hand and walked away, and Konnor stood in a stupor and with a pain around his heart. He realized that Tamhas was right. He'd be gone sooner or later, and he'd hurt her when he left...and surprisingly, this time, he'd hurt himself, too.

And he may never recover.

CHAPTER 22

That night, after dinner, Konnor walked Marjorie to her bedchamber. She lingered before her door, wondering...hoping...searching for a kiss.

They'd had such a wonderful day yesterday. She hadn't seen Colin so excited for a long time. Konnor had managed to cheer him up, and even today, Colin had kept playing soccer, the game from the future.

And today, after the midday meal, she'd trained with Konnor again for the rest of the afternoon. Konnor was... Oh Jesu, how he made her heart sing. How that scene made her wish the impossible—that Konnor would stay. That Konnor could belong to her time. That he could play soccer like that with Colin every day. Wouldn't that be a wonder?

His eyes shone like an endless night sky in the flickering light of the torch. His Adam's apple bobbed up and down as he swallowed, his gaze on her lips. He made her arms feel soft and warm, and he made her knees weak just by looking at her.

"Good night, Marjorie," he rasped.

"I dinna think I can sleep without a kiss good night," she whispered, surprised by her own audacity.

Then without waiting for him, she stepped forward and kissed him.

She kissed him!

He pressed her tighter against him, as if he were a drowning man and she were his last hope. His lips urged her more than yesterday, his tongue a sweet, lashing desire. She lost all sense of time and space.

Only he existed—and the hot, hard flesh of his body under her palms. His lips. And his tongue. And that clean, masculine scent.

He stopped first this time, but he didn't let her go. Instead, he pressed his forehead against hers and breathed.

"If I don't stop now," he rasped, "I'll never want to stop, Marjorie."

Then dinna, she wanted to say. But her shields went up again, cooling her senses. Oh, she wanted to smash them and let them burst into shards like a cup made of glass.

But those shields had protected her against any pain without fail for twelve years. And she couldn't imagine living with her heart so exposed and vulnerable. Because no matter how much she wished for him to stay, he wouldn't.

"Aye, 'tis best," she said and stepped back. He eyed her, his gaze intense and heavy. "Good night, Konnor."

That night, there were no nightmares of danger chasing her and a dark, strong man entrapping her. No. She dreamed of hot, gentle lips, and big arms that protected her, and of a happy, married life that she'd never have.

The next day, Konnor looked much better. He still limped, but he said exercise was good for his leg. They trained until the midday meal, after which he went to help hammer in the sharp spikes on the northern wall. Something about being in his proximity made the sun shine brighter, and the air fresher. It filled her belly with a strange feeling, like a flock of starlings launching into the sky.

Later that night, when they walked towards the tower

together, dark thoughts came into her mind. When would the MacDougalls attack? Would Konnor survive? She'd need to keep an eye on him during the battle. If he did survive, if they won, how soon would he leave her?

Sooner or later, he would. Cold crept into her body and prickled through her limbs. What did she expect? He'd never promised to stay with her forever. He had a life back there, in the future. His mother needed him. And she had to stay here. She had her people to think of. But she'd be lonely. She'd think of him every day.

Warm summer rain drizzled over the castle, and the scent of wet, lush earth hung in the air. The courtyard was dark, save for a few torches on the walls. The distant hum of voices came from the great hall, where people were still having dinner.

"Why were ye never marrit?" she said.

Konnor stopped in his tracks and turned to her with a frown.

"Why do you want to know?"

"'Tis just…" She exhaled, blinking against the tears accumulating in her eyes. "I will never be marrit."

His face darkened. "I wish you'd stop with that. You're every man's dream. Beautiful, strong, kind, and smart."

He took her hand in his, burning her with the heat of his skin, and put her fingers against his lips. A sweet shiver went through her.

"But no one could want me after… Ye ken."

"Any man with eyes and brains would want you. And those who don't, don't deserve you, do you hear me?"

She exhaled and nodded. His words were like a balm on her ragged soul.

Konnor sighed. "The truth is, I don't know what it's like to be a good husband or a good father. Romantic love is a lie. It's an illusion that just leads to heartbreak. My mother loved my father, and he died. She loved Jerry, and he abused her. And after all the violence I've seen and the things I've done, I don't think a man like me should get married or should become a father."

Marjorie shook her head. "A man like ye? A brave, kind man of honor? A smart, educated man with military experience? Ye'd make a wonderful father and husband, even if ye didna have an example."

A man who melted her heart like the sun melted wax...

Marjorie opened her mouth to tell him that it didn't matter to her, not one bit, when feet pounded against the dirt of the courtyard.

"Mistress! Mistress!" Malcolm yelled.

She whirled around. "What is it?"

"The MacDougalls. They're on their way. The signal came from the lads."

Marjorie's back broke out in a cold sweat. "Where?"

"South, mistress. By the turn to Kinnavar."

Marjorie exhaled softly and nodded. "A hard ride away."

So close... So close to Colin! To her... Her whole body began to shake. "Are the lads on the way back? We must start preparations for the siege. Call everyone—"

"Wait," Konnor said. "They're just preparing to sleep for the night and will probably attack tomorrow, right?"

"Aye."

Konnor took both her shoulders in his hands and looked into her eyes. "So we should take them by surprise. Attack right now, in the dark."

Attack at night? She could see the logic of his proposition, but her insides trembled with fear. She was too weak to fight the real warriors. The castle walls would protect her.

"I know what you're thinking," Konnor said. "I can see it in your eyes. You're wrong. The walls will only slow them down. The element of surprise is what will win you this battle." He looked up at Malcolm. "Do you know how many men they've brought?"

"Nae. The lads who were scouting will tell us."

"But how many do you think?" Konnor said.

"A hundred at least. 'Tis how many they need for a siege."

"That's double the men we have. Marjorie, you've been preparing them and training them, and you're more than ready. We need to attack now. Surprise them."

"But we've been preparing the castle all this time…"

"And the walls will keep you safe here. I'll go with your warriors to surprise the enemy. I know you're a fierce warrior, and I'm sure you can take down any MacDougall foolish enough to get close to you, but I will die before I let anyone harm you. I swear."

Let them go without her? Surely she was stronger than that?

But the idea of facing the MacDougalls in the open covered her skin in goose bumps. She remembered rock-hard arms around her waist, beating her hands and legs helplessly, the hard bounce of the horse's withers against her stomach. Marjorie's whole body went cold. What if it happened again?

Worse—what if it happened to Colin?

Marjorie's stomach tightened, and she shook her head. "But I canna leave my men… Ye can barely hold a sword!"

"Marjorie," Konnor said. "I can do this. This is the best chance we got. They won't expect an attack, so we'll run through them like a knife through butter."

He took her face in both of his hands.

"I'll take a few of your men and hit the MacDougalls tonight, before they can reach the castle. That way their numbers will be depleted. Maybe we'll even scare them off."

She cried, tears dropped quicker and thicker than the rain.

"Nae. I canna have ye risk yer life for me. I need to be there, too."

She should be strong. After all those years of training, she couldn't sit behind the walls again. She should be strong. If anyone should get revenge, it should be her.

"You need to stay here, Marjorie," he said, his voice like

steel. "Your safety is the priority—yours and Colin's. I won't let you endure any sort of violence... I won't let the MacDougalls touch a hair on your head again. Do you hear me?"

It would be so easy to just say aye, to let him fight her battle. To tell herself she had Colin to think about, and there were still preparations to be made here in the castle, stakes to be made and put in place, swords to be sharpened.

Taking her silence as agreement, Konnor leaned down and kissed her—a quick peck on her lips.

He looked up at Malcolm. "Let's go. Pick your best men. We go as soon as everyone's ready."

She watched them go, and her heart thumped like a fist. What was she doing? She should go and tell them she was coming, too. Take her sword and put on her armor, and finally let her claymore drink some enemy blood.

But the walls looked familiar and secure. And as she thought about the hands grabbing her, panic gripped her whole body in a vicious vise.

No. She'd stay here. At least, she'd be safe.

She watched Malcolm gather the men—he took about twenty of them. They stood in the darkness of the night court-yard, in the rain, their swords and the small chains of their mail coifs glistening dully in the light of the torches. Malcolm was barking instructions and the men listened to him carefully. Konnor did, too.

Marjorie stood on the wall looking down at them, her heart thumping. *Coward. Coward. Coward.* These men would go and risk their lives for her and for Colin. Konnor would.

Konnor! Who wasn't from her clan, or even from her time.

Tamhas appeared by her side, rain dripping from his rare stubble.

"'Tis a smart move, mistress," he said. "I'm glad ye're nae going with them. I'll stay with ye and make sure ye're safe."

She gritted her teeth and almost felt them crumble. She wanted to say she didn't need his protection.

The gates opened, and the men poured out into the black-ness of the night. Konnor looked up, and even in the dark, his eyes found hers. A wave of something washed through her—tenderness, warmth, and longing. He touched his forehead with his index and middle finger and made a short gesture forward with his hand... It looked like some sort of military salutation, probably from the future. Or a goodbye.

Tamhas kept talking about her safety, her protection, Colin's well-being, loyalty, and some other things she couldn't even register in her mind. She watched Konnor's silhouette go farther and farther into the distance beyond the walls until he dissolved into the darkness completely, as well as the other men.

"I ken ye're impressed by him, but I've been with ye yer whole life. I'll die for ye, mistress. I've kent ye since we were children..."

She kept staring out into the night. She didn't know how much time passed, but it felt like Tamhas went on forever. What if she never saw them again? What if she'd just sent Konnor, Malcolm, Muir, and almost two dozen men to their deaths?

What was she doing?

She was letting herself be weak. Once again, she was the lass who had been assaulted and beaten and broken, even though every single day for the last twelve years, she'd fought with herself—for herself. She'd fought for her honor and for her life.

And most importantly, she'd fought for hope.

She'd never felt such deep despair as when she'd been a captive in the MacDougalls' castle. When she'd started train-ing, she hadn't realized it, but every time she'd swung her sword and imagined an enemy, she'd fought for her future. For the hope of recovering the lass she'd been before the night-mare that changed her.

And now, if she sat and waited and let others fight her

battles, she'd never get a chance for that. She'd never be the strong warrior she wanted to be. She'd never be a good example for Colin.

She'd never have hope for a better future—not just for her, but for other lasses and women of her clan.

It was enough. Tonight, she would finally fight a real battle for the first time. It was time to rise.

"I'm going with them," she threw across her shoulder to Tamhas, and without waiting for him, she hurried towards the tower and her chamber to put on her armor so she could give the MacDougalls what they deserved.

CHAPTER 23

Konnor crouched behind a pine and watched the mostly sleeping camp. The rain was pouring down now, drumming against the leaves and grass. Many of the warriors slept in tents, hiding away from the weather. Sentinels sat by the fires burning here and there, huddling in their coats. The noisy, heavy rain, although wet and unpleasant, was another thing on their side.

Someone crouched next to him, and he looked to his side.

Marjorie!

"What are you doing here?" he hissed.

"I'm here to fight," she said.

"Go back to the castle this minute!"

Tamhas appeared and squatted by her side. "Ye think I didna try? At least we can agree on this. Her place is safely behind the wall."

"Shut up, ye two," she whispered.

Being very much aware of Marjorie next to him, he felt just like before his first battle in Iraq as a young pup. Almost shitting himself, his fists clenched around his weapon like iron clamps. Only this time, it wasn't his life he was afraid for.

It was hers.

The woman he was falling in love with.

The thought made him very, very still. He stopped breathing.

Love?

He shook off the surprise. He'd think about it later. He needed to focus on the battle now.

Malcolm had given him some Scottish armor and a *leine croich*. Iron armor he'd seen in numerous historical action movies were too expensive for regular Scottish people. But Marjorie did have a pointed iron helmet for him and chain mail to protect his neck and shoulders. He felt like an extra on *Braveheart*, and Mel Gibson could jump out of a bush at any moment.

Except, down there, the men in the little clearing in the woods weren't actors. Or doubles. Or extras. They were real warriors with real freaking sharp steel and years of battle experience. Which Marjorie didn't have. Konnor did, but not with swords. He should insist she return to the castle before it was too late. Tamhas would help. He could tie her up and take her home by force. But she'd hate him. And he couldn't stop a woman like Marjorie from doing whatever she'd set her mind to. All he needed to do now was keep her safe whatever it took. Even if it cost his life.

She was frowning, her lips tight, her chest rising and falling quickly under the leather armor she had on. She'd told him her father had splurged on it a while ago to protect her, and Konnor was glad for it.

What was she thinking? Was she actually ready to wound and kill after so many years of theory? He'd never forget the first person who'd died by his hand. He wished she wouldn't carry that memory.

"How many do you think there are out there, Konnor?" she said.

"A couple of hundred, probably."

Ten times as many as them. The enemy had two siege

ladders, so they would move slowly tomorrow, especially after the rain.

"Aye, looks right to me," she said. "Well, 'tisna anything the Bruce would shy away from. He defeated armies of two thousand men with only eight hundred of his own. 'Tis because he had the element of surprise and clever tactics."

Dressed in her helmet and chain mail, she looked at him with such hardness in her eyes that she resembled the goddess of war herself.

"We're Highlanders, and Loch Awe is our land. 'Tis how we fight. Together with nature, nae against it. Using our heads and cunning and nae thinking with our cocks."

Konnor's jaw dropped to the ground. Marjorie was a badass.

But again, he already knew that.

She looked around at her troops, all of whom were watching her.

"*Cruachan*," she said. Then a little louder. "*Cruachan!*"

The whole group echoed her, in a hushed, "*Cruachan!*"

Even though quiet, it rang through Konnor like the sound of a tuning fork in synch with something deep in chest. A war cry, he realized.

They rose to a half crouch and all crept silently down towards the MacDougall camp. Konnor stood close to Marjorie, his sword at the ready.

They sped up as they got closer. And with the speed, something took them over. Konnor had never felt this in any of his experiences in Iraq. Like a common blanket of battle rage, one spirit of war united them. It settled in Konnor's bones and muscles. With a final "*Cruachan!*" they smashed into the enemy camp like one wave.

Konnor made sure to stay close to Marjorie. And it was her kill that he saw first. A sentinel rose, astonished. He didn't even have time to raise his sword before she pierced his chest with her claymore.

Her bared teeth glistened as she did it. Beautiful and terrifying, she didn't stop. Her cat eyes shone with fury. His Celtic goddess of war, indeed.

Konnor met his first opponent—a man who had just taken his sword out—and Konnor, letting his body remember the intense training he'd gotten from Marjorie, swung his sword. He met the sharp resistance with a loud *clang*. But the man was weak, probably still from the sleep, or from the drink. Konnor swung again from the other side. *Bang*. Another block. With one leg too close to Konnor, he was in an inferior position. Konnor thrust the sword and stabbed the man right in his stomach.

It took more strength than he'd realized, but the man clenched the blade with both hands and fell with a pained-and-surprised expression. Konnor sighed. His first victim. Like every time, a pinch of guilt stabbed at him, but he didn't have time to contemplate. Another man was already upon him.

It was a bloodbath. Many were killed in their sleep, many barely managed to take up their weapons. But soon, the remaining MacDougalls were awake and armed.

They came out of their tents roaring war cries. Marjorie crossed swords with another warrior. Konnor wanted to help, but he had his own battle to fight.

A big man came at him with a sword. The MacDougall thrust his sword at Konnor, who met the blade with his own. He took another swing, and iron clashed too close to Konnor's throat. He stepped back. The man, sensing weakness in Konnor, came at him with a series of downward strikes. Konnor deflected them, his training coming in handy.

The man, sensing victory was close, raised his sword with both hands. Using a fraction of the moment when his opponent's torso was exposed, Konnor thrust his sword into his enemy's belly. The man went still, his claymore falling to the ground before he landed next to it.

Something sharp bit into Konnor's shoulder, and he

jumped back. Already another MacDougall, much younger and stronger, was at him. Konnor didn't even have time to raise his sword. The enemy's blade came at him, ready to pierce his heart.

Death looked into Konnor's eyes.

But before the blade reached Konnor's chest, the man stopped in his tracks and fell on the ground. Marjorie removed her bloody claymore from his back.

She nodded. "I believe we're even."

She'd just saved his life. Her face was sprayed with blood, her eyes shining, her back straight. She'd never looked more powerful, more beautiful, and more alive. Konnor forgot how to breathe, how to move, how to live for a moment. She was the sun, and he was a man who'd lived in an eternal night.

And she needed him. He needed to protect her, to do everything to have her live, even if it meant to take a blow meant for her. He looked around. More enemies came at them, and Konnor stood in position to take his next opponent. "*Cruachan!*" he cried, and Marjorie beamed at him.

But the more people woke up and came at them, the more enemies the Cambels had to face. Soon, it was clear they were being pressed back.

He pierced an enemy's throat and kicked him back. He exchanged a glance with Marjorie, who'd just wounded another man and stood panting, her sword dripping with blood. "We need to retreat, Marjorie," he said. "Command the retreat."

She looked around, her eyes determined. "Aye." She took in a lungful of air. "Retreat! Quick! Retreat!"

"Retreat!" Konnor echoed.

He made sure Marjorie turned around and ran, and then he followed her, putting himself between her and the enemies. Their people ran back as well, and Konnor saw Muir, Tamhas, and Malcolm, as well as others. He estimated there were fifteen of them alive.

The enemy warriors started following them but soon

stopped, and Konnor knew they were getting instructions from their commander, taking horses and equipment, and they would arrive at Glenkeld with full force.

And then it would be a matter of whether the castle's fortifications would hold the MacDougalls back or not.

CHAPTER 24

Marjorie's chest strained for breath, her shoulders and arms aching after the battle. Her head pounded from a couple of hard punches she'd received. Her face was cut, her ribs burned, and she was bruised in several places.

Konnor stood by her side on the wall, watching the MacDougall army approach. Konnor had swung his sword well on the battlefield, and she was proud. He was like a Highlander. What he lacked in experience, he made up for with cunning and dexterity.

She watched the MacDougalls arriving at Glenkeld in full force. The rain had stopped, and the sky began to clear in the east behind the trees, spilling everything in a whitish stone-gray hue. Pine trees in the nearby grove looked almost black.

This night, she'd been christened as a warrior on her first real battlefield. She wasn't a weakling anymore. Her hands had not shook. It was thanks to Konnor, who'd given her the strength and security to believe in herself. She hadn't realized how much strength she'd built up after all these years.

Thanks to Konnor's idea, Cambels had taken out about six dozen men, but there was still no way they could win a battle in an open field. She could see now there were many more of them. Three hundred or so.

It was the matter of defenses now.

Her archers hid behind the hinged wooden shutters between the stone merlons on the walls. While Marjorie and her group had been fighting, the men who'd remained in the castle had covered the wooden hoardings on top of the towers and the roofs of the buildings with animal hides to make them fireproof. The northern wall was as secure as it could be, given the limited time and resources they had. In the courtyard, six cauldrons full of hot sand hung over the campfires, and a heap of sand lay nearby to replenish them.

The castle had to hold.

The mass of warriors were approaching. A siege tower loomed in the middle of them with a battering ram by its side. People carried long siege ladders. Marjorie shivered at the sight of these siege weapons.

But then the army came close enough.

She saw *him*.

The face she'd never forget. The face she saw in her nightmares. The father who'd let his son treat her like a dirty rag.

John MacDougall.

Chief of the MacDougall clan, John MacDougall, sat up front on a horse. He was in expensive chain mail and armor that glistened in the milky light of dawn. His white hair was gathered in a long tail that ran down his back.

A shiver went through Marjorie at the sight of him. When she'd seen him last, all those years ago in Dunollie, he's been much younger. Strangely, he seemed shorter now and less powerful, though his shoulders were still mighty and broad, and he sat on the horse with the grace of a highly experienced warrior.

His eyes met hers.

Oh, nae.

"Marjorie," John said, a surprised frown on his face. "Was it ye who attacked us?"

In the darkness of the night and in the chaos of a surprise attack, he probably hadn't recognized her, or he hadn't seen her. *That's right, ye pig.* Triumph spread through her core like an avalanche of fire. "Didna expect that, did ye?"

The surprise on his face changed to a threat. "Even better, ye silly lass. Do ye think ye can take *me*? Give me my grandson, and I will leave ye alone."

The goddess of winter, Beira, must have passed through the air, because Marjorie turned into an ice statue. "He isna yer grandson, ye slug! He is my son. A Cambel. MacDougalls will never touch a hair on his head."

"What he is, is a bastart. I will legitimize him and make him my heir. He's the son of my only son. All my daughters gave me nothing but lasses."

"Over my dead body," Marjorie growled through her teeth. "He doesna ken about ye, and he never will as long as I have a say in this."

She hoped Colin was sleeping, but what if he heard her? She'd concealed the truth of his violent conception from him to shield him from the knowledge, but she might need to tell him the truth and explain to him what happened.

"Is that yer last word?" he said, looking at her from under his eyebrows.

"Aye."

"Then over yer dead body it shall be."

He put his helm on and drew his sword. "*Buaidh no bas!*" Victory or death.

"*Buaidh no bas!*" the clan behind him echoed.

"*Cruachan!*" Marjorie roared.

"*Cruachan!*" Dozens of voices pierced the air around her.

MacDougalls launched forward, splitting into two rivers— half of them heading to the northern wall, while the other half ran with siege ladders towards the front wall.

"Archers, ready!" Marjorie cried. "Loose!"

Three dozen arrows flew through the air in a high arch and descended into the swarm of people below. Warriors fell with pained grunts.

"Again! Loose!" Marjorie cried. She turned to the inner side of the wall and yelled to the courtyard. "Sand! Bring the sand here and to the northern wall!"

While arrows flew, down in the courtyard, two men per cauldron picked up the hot sand and made their way to the top of the walls. The siege tower moved towards the castle, as well as the battering ram.

"Shoot the men with the ladders!" Marjorie cried.

She turned to Malcolm and Konnor. "I'll go to the northern wall. Can ye hold the attack here?"

"I'll come with you," Konnor said.

"Aye, I'll hold command here," Malcolm said.

Marjorie and Konnor hurried along the wall, through the tower, and onto the northern wall. The MacDougalls were trying to lean the siege ladders against the wall, but the spikes at the base were hindering them.

"It's working!" Marjorie said. "Konnor, it's working."

Konnor nodded, his eyes intense as he stared down at the attackers. They had archers, too. While John MacDougall was at the main gate, his first commander was probably here.

"Take aim," a man on a horse in full armor cried, and a hundred or so archers lined up a few yards away and nocked arrows on bowstrings.

"Take shelter!" Marjorie yelled, and the warriors knelt behind the shutters and behind their shields. Konnor sank to his knees and pulled her with him, covering them both with a shield.

"Loose!" came the call from behind the wall, and arrows thunked around them, jumping off the stone floor, piercing the wood. Konnor grunted as an arrow hit his shield.

While the MacDougall archers reloaded their bows,

Cambel bowmen had enough time to take a quick breath before the enemy would shoot the arrows again. Enough to take another shot and stop them. "Aim for archers," Marjorie cried, rising to her feet. "Take aim! Loose!"

Arrows flew. The back and forth of arrows continued for a while. After some time, Marjorie looked down and froze. The MacDougall warriors were cutting down the wooden spikes. They'd cut enough to place the first siege ladder, and it was already rising.

"Pour hot sand on the bastarts!" she yelled. With heavy grunts, the men lifted the cauldrons and turned them over. Steam rose, and the air filled with the scent of hot stone. Men yelled in pain as sand fell on them and burned their skin.

As the men with cauldrons ran down for more sand, the iron hooks of the first ladder landed, clawing at the stone merlons. The attackers had a hard time climbing over the blade-sharp spikes that decorated the crumbled part of the wall. They hurt themselves and tried to avoid them, which slowed them down. If the spikes hadn't been there, they would have easily climbed up and flooded the wall, but now there would only be one at a time.

The first enemy came, and Konnor stabbed his chest and pushed him back. The man fell with a yell. The next ladder swayed in the air on the other side of the wall, and Cambel warriors pushed it back before it could hook at the merlons.

The battle continued. More and more warriors came, but Marjorie's men fought well and held the wall. She looked at the main wall and gasped. The siege tower stood directly by the wall, and MacDougall warriors poured from its wooden top. More men climbed the stairs of the tower to the platform at the top. Marjorie rushed to that wall to help fight the onslaught.

The castle shuddered with a loud, wooden *knock*. The battering ram!

"*Cruachan!*" she called to raise her warriors' spirits. As she sprinted to the other wall, Konnor ran by her side. They slashed into the battle on the wall.

Thud. Thud. She wielded her sword against the shield of a warrior. She kicked him and pivoted in an unexpected move. She slashed at his unprotected side and kicked him off the wall.

She fought and fought. The *clang* of metal against metal, screams, and groans of pain rang out all around her. They'd defended the wall well, and there weren't many MacDougalls left climbing, but the ram continued battering the gate.

Boom. Boom. Boom.

A loud *crack* thundered through the air, and the MacDougalls yelled in a triumph.

No, no, no! They poured into the courtyard. Colin! He was locked in his bedroom, and Tamhas stood protecting him. She needed to send more men there.

They could win this. The MacDougalls had lost a significant amount of their forces, and now the Cambels had a real chance of victory. She just couldn't let anyone get to Colin.

Marjorie rushed down into the courtyard with Konnor right after her. They dove into a battle there. She had no idea how long they fought, but it felt like an eternity.

And then she saw John MacDougall.

He was ten feet away and walked towards Konnor, who'd been separated from her and was finishing off the man he was fighting. MacDougall's sword dripped blood, and his chain mail glistened in the dull dawn light. His white hair was in disarray.

Marjorie ran, her blood seething in her veins. He swung his sword at Konnor, but before he could strike, Marjorie roared.

"MacDougall!"

He stopped and looked at her. His face fell in astonishment, and he stepped back. Marjorie stopped before John with her sword in her hands, assuming a fighting position.

She snorted. "Oh, aye. Did ye think I was going to shrink

and die like a crumpled wee flower? Nae. Never. How do ye like this?" She indicated at the battlefield with her claymore. "I'm a sword forged by the fire ye've set under me."

John's expression changed from surprise to anger.

"Ye are nae a sword. Just a wee lass playing the games of grown men. Ye couldnae do anything *then*. Ye canna do anything *now*."

Marjorie shrank back internally. The helplessness she'd known all too well from twelve years ago weighed her down. Her ribs tightened around her lungs, and her insides felt as though they'd been scraped away, leaving her hollow.

"Ye think ye will stop me?" John MacDougall roared. "Come and try, wee bitch."

Wee bitch—that was what Alasdair had called her. Her arms hung helplessly. Konnor, probably seeing her expression, raised his sword, his face distorted in a furious mask.

But she couldn't let him. She couldn't let anyone finish her battle for her. She'd hidden behind the castle walls long enough. Whether she died today or the MacDougall did, it didn't matter. What mattered was that she'd fight her own battles.

"Dinna ye dare, Konnor," Marjorie called. "He's mine."

Konnor grunted and stilled. The MacDougall looked at him like he were a helpless pup.

"Aye, lad. Go and play with the others. This doesna concern ye."

Marjorie's heart thumped in her throat. Alasdair was dead. But his father stood before her. As the chief of his clan, he could have returned her home, could have set his son straight, could have ended the madness of everything Alasdair had done right under his nose.

She held her claymore in both hands. They tingled with the need to fight the last man alive responsible for her broken life and for her broken self.

She would be the flame-forged blade. For her son, for

herself, and for Konnor, the man who had come from another time to fight at her side.

Her arms filled with energy, like lightning flowed through them. Her claymore became an extension of her arms. Her cheeks hot, her muscles straining against her skin, she planted her feet wide.

The MacDougall limbered up his neck and rolled his mighty shoulders. Despite his age, he was a dangerous opponent. He took his sword in both his hands. A guttural roar escaped his throat, "*Buaidh no bas!*" He launched at Marjorie.

She cried, "*Cruachan!*" and darted forward.

Their swords clashed. The impact knocked Marjorie back, stealing her breath. She gasped and attacked again, only to meet the rock-hard resistance of his claymore.

Marjorie and John MacDougall circled each other. She searched for weaknesses in him, her muscles taut. He was big. She was small. He was stronger, but she was faster.

Malcolm's words echoed in her head, "*In a real battle, that unexpected move might be why ye win.*"

That was what she needed to do. Surprise him, just like she and her people had surprised the MacDougall camp.

She kept moving in slow circles to disorient John. He came at her, striking down onto her sword over and over. Her arm absorbed the impact, and it resonated painfully in her bone marrow. The sound of metal rang in her ears.

There was a small moment of opportunity, and she stroked with her blade from the side, ripping into his chain mail. MacDougall roared with pain and slashed at her with his claymore. Marjorie stepped back, but not fast enough, and the blade went through her leather armor and bit into the flesh of her shoulder.

"*Arghhh!*" she cried. Unexpected pain burst into flames. The shock of it, her first real battle wound, caused her to fall still for a moment. That was a mistake. Because MacDougall did not stop. He slashed low. Only the instinct honed over years of daily training helped Marjorie block his blade with hers and avoid her thigh being cut open.

MacDougall raised his sword to give her a death blow, but Marjorie spun out of the way and it hit the ground beside her. She thrust her sword upward, ripping open his chain mail and sinking it between his ribs.

The man roared. She pulled her sword back and pointed it at his neck, about to kill him.

But she stopped.

Did she have to kill him? She could take him prisoner. But she'd won the fight. She'd wounded him. She was strong. That was all she'd wanted to prove to herself—and to the MacDougalls. She didn't need to take his life or his freedom.

She kicked his sword out of his hands and looked around. The battle stopped. Archers stood on the walls, their arrows pointing at the remaining MacDougalls. The men were exhausted, but many glanced at her and John MacDougall with a question in their eyes.

"Leave," Marjorie spat. "Take yer men and leave if yer life is dear to ye. And never come back to our lands ever again."

"Ye dinna decide over my life. Ye won, wee bitch. Finish me. Kill me. Dinna ye want me dead after what we did to ye?"

Marjorie's arm jerked a little.

"Oh, I want to kill ye. But I wilna take my son's grandfather's life. Take yer loss and crawl back to yer castle, and live with the knowledge that ye'll never see yer grandson. That the wee bitch won. That she's stronger in every way than ye."

Taking someone by force and torturing them wasn't strength. Strength was coming back from it and choosing not to take a life. Making the choice was the strength.

The strength was hope.

And she had it now.

CHAPTER 25

Colin peeked from behind the merlon at the retreating remnants of the army that had just attacked his home. Arthur, his wooden sword, shook in his hand. He couldn't believe what he'd just heard as he watched the big man with white hair attack his mother.

"Ye'll never see yer grandson."

That was his other granda—an enemy of his clan. A MacDougall.

His family had never told him who his father was, but Colin wasn't a simpleton. He suspected something bad had happened to his mother.

And now he knew that this MacDougall's son had done bad things to her. He knew his mother was strong, kind, and capable. But sometimes, he'd see her stare into the distance with a sad look in her eyes.

Colin knew now that she looked like that when she remembered the bad things that had happened to her. He wished with everything that he could shield her from the memories, even with his wooden sword.

After all, his mother and Glenkeld were in danger because of him. His evil granda could come back and hurt his mother to get to him. He should be like Uncle Ian and his great-granda Colin. Brave. Capable. He should protect his mother and his clan.

No one would suspect a wee lad like him to follow them. He could get close and kill the MacDougall when he didn't suspect it.

Colin looked around. Everyone was busy. His mother was helping with the dead and wounded. Isbeil commanded the clan about, directing the wounded into the great hall. Tamhas, who had left his post by Colin's door when the MacDougalls retreated, was helping carry the fallen warriors. Konnor was bandaging a wound on someone's leg. There was no one on the walls anymore, save for dead bodies.

His granda's sword!

He hurried into his bedchamber. After Konnor had fought Colin's attackers, the sword had been cleaned and oiled and hung on the wall, glistening like new. Colin stood on a chest and took the hilt with both his hands. With a grunt, he lifted the weapon, only to have it sink back down and fall on the floor. It was almost as long as he was. No. He needed something smaller and lighter.

A dagger!

Colin hurried back to the wall. He saw a dagger lying next to a dead warrior. He grasped it, hid it behind his belt, and quickly sprinted down into the courtyard, through the broken gates, and after the MacDougall army, unnoticed by anyone.

KONNOR FROWNED AS HE WATCHED A TINY FIGURE RUN through the castle gates and crouch behind a bush. He'd come to take any wounded from the northern wall down into the great hall where Isbeil could help them.

Given the disadvantage in numbers, Konnor was relieved at how few casualties they had. Most of the dead bodies belonged to the MacDougalls. As far as Konnor could see, Glenkeld had lost about fifteen men, though every single one who was still alive had wounds of some sort.

The small figure peeked from behind the bush, rose, and sprinted after the MacDougall army. A boy. There was something familiar about him... A white stick swung violently attached to the boy's waist as he ran. A sword?

A wooden sword?

That couldn't be...

Konnor's blood chilled. Someone went past him. "What the feck are ye looking at, man?" Tamhas asked him as he walked towards the nearest body. "Dinna have nothing to do?"

"Where *the fuck* is Colin, Tamhas?" Konnor growled.

"In his chamber, of course." But his voice didn't sound confident at all. Tamhas stopped and followed the direction of Konnor's gaze.

Without saying a word, Konnor ran to check Colin's bedroom.

Empty!

Tamhas stopped behind his shoulder. "Nae, nae, nae!" He darted towards the round stairs and down. "I left to help with the wounded when the MacDougalls started leaving."

Konnor dashed after him, his heart beating heavily in his chest. His legs didn't move fast enough, as though his feet weighed a ton and felt as cold as ice.

Tamhas ran towards the stables, and Konnor followed him, but all the horses were unsaddled.

"Goddamn it," Konnor growled. "I'm going after him on foot. He isn't that far."

"Aye, man. I'm coming."

Konnor's muscles were tired from a sleepless night full of physical strain, battle, and nerves, but he gathered the remnants of his strength and willed his body to ignore the burning pain in his ankle. He sprinted after the boy.

The grass flashed under his boots, and a breeze chilled his

sweaty body under the tunic and the *leine croich*. There, he saw Colin about a mile in front of him, a small figure, about to run into the forest. He and Tamhas ran faster.

Konnor hoped the MacDougalls wouldn't see the boy. If they did, and John MacDougall realized who the boy was, that was it. There was no way he'd let the boy go. The battle would start again, and no matter how wounded John was, there was no way the Cambels could win out in the open like this.

They'd lose Colin.

Konnor couldn't imagine what that would do to Marjorie.

He had to retrieve him. He and Tamhas had to. Konnor sped up.

By the time they reached the first trees, Konnor was out of breath, and sharp pains from running stabbed his stomach. Tamhas and he stopped and hid behind the trees and peeked.

"There he is," Konnor said.

A white tunic flashed between the trees half a mile or so before them.

"Let's go, man," Tamhas said.

Panting, they both resumed the pursuit. Konnor's whole body felt like it were on fire. He was so tired. At some point, his mind went blank with exhaustion while his body kept running. He blinked the sweat from his eyes and saw that about two hundred yards before them, one of the MacDougalls had caught Colin and dragged him forward by his shoulders.

Konnor went cold. His foot caught a root, and he tumbled down, scraping his palms raw.

"Go!" he yelled to Tamhas while he was getting up.

Goddamn it! He didn't believe in magic, or God, or much of anything, but at this moment, he prayed. To God, to the universe, even to Sìneag the Highland faerie. *Please, let us save the boy. Please, let us get him back.*

Tamhas sped up, his long, dark hair flying on the wind behind him. He drew his sword.

"Stop!" he yelled, and the MacDougall stopped and turned. His eyes widened.

"Tamhas!" Colin cried.

The MacDougall brought his dagger to Colin's neck. "Stay back," he said, "or I'll cut his neck. I ken who this is. The MacDougall's bastart grandson. I will take the lad to him. He wants him alive, but he wilna mind if the lad is scratched a wee bit."

Konnor stopped and panted, trying to steady his breathing. He drew his sword and pointed it at the man. He wasn't tall, and he didn't look strong, for that matter, but he did have their boy.

"One movement, and I will cut his neck open."

Where was the rest of the MacDougall army? Konnor and Tamhas could take the man easily. He glanced farther into the forest and saw the backs of men and carts moving away in the distance between the trees.

Konnor looked at Tamhas, who caught his eye. Konnor made a barely noticeable movement with his head, indicating to Tamhas that he should circle the man from the left side while Konnor did the same from the right. Tamhas gave the tiniest nod.

But the MacDougall's nostrils flared, and he whistled.

Oh, for the love of—

The men who were last in the procession looked back at him, and three of them hurried towards their companion.

Hell. Four against two, and one hostage.

One of them had a long spear with a single-edged blade and a sharp end. The other one held a long-handled ax, and the third had a mace.

The spear gave the first one the advantage of distance, and Konnor had seen how a mace could smash helms and armor. It could crush a man's skull easily. The ax was a simple weapon, but its long pole also gave the enemy the advantage of distance, while having a larger blade to injure a man.

This didn't look good.

The first man poked the glaive at Tamhas, who jumped back just in time, and the other man brought his mace high above his head and launched at Tamhas. Konnor didn't have time to help him, because the man with the ax darted at him and brought his ax down towards him.

Konnor ducked. The blade swooshed passed his face, and he felt the small puff of wind as it went by. Close.

The man was at a disadvantage while fighting in close combat. Konnor's only chance was to get near. He darted forward, stopping the pole of the ax with his sword. The impact resonated in his bones. With his free leg, he kicked the man, who then staggered and fell back. But the ax's handle was long, and even while lying on the ground, the man came at Konnor with the ax and would have wounded him in the leg if Konnor hadn't jumped back. Risking his arm, Konnor grabbed the handle just beneath the blade and yanked the ax forward, taking it from the man's hands. With one smooth motion, he jabbed the man with the wooden end of the pole in the face, and he stilled, unconscious.

He looked at Tamhas. The man was still fighting two enemies and was backed against a tree.

The first man, the one who had Colin, was backing up towards the army.

Damn it.

Konnor was torn between helping Tamhas and getting Colin. Tamhas was still all right, but if the McDougall warrior managed to join the army with Colin in his possession, they wouldn't be able to retrieve him.

No, Konnor had to act now.

With the long ax in one hand and his sword in the other, Konnor advanced towards them. He looked at Colin, who stared at him with wide eyes. If Colin would move just a little bit, Konnor could thrust the blade of the ax into the guy.

Konnor locked his eyes with Colin. "Look, Colin, buddy, do you remember our game of soccer?"

He nodded.

"Shut up!" the MacDougall said, confusion in his eyes.

"I can score. I just need you to clear the goal for me."

He blinked, then his face became calm and concentrated. He gave a barely noticeable nod, opened his mouth, and bit down on the man's hand.

The man screamed and released his grip, which allowed Colin to twist out of his grasp. At the same time, Konnor tossed his sword aside, gripped the pole of the long ax with both hands and thrust the sharp, upper edge of the blade into the man's face.

Blood sprayed, and he dropped to the ground like a sack of potatoes. Colin ran into Konnor's arms, and he hugged the boy.

Oh thank God! He felt so small and yet firm and trembling in his arms. Konnor pressed his cheek against Colin's unruly mane of hair.

He turned to Tamhas and stopped in his tracks. One opponent lay immobile on the ground, while Tamhas was pressed against the tree, holding a bloody gash on his side. The last warrior brought his mace high above his head for the last, deadly blow. Tamhas's sword lay on the ground by his foot. He was defenseless.

Konnor let Colin go and darted at the man with a loud whistle. The whistle worked, and the MacDougall glanced.

Tamhas—good man—launched at the man's stomach, using his head like a battering ram. The man doubled over but hit Tamhas's back with his mace. Tamhas screamed in pain.

Konnor was now close enough, and with one clean movement, he cleaved off the man's head. Blood sprayed in a fountain of gore, and Tamhas fell with the man's body on the ground.

Konnor crouched by his side and laid him flat on his back.

He looked at the gash and at Tamhas's pale face. The man was breathing hard and wheezing. Colin sank to his knees by Tamhas's side, his green eyes wide.

"Tamhas?" he said.

Damn it. The man didn't look good. Konnor pressed his fingers against Tamhas's neck to measure his pulse. It was weak. *No!*

The man looked at Colin and closed his eyes, his face relaxing with a relief. "Thank Jesu!" he mumbled. "Good man, Konnor." He looked at him. "Thank ye for saving him. Ye two should go back now, before the army notices ye."

Konnor's gut clenched. He knew the man was right. But he just couldn't leave a fallen soldier behind.

"Let me see how badly you're wounded. I can help you."

He took Tamhas's hand off the wound and swallowed a gasp as sharp needles pierced his gut. Blood pumped out of the open wound, and he could see the man's pink intestines.

Colin saw it, too. His face paled, he turned and vomited.

Konnor pressed Tamhas's hand back against his wound. The truth was, he didn't have long. Damn it. Konnor's hands shook as he took Tamhas's other palm in both his hands. He glanced at the forest, but no one else had noticed them yet.

"Look at me, brother," Konnor said. Tears prickled in his eyes, and he blinked, willing them away. He'd seen other men die in battle. It hadn't happened often, thankfully, but Iraq had been a bloody battlefield. "I'm here with you. So is Colin. We're not leaving you."

Tamhas's eyes darkened and focused on Colin. He smiled. "Lad. I loved ye like ye were my own. Take care of yer mother, aye? She's one of a kind."

He looked at Konnor. "I hated ye because she looks at ye as I wish she would at me. I've wished that my whole life. And yet ye came and it only took a couple of days for her to fall in love with ye. I ken she'll be safe with ye. She'd never be mine, no matter how much I've wanted it. But I ken ye'll make her happy. Tell her I loved her."

He stilled, looking at Konnor with unseeing eyes. Colin wept quietly by Konnor's side, and he hugged the boy and brought him close. He let a tear crawl down his cheek, too, for the man who'd given his life protecting the son of the woman he loved.

His last words burned painfully at Konnor's heart. *Make her happy.* Clearly, Tamhas didn't know Konnor. All Konnor could do was hurt women with his coldness. But he'd laid his life down before he'd let anyone hurt Marjorie.

They needed to get back to the castle quickly. Someone from the MacDougall army could notice the absence of their men and catch Colin and Konnor.

He rose to his feet. "Come, Colin. Let's go back. We'll get someone to come back for Tamhas's body later. Let me take you to your mom. You've seen enough bad things happen today."

CHAPTER 26

The minute Konnor appeared in the courtyard, Marjorie saw them. She ran towards them with wide eyes and took Colin in her arms with a gasp. Tears ran down her cheeks as she hugged him so tightly, he groaned. She held him at arm's length and looked him over, then she shook him.

"What were ye thinking!" she yelled so loudly everyone in the courtyard turned their heads to her.

"I wanted to avenge ye against the evil granda I didna ken I had."

She groaned and brought him back against her. Then she looked at Konnor. "Where's Tamhas?" she asked.

Konnor lowered his head and shook it. "I'm sorry, Marjorie. He died protecting your son."

"No!" she cried, then closed her eyes and pressed her lips against Colin's head. "No... Nae Tamhas..."

Colin's shoulders shook as he cried. Tears streamed down Marjorie's face as she hugged her son. Konnor wanted to scoop them both into a hug and shield them from everything, but all he did was stand stiff as a goddamn statue.

They mourned the man who'd been good to both of

them. The man who'd died for them. The man who could have been Marjorie's husband and a great stepfather for Colin.

Konnor wished he could have saved him.

Marjorie wiped her tears and leaned back, pressing out a cheerful smile on her face. "Come, sweet, we canna help Tamhas nae more, but we can try and save those who are still alive. Let's go and see if Isbeil needs help. Aye?"

Colin wiped his face with the back of his sleeve and nodded.

A gash on Marjorie's shoulder darkened the tunic with caked blood. "Marjorie, ye need to go and see Isbeil about that wound," Konnor said.

"Dinna fash." She glanced at him. "There are others who need her more."

"Then let me take a look—"

"Konnor"—she stopped and looked at him firmly—"my son needs me now. A wee scratch can wait."

Konnor clenched and unclenched his fists as he watched her straight back as she walked away, anger and worry thundering in his gut. She was a strong woman, and there was no changing her mind if she'd made it up. And of course Colin needed her. But she needed someone to take care of her, too.

There was nothing he could do about it now, so he made himself useful. The day passed with them tending to the wounded, gathering and cleaning weapons and armor, and clearing the castle as much as possible. In the afternoon, Konnor stared at Marjorie's door. He'd given up his bedroom for the injured. Thankfully, he only had a couple of scratches, although his ankle was killing him. He listened, and when he didn't hear anything, he knocked.

"Aye?" Marjorie's voice came from behind the door.

Konnor opened it.

She sat with her back to him in an undertunic that had slid off one shoulder, exposing delicate flesh, beautiful bone structure, and a caked gash. She was wiping the wound with a wet cloth.

Heat ran through him at the sight of her exposed body, and it mixed with the worry and anger at seeing her hurt. What was wrong with him that he felt desire even seeing her wounded?

All he could do was stare at her long, wavy hair spilled across her uninjured shoulder, free from the braid it had been in during the battle. She sat on the bed, one leg tucked under her, her back straight. Seeing her like this felt so intimate, so personal, like he was invading her privacy. He stared at the floor, forbidding his gaze to slide an inch higher.

He cleared his throat. "It's me," he said. "I'm not looking. I wanted to make sure you're okay."

The sheets rustled. "Thank ye, 'tis verra kind. I'm decent now."

Konnor fixed his eyes with hers. She'd pulled the sleeve up to cover her shoulder and was now sitting with her face to him.

"Konnor," she said, and his name trembled on her lips. "Thank ye for saving Colin. I was so angry and relieved when I saw him, I didn't even think about thanking ye."

"No need to thank me," Konnor said, warmth spreading in his chest. "I'd never let him get hurt—or you. Is he okay?"

"Aye. He's sleeping now, poor lad. He'd like to be more grown than he is, but he's still more a boy than a man."

Konnor nodded. He was. And he'd seen more than a child should. But then so had Konnor at that age.

"Do you need any help cleaning the wound?" he said.

She hesitated. "I suppose... I canna see what I'm doing on my shoulder."

"Sure." Konnor shut the door behind him and proceeded into the room.

A rainy afternoon came in through a single narrow window, but it was the fireplace that gave most of the light. Marjorie's eyes were dark in the golden-orange glow reflected on her face.

She was so still as she watched him approach, a strange combination between a puma on a hunt and a deer. Both huntress and prey, ready to move at any moment.

Konnor sat by her side and took the cloth. He poured the brownish water from the small basin into the chamber pot and poured fresh water from the jug standing by the bed. He'd much rather use a disinfectant than water from the well, but the only disinfectant he had with him was a pouch of moonshine.

"Are you sure you're okay with this?" he said.

"Aye," she whispered and cleared her throat.

The vein on her neck pulsed, barely visible.

"Okay. Tell me to stop at any time, and I will."

She nodded, inhaled sharply, her nostrils flaring before she pulled the tunic down her shoulder. Konnor swallowed as her delicate collarbone came into view, and the crease between her arm and her breast. He could see the tiny blue veins under her skin. His mouth went dry. How could he be so turned on by seeing so little?

"Do ye like what ye see?" Marjorie whispered.

Busted. Konnor looked up.

"I didn't mean to—"

"Do ye like it? Do ye think me beautiful?"

Konnor licked his lip. "You're exquisite."

Her eyelashes trembled, and her eyes watered. "I've never heard that before. Truly?"

"Truly."

Their eyes locked, and heat ran between them. Longing like nothing Konnor had ever felt before pulled at his heart. He dipped the cloth in the water, squeezed the liquid out, and gently touched the gash. She winced a little but didn't move.

"I don't see any dirt. It looks clean," he said as he wiped. Blood stopped oozing, and it was already drying up.

He put the basin aside and reached for the pouch with moonshine. "I'll disinfect it before dressing it. This will sting."

Marjorie looked down, and her eyes widened. "I ken. 'Tis good to clean a wound with uisge. But desi— What?"

"To clean your wound from germs."

"From whom?"

Konnor chuckled. "The bad stuff that gives you an infection."

"Ye're speaking yer words from the future with me again."

He took a fresh, clean cloth and poured the moonshine on it. "Ready?"

"Aye."

He pressed the cloth to her cut, and she hissed. He held it a bit longer, then in another place where she needed it.

"Mother of—" Marjorie spat.

He removed the cloth and blew on the wound. Marjorie closed her eyes, tilted her head slightly, and sighed. She opened the side of her neck to him, the thin, graceful neck he yearned to kiss and nibble. The neck that would smell so much like her. The skin that would be soft and silky under his fingers. His cock hardened.

"I'll just dress it."

He took a fresh cloth and wrapped it around her upper arm and shoulder tightly. As his fingers brushed against her skin, he tightened his jaw. He was right. Smoother than silk. Warm and delicate. He ached to taste her.

"Done," he rasped as he tightened the last knots.

He better go, or he'd want to touch her again. He took the edge of her tunic and pulled it up to cover her shoulder. She eyed him from under her eyelashes, her eyes golden green, dark, and sparkling. His fingers lingered on her flesh. The touch melted their skins together and stole all air from Konnor's lungs.

"Marjorie, I should go before—"

"Dinna go."

Jesus Christ. He wanted to throw himself on her then. Instead, he closed his eyes, gathering all the self-restraint left in his body, and breathed. He looked at her again. Her chest rose and fell quickly, and her lips were parted and red.

"The trouble with that is I want you," he said. "I want you so much, but we can stop at any time..."

She looked at his mouth. "I dinna want ye to stop."

MARJORIE LICKED HER LIPS. THE HUNGER IN HIS VOICE LEFT her speechless. All she could hear was the violent thundering of her heart. The skin of her shoulder burned where Konnor's big, warm hand touched her. He sat so close to her, a massive wall of a man. His mere presence flamed her cheeks with heat and made tremors run through her hands.

She'd just been through the most transformative moment of her life. If he hadn't been here, none of that would have happened. They would have waited until the MacDougalls attacked. The siege would have likely been successful. She would never have beaten John MacDougall.

She would never have found her strength.

She was a new woman. Nae, not a new woman. She'd found the inner strength that had always been there—just forgotten, lost, and abandoned.

And this Marjorie, the battle-clad Marjorie with wounds and cuts and scratches, she wasn't afraid to take what she wanted. And what she wanted was Konnor. Before, she'd never thought she'd lie with a man. Now, she didn't want to lie with anyone but him.

"Marjorie..." he said.

She shifted to sit closer, and their knees touched and brought more heat into her body. "Heal me with yer touch," she whispered, suddenly feeling a tear roll down her cheek. She cupped his jaw, the small beard soft against her palm. "Wash the dirt of his hands and body away with yer hands."

His lips tightened with hurt. "Me? I'm not—"

She laid one finger on his lips. "Nae a word more. Ye are nothing like yer stepfather. Ye are the opposite of him."

And before he could say anything else, or change his mind, she shifted forward and put her legs around his hips, straddling him. She kissed him, and the touch of their lips sent a delicious wave through her, impairing her thoughts.

She wound her arms around his shoulders, and he wrapped his around her waist, pulling her closer to him. His teeth nibbled and his lips caressed, impossibly tender, his tongue swiping and gliding. The heat in her body rose, incinerating her.

"Are you absolutely—"

"Silence," she interrupted him and resumed the kiss.

He made a low sound at the back of his throat and tightened his arms around her. He ran his hands up and down her back, warm and pleasant. His scent was in her mouth. The succulent, manly scent of him that made her sag.

She ground herself against him, feeling drunk and disoriented. Her clothes were tight and wrong on her, and she ached to feel his warm skin against her, to have his weight on top of her.

She pulled up the ends of his short tunic and raised them over his head. Jesu, Mary, and Joseph... Did the ground just move, and the bed shift with it? Marjorie ran her fingers up along the tight muscles on his stomach and up his chest. He was as hard as iron and as hot as a furnace. And she felt the safest she'd ever been in her life.

"You're so beautiful," he said, looking into her eyes. "I can stare at you all day long."

"Then see me whole."

Was she seriously going to do this? With her heart thumping, she pulled the edges of her undertunic up and over her head. As her breasts became free, they brushed against Konnor's chest, and her nipples hardened from the pleasure that spread through her.

Konnor looked down and gave a low, animal growl. "What are you doing to me?"

He kissed her again, hungrier this time, his lips brushing against her with need. He lay back on the bed and pulled her with him. He cupped her breast and massaged it, playing with her nipple. An acute bolt of pleasure shot through her, and she whimpered like a kitten.

Her blood on fire, she pressed herself against him like she would die if she didn't. He glided his palms against her, leaving traces of fire. Her breath ragged, she swam in the sensations like a drunkard wanting more.

Konnor's fingers reached the edge of her breeches, and he froze. She looked at him. His eyes were black, naked lust shining in them, but also a question.

"Marjorie?"

"Aye, Konnor."

A hot need pulsated between her legs. All she wanted was him—his hands, his body, his skin against hers—as much as possible. She wanted to dissolve in him, become one. Body to body. Soul to soul.

"I need this," she whispered. "I need ye. Help me erase the memories. Help me become whole again."

He swallowed hard.

"Sweet Marjorie, it's you who helps me heal."

Oh, she wanted him to heal... Mayhap, if he healed enough, he would reconsider returning to his time? Mayhap, he'd want to stay and say more of those words he'd told her, like calling her Highland queen.

Then every day could be like this, full of bliss and happiness and love.

He let her roll next to him without breaking an inch of body contact. He released the straps that tied the breeches on her hips and slowly pushed them down. A sudden wave of fear came over her. She felt vulnerable and weak, being so exposed to him. Should she tell him to stop?

No. It was Konnor with her. He could never hurt her. And she wanted this more than she wanted to take her next breath.

Soon, her breeches lay on the floor next to the bed, and Konnor ran his knuckles slowly up her naked leg, bringing every inch of it to life.

"God, you're perfection," he whispered. He left soft, wet kisses down her neck. "I want to kiss you here. And here. And here."

He went to her breasts and took one in his mouth. He licked and sucked her nipple, and a storm of pleasure rushed through Marjorie. She gasped, making sounds she'd never heard herself make in her life. He went to the second breast, his hand still on the first one, and repeated his sweet torture there.

When she thought she couldn't take it anymore and would burst in a geyser of sunlight and sweetness, he withdrew and continued his way down, leaving hot kisses on her stomach, caressing her hips at the same time. Her inner muscles clenched in anticipation—like before a jump into the loch for the first time—both scary and exciting.

He massaged her thighs, squeezing her flesh as he went. Marjorie felt her entrance grow wet, and her face heating in embarrassment. But before she could say anything, his mouth was on her there.

She sucked in air as the sensation took her. He spread her folds with his fingers and played with his tongue.

"Konnor..." she whimpered, putting her hands on his shoulders to push him away.

Oh, how embarrassing.

But he was like a stone wall, and she didn't want him to stop, not really. The most beautiful pleasure spread through her in waves of sheer bliss. How could she possibly feel so good down there when all she had known had been pain?

"Konnor..." she moaned, and there was a hot plea in her voice.

He gave a low rumble of lust against her flesh, moans that made her feel like a goddess. He flickered a spot with his tongue, and something began to build within her, tightening and accelerating and expanding at the same time.

He withdrew, leaving her wanting more, much more.

"Sweet Jesu," she said, her words resembling a moan. "I never kent my body could do this."

Her glance went down his breeches where a considerable bulge showed between his legs.

"Take me like a man takes a woman," she said. "Make the darkness go away."

Konnor swallowed, and his eyes shone. "My beautiful warrior queen, I will help you forget everything bad that ever happened to you."

"Aye," she whispered.

He straightened, still on his knees between her thighs. Without taking his eyes off her, he undid his breeches and pushed them down. His erection sprang free, straight and big, and Marjorie's breath caught at the sight. She'd avoided looking at Alasdair, and the other penises she'd seen by chance when men bathed in the loch hadn't been erect.

Oh God, would he even fit inside of her without hurting?

He kicked his breeches off and pushed them to the floor. He lowered himself on top of her and supported himself with his elbows on both sides of her shoulders. His weight was pleasant and welcomed on top of her, and she wrapped her arms around him. He cupped her face with both his hands and looked deeply into her eyes. There was heat, and anguish, and adoration in his gaze, and something that resembled love. Her heart squeezed.

"I have never wanted a woman more than I want you," Konnor said. "My Highland queen."

There it was again, the words that brought her hope. He kissed her, spurring a new wave of desire through her veins. There was such hunger, as though he'd die if they stopped. She wrapped her arms around him, pulling him closer to her, wanting to dissolve in him and become one.

He positioned himself at her entrance, gently stretching her. He withdrew slightly and locked his eyes with hers. He sank into her slowly, gently filling her like an empty vessel, she nearly fainted from the pleasure spreading through her. He dove deeper, till he reached the very end, and there was no pain, nothing but profound connection and bliss.

"Marjorie," he whispered hoarsely.

She drowned in the blue intensity of his eyes, diffusing in him. But it wasn't enough. She needed more. She urged him to go on by digging her fingers into the tight flesh of his buttocks. He withdrew and plunged again, faster, and Marjorie gasped from the bolt of pleasure. He withdrew and thrust back into her, and she moved her hips to match his rhythm. He groaned softly, and his plunges grew faster, and the same feeling of tightening and building up took her over. She breathed erratically, and so did he. He devoured her with his gaze as though he'd seen spring for the first time in his life.

And then she fell apart in cascading waves of pure sunlight that ate every last piece of darkness. A pleasure that she'd never known slammed through her. She was unraveling, peeled open, cleansed, and finally free. Her mind went blank as she convulsed over and over in delicious, soul-shattering shakes.

Konnor stiffened together with her, cried out her name, bucked and lost himself, spilling his seed on her stomach and finding his release.

He collapsed by her side, taking her into his arms. He pulled the blanket on top of them, and as she was drifting into sleep, a realization shot through her in an arrow of aching pain. She was falling in love with Konnor, the man from the future.

She prayed to Jesu and Mary that he would change his mind and stay with her. A life of love and happiness with Konnor and Colin was the hope she fought for now...

CHAPTER 27

Konnor brought Marjorie closer to him. He was warm and heavy and melted together with her. He'd never seen anyone as beautiful as her during her release.

He'd call her a queen.

No. She was more like a goddess. A Highlander goddess, free and perfect and powerful. There was this light in her, this strength he didn't think he had.

Seeing that he done that to her, that she'd unraveled because of him, that he was the one who'd given her this positive experience after what she'd been through...

He nuzzled against her head and took a lungful of the scent of her hair. He felt like he were flying, like he'd just brushed against the sky.

He put his leg over her hip to bring her as close as possible. What if every day could be like this, be full of this closeness and this light? Full of taking care of her, playing soccer with Colin, doing something useful with his hands. What if every day could feel like he'd just touched a miracle?

Him? A miracle?

Something dark twisted in his gut. He wasn't supposed to touch a miracle. If anything, he was on his way to hell.

A shard of fear pierced his heart at the thought. Nothing could change the facts. Nothing could change who he was. He knew nothing of happiness and love. He had no idea how to be a good father and a husband. There were no miracles for him.

As though sensing the shift in him, Marjorie stirred and twisted in his arms to turn and face him. He met her luminous almond-shaped eyes and kissed her briefly on her soft, sweet lips. She reached out and ran her fingers through his hair, and he closed his eyes, enjoying the touch.

"Konnor," she said.

"Don't," Konnor said. "Please. Don't."

She kept silent, and when he opened his eyes, he hated himself. Her carefree, sunny expression was gone. Her shields were up, guarding that magic from him.

"What?" she said. "Ye dinna ken what I was about to say."

Their bodies disconnected, and cold crept into Konnor's heart. He sat up, sorry he was leaving her silky, taut body.

"Whatever you were going to say, I should never have done this. I should never have listened to this urge. I should've stayed away from you."

She sat up, too, holding the blanket to her chest. The hurt in her eyes twisted his heart.

"Do ye regret what happened?" she said.

"Marjorie, whatever happened, nothing is going to change the truth. I can never be the man you deserve. And nothing is going to change the fact that I'm leaving."

She blinked, her eyelashes trembling. She reached for her tunic on the floor and yanked it on to cover herself. Then she left the bed and went to stand by the window.

"Aye, I ken ye want to leave. Ye never said ye would stay." She turned and faced him with her arms wrapped around her stomach protectively. "But I thought... I hoped after what ye said to me about helping ye heal, and what ye called me, and after what ye did—what *we* did..." She gestured at the bed.

Konnor found his breeches and put them on. He couldn't

stand hurting her like this. He ached to take her in his arms. To soothe her. To give her that sunlight that had shone through her eyes again.

He walked around the bed. She stepped back.

"That's why I should never have given in to this. I don't want to hurt you. And I am. And I hate doing this."

"Then dinna," she whispered, tears glistening in her eyes.

Guilt twisted Konnor's gut. "I have to go, Marjorie. I told you I'd stay to protect you, and now that you're safe, I must go back to my life. My mother... She depends on me. I have my company to run. We have no future, you and I, no matter how much I—"

The word *love* almost slipped off his tongue.

"No matter how much I care about you, I'll never be the right man for you."

"Not a right man for me? Ye brought me back to life. Ye changed me. Ye returned my strength and confidence to me. Ye saved me and my son. Are ye saying all that is nae good for me?"

"Love only leads to pain, Marjorie. Love is a lie."

Silence hung between them, heavy and so saturated that Konnor could cut it with a knife.

"I don't know how not to hurt a woman's heart. How to be a good father. I grew up with this darkness. This violence." He dragged his hands through his hair, pulling the skin of his scalp back.

"If I ever hurt you..." Konnor shook his head. "I couldn't live with myself. I just can't."

Marjorie stepped to him and took his hands in hers. She kissed his knuckles and looked at him.

"Ye wilna hurt me. Ye wilna become yer stepfather."

Konnor shook his head, his eyes stinging. "You don't know that. Marjorie, I do care about you. I meant every word I said. You're the most stunning woman I've ever met."

Her eyes watered.

"But I can't stay," he continued. "I've been straightforward with you from the beginning. I must return to my time. My place is there. And your place is with a man who can be a great example for Colin and who won't break your heart. I cannot give you the love you deserve."

A tear ran down from her eye, and Konnor wiped it with his thumb.

"I hate ye," she whispered. "I ken yer mother needs ye. I understand that. But I still wish I'd never met ye. Ye opened me up to this possibility of happiness. Something I thought was never meant for me. Ye were wonderful with Colin and ye made me hope and put my guard down and feel things I've never felt for anyone." She slapped his chest, stinging him. "And now ye're leaving."

She shook her head, biting her lower lip.

"I kent I should never trust a man. But I broke my rule for ye. Ye canna be trusted. I gave ye the power to hurt me even more than he did—and ye're using it."

Konnor's heart sank to his feet. Pain like an arrow piercing his chest shot through him. He hated himself. He wished he could give Marjorie every happiness that she deserved. And he hated that he was the source of her heartbreak.

"Marjorie..."

She pulled her breeches up angrily and tied them at her waist.

"Dinna say my name." Her eyes shot daggers into him. "And if yer life is dear to ye, ye'll go. Now. I canna stand a moment more of seeing ye."

She pulled on her shoes and marched towards the door. She turned to him. "I'm going to the great hall. When I get back, ye better be gone. Dinna return, or I will fight ye, and ye will be sorry."

She walked out and slammed the giant door behind her. And as her angry steps receded down the stairs, Konnor stood. He had no will to move. But he had to.

"Goodbye, Marjorie," he whispered, staring at the closed door and wondering how he was going to breathe in a world where she didn't exist.

He went to his bedroom, where three wounded lay sleeping, and quietly changed to his cargo pants, his T-shirt, and his jacket. He'd been here, what? A week or so? He'd lost count of how many days. The modern clothes felt foreign on him, as though they belonged to another life.

To another man.

He considered stopping by Colin's bedroom and saying goodbye, but he didn't want to wake the boy.

From the pocket of his military jacket, he fished out the watch Andy had given him. It was 5:34 p.m. The second hand on the watch ticked, cutting the time, stealing it bit by bit from Konnor.

He didn't want to leave Marjorie and Colin. But he couldn't leave his mother alone.

And even if he didn't have his mom, nothing could change the fact that he just wasn't great husband or father material. A little game of soccer and him saving the boy hadn't changed that. He was a soldier, and it was a soldier's duty to protect and save people. And soccer... Big whoop. Anyone could kick a ball around with a boy.

Still, he'd miss Colin. He climbed the stairs to the next floor and opened Colin's bedroom door. It was dark inside with the shutters closed. The boy lay in the bed and slept peacefully under the blanket. Konnor found himself itching to tuck him in and kiss his forehead to say goodbye.

He put his watch on one of the chests in the corner and threw a last glance at Colin's unruly head of hair. Why did it feel like betrayal that he was leaving him and Marjorie?

He walked through the courtyard where dead bodies lay along the wall. A razor blade was cutting out his heart with each step he took. He wanted to say goodbye to Muir and Malcolm and the other warriors he'd fought shoulder to shoulder with. He wanted to help bring Tamhas's body back.

But it would be better if he left now.

As he walked out of the gates, someone called after him.

"Konnor!"

He looked back. Isbeil wobbled towards him. For the first time since he'd met her, she looked tired. Her eyes were sunken deeper into her sockets, and her aged skin had an ashen undertone.

"Leaving, are ye?" she said when she came to stand and face him. Her black eyes, though bloodshot, pierced him sharply.

"Yes."

"Hm. I thought more of ye."

"I never promised to stay."

She nodded. "Aye. 'Tis true. Are ye saying the faerie that commands the magic of time travel was wrong about ye?"

He swallowed a lump the size of a boulder. "Unfortunately, she was. I have to go. I've fulfilled my duty here. Marjorie is safe, so is Colin. I have a person in my life who's waiting for me, and who needs me."

"Be well, Konnor. Something tells me, though, I still may see ye."

Konnor shook his head, and on a strange whim, leaned down and hugged the tiny woman with one arm. She smelled of herbs, blood, and something waxy, like old wood. "Take care of her, will you?" he murmured.

When he released Isbeil, her eyes watered.

Without another word, Konnor turned and left the castle. With each step, he felt like the ground itself clawed at his feet, making it difficult to move forward. He followed the stream that went into the woods and continued down into the ravine to the east.

Twilight had descended by the time he made it to the ruin. He studied the remnants of the ancient tower, the rubble around it, and finally the damned time-traveling rock itself.

Compared to a few days ago, he felt like he was returning as a different man—broader, bigger, and lighter. Expanded.

But with a huge, open wound and his heart ripped out from his chest.

A figure in a long cloak sat on one of the stones of the tower and held something in her hands. Marjorie, he thought, his gut squeezing with excitement.

"Loves me, loves me nae..." A white petal flew in the air. "Loves me, loves me nae..." Another petal fell.

The figure raised her hooded head.

"Sìneag..." Konnor murmured, his stomach dropping with disappointment.

She stood up and walked to him, an oxeye daisy with only one petal left in her hand. She held it in front of him and plucked it demonstratively. "Loves me," she said and beamed. "I think she loves ye, Konnor."

Rub salt in the wound, why don't you? The scent of lavender and freshly cut grass enveloped Konnor as she came near. She threw the remnant of the daisy away and looked at him with her shiny, sparkling eyes. The tiny freckles looked dark brown in the twilight.

"If she does, she shouldn't," Konnor said. "I'm leaving."

She narrowed her eyes and cocked her head as though she couldn't decide where to put a flower in a bouquet.

"Are ye sure about that?"

He ground his teeth and said with more confidence than he had, "Yes."

"If ye leave, ye'll only have one last trip left. Are ye truly sure?"

Was he? Isbeil's words came to mind. Was she right? Was this not the end of his and Marjorie's story?

Would she come after him? To forgive him and say good-bye? Hope bloomed in his chest at the thought, cool and soothing. He looked back into the gray woods. Watched the branches moving in the wind ever slightly.

Wait... Was it her face?

No. Just the shadow of a bush swaying.

She wasn't coming. And even if she were, all he could offer her was more disappointment, because he would still leave. Wouldn't he?

He let out a half sigh, half growl, angry with himself now, because he dared to consider another option.

No. No more lingering and hoping and waiting. GTFO.

"Yes, Sìneag," he said. "I'm sure. This is best for everyone."

Sìneag's eyes grew sad. Without casting another glance at her, he marched towards the flat stone that had already started to glow and slammed his hand right into the handprint. A buzzing went through him and surrounded him like a tornado. The cool rock under his palm disappeared, and he started falling into the emptiness, but he still looked back, hoping to see Marjorie for the last time.

But there was no one there.

CHAPTER 28

T*hree days later...*

"MA, PLEASE PLAY SOCCER WITH ME," SAID COLIN COMING to her with Konnor's hay ball tucked under his arm.

There were no enemies here now. The waves of the loch splashed by her shoes, created by the breeze. Green, violet, and brown hills were calm under the leaden sky on the other side of the loch. Trees and bushes rustled in the wind behind her, and sheep grazed by the castle to her right.

Aye, she was alone with her son outside the castle walls. And she felt quite safe and secure. If she could protect Glenkeld against the MacDougalls, if she could defeat John MacDougall, what was there to fear in a wee walk outside the gates?

But despite the calm picture, Marjorie was in pain. Konnor's dear face was on her mind. Oh, how she missed him. Oh, how his rejection stung. She took in a lungful of air saturated with the scent of sheep, and lake water, and greenery.

Playing soccer would plunge her right back into that beautiful day when Konnor, Colin, and she played together. And that would torture her, reminding her again and again of what she'd never have.

The man she loved. A family with him. Happiness with him.

But her son didn't need to suffer just because she was. He deserved better, and she'd give him every happiness in the world.

She pressed on a smile. "Aye, of course I will."

The strange bracelet that Konnor had left for Colin shone on his chest. The bracelet was too big for the lad, and he'd put it on a leather string around his neck and wore it together with his cross. Marjorie was pretty sure it was something like a wee clock or a sundial, but it looked like magic, with the wee hand moving on its own, producing the *tick, tick, tick* sound. The surface was the smoothest steel she'd ever seen, smoother than the blades of a new sword. The thing was beautiful, masculine, and brought a sense of wonder.

When she touched its cool, sleek surface, she felt she not only touched Konnor, but she touched the future as well.

Colin had been ecstatic about the thing and called it "the ticker." He even slept with it. He didn't take it off when he bathed, and the miraculous object still ticked even under water.

It was the last thing she'd ever have from Konnor.

"All right, son. Where shall we have the goal?"

Colin pumped his fist excitedly and picked a large rock from the shore. "Over there, look." He pointed with his chin about ten feet farther up the shore. "That bush can be one part of the goal, and the boulder can be the other."

"Aye, good," Marjorie said and walked with him towards there.

She was the goalkeeper, again, and Colin turned out to be an excellent shot, it was also easier to kick the ball rather than the cluster of hazelnuts. They played for a while, until Colin suddenly stilled, his foot frozen midair over the ball as he stared at something behind Marjorie.

An icy shiver went through her, panic pulsing in a paralyzing wave. Thoughts flashed through her mind like angry wasps.

She was alone outside the castle with her son.

If the MacDougalls had sent someone to kidnap them, the watchmen wouldn't see them right away.

She'd rather die than let anyone take Colin.

Her hand shot to the dagger on her belt, and she pivoted to face whoever was behind her while unsheathing the dagger at the same time.

She pointed it at a man who sat on a horse and stared at her with wide eyes. He was giant. Tall, broad-shouldered, square-jawed, and red-haired. He was dressed in a weathered tunic, his breeches dirty in places and with patched holes.

Where had she seen him before? His face was blank in astonishment as he watched her and Colin.

"Marjorie?" His deep voice cracked in wonder and relief.

She blinked. He dismounted and took a step towards her.

"Stop!" she cried, still pointing her dagger at him.

The man held his hands up and stilled. Why did he look so familiar? Those high cheekbones, the almond-shaped eyes of a warm-brown color... He had a long, almost shaggy beard and his hair looked like it hadn't had a woman's touch for a very long time. And his eyes... There was pain in them, and sadness, and a desperate, desperate hope.

She'd seen those eyes before, but the man they belonged to was dead.

"'Tis me, Ian," he said.

The ground lurched under her feet and slipped away. She waved her free hand in the air, looking for something to lean on but found nothing. She stepped back and found her balance again.

"Ian..." she whispered.

She looked to her right, to where the small Cambel cemetery was, to where Ian's grave was with a headstone dedicated to him.

But if time travel was real, there was more magic possible. She turned to Colin, who kept staring at Ian with a frown. She gestured to him, and he hurried into her arms. Once he was in the security of her hug, she looked at the apparition before her.

"Are ye Ian's ghost?" she said.

His eyes clouded with an inner turmoil, and he pressed his lips tightly together in his beard. "In a sense, I am. The Ian ye kent died, Marjorie. But I'm flesh and blood."

Her vision blurred with tears, and her hand holding the dagger shook violently. "Ye didna die?"

"Nae."

She released the air in her lungs, but something in her refused to completely believe him, and she still held the dagger.

"Where have ye been?"

He swallowed. "The MacDougalls sold me into slavery to the caliphate. I've been a slave over there all these years."

Her arm fell. *A slave! Ian had been a slave...* A tear left a burning trail down her cheek. She dropped her dagger in the soft grass and marched towards Ian.

He took her in his huge arms, and she fell into them, crying, inhaling his dusty, dirty, dear scent.

"Ye came back," she whispered as he tightened his embrace. "Oh, thank God! Oh, thank God..." She leaned back. "Colin, come meet yer uncle Ian."

Colin came sheepishly, his eyes carefully estimating Ian. Marjorie let go of Ian and came to stand behind Colin and put her hands on his shoulders. "Ian, 'tis my son, Colin."

Ian's eyebrows rose. "Yer...son?"

"Aye," she said with her head raised.

Ian nodded respectfully as way of greeting. "Pleased to meet ye, lad. I'm so glad to have lived to see ye with my own eyes."

"Hello, Uncle," he said simply.

Marjorie sighed and felt a huge smile cut her face in two. "Come now, ye must be hungry and in need of a bath. I'll order one for ye, and ye can sleep in—" Her voice stumbled as she almost said he could sleep in Konnor's chamber. But it wasn't Konnor's anymore. "In the guest chamber next to mine."

Ian beamed. "Aye. Gladly, thank ye."

As they turned and walked to take his horse and go into the castle, Marjorie squeezed his hand. "Ye must tell me everything that happened to ye."

Colin kicked the ball towards the castle and ran after it. As Ian and Marjorie followed him, her cousin's face darkened. "I canna tell ye *everything*. Some of it isna for a tender lass's ears."

Marjorie laughed. "Tender lass? I dinna ken of whom ye speak. I have just led a strong defense against a MacDougall army six times bigger than my forces. And I won."

He looked at her with a blank expression on his face. "Ye? Alone?"

"I wasna alone. I had fifty men." And one of them from the future, without whom she probably wouldn't have made it. "But my father, and Uncle Neil, together with all my brothers and many other Cambel men, have been in the northwest, fighting for King Robert the Bruce."

"Marjorie, I dinna ken what to say..." Tears welled in his brown eyes. "I remember ye broken, curled into a ball, with nae will to live or go out to see the sun. And now ye have a son, and ye fight the battles that nae every man can... Lass, I'm so proud to be yer cousin. Ye're a true Cambel."

Gratitude spread through her chest like the warm rays of sunlight. "Thank ye, Ian."

They reached the castle and went through the gates. Colin

took Ian's horse and led it into the stables. Ian looked around and took a deep breath, then he let out a long, long exhale.

"I didna think I'd ever see Glenkeld again," he said. "Have ye been to Dundail lately?"

Dundail belonged to Ian's father, Duncan Cambel. It was about a day's ride away. It was Ian's home when he wasn't fostered with the Cambels in Innis Chonnel or Glenkeld.

"Nae since we were children," Marjorie said. "I ken yer father has been unwell recently. He hasna been on many battles ever since yer burial. He is in Inverlochy now. A rider came yesterday to say my father and brothers are there taking a brief rest."

"Then 'tis where I go on the morrow."

Marjorie nodded and smiled. "Aye. I'd like to see my brothers' faces once they see ye, but I must stay here to guard the castle."

She took him to the tower with the bedchambers.

"Where's yer husband, Marjorie?" Ian said.

"Husband? I have nae husband. Colin is Alasdair's."

Ian shook his head once. "Ye're a remarkable woman. After what he'd done to ye, ye love his son."

"Alasdair's seed conceived Colin, but there's nothing of that monster in my son. He's a Cambel. And I'm proud to be his mother, no matter what. It only made me stronger, Ian. It made me who I am."

And as she said that out loud, she realized her biggest fear, of being a coward, was gone, too. She wasn't a coward. She never had been. The fact that she'd been kidnapped wasn't a sign of her weakness. She'd fought as much as she could, and she hadn't submitted to Alasdair, no matter how much violence he'd wrought upon her. She didn't give up—not on herself, not on her child.

She hadn't even given up on love. Only that had gone to shite.

"Aye, I dare say it did, lass," Ian said. "Do ye nae want to get marrit?"

She looked at the courtyard thoughtfully. The men carried rocks up the towers and onto the northern wall. Now that they had time and peace to repair it, Marjorie wanted it done as soon as possible. They'd reclaimed the rubble from down under the wall to save money, and the clansmen who were normally engaged in sword training were doing the repairs.

"I didna for a long time. And then I met someone." She nudged a small stone with the edge of her shoe and kicked it away. "I...fell in love with him, and despite the heartache of my experience, I started seeing the possibility of being happy. He did that for me."

"Is he a good man?" Ian said. "Not that ye need my approval, but I will break his neck if he as much as looks at ye the wrong way."

She sighed. "He is a good man. Colin opened up to him, too. He saved both our lives."

"So where is he now, this good man?"

Marjorie hugged herself. "Far away."

"And ye love him?"

"Aye."

"And he loves ye?"

"I dinna ken. I thought he did."

Ian ran his fingers through his long, shaggy hair. "I've been a slave for many years, Marjorie, and I thought every day might be my last. I saw the Highlands and ye all in my dreams. I faced death daily. The one regret I had about my life was that I never kent true love. Never had a woman to care for, a bairn to live for. If ye met yer true love, lass, dinna throw it away. Or ye may regret it."

Marjorie bit her lip, fighting back the tears. He was right. If she didn't have Colin to think of, she might have tried to find a way to travel in time to Konnor, but she had her son to think about first. And nothing was more important than Colin and his well-being.

"Aye," she said. "Unfortunately, that isna possible. He's so far away, he may as well nae exist." She grasped Ian's hand and squeezed it. "But it dinna matter. Ye're here. Ye're alive and well. Do ye ken what ye want to do now?"

"Aye. Find my father and live my life quietly in Dundail."

"Ye chose the wrong time to try to live yer life quietly, cousin. The kingdom's at war."

"Doesna concern me. I wielded my sword for too long in the caliphate. I promised I wouldna kill another man in my life."

Marjorie nodded. It was his decision, but she doubted he'd be able to keep that promise.

"All right, go rest. I'll ask the servants to bring a bath and hot water for ye, as well as a warm meal. I'll send men out on a hunt, and we'll have a feast tonight in yer honor."

"Thank ye, cousin."

As Ian went into the tower and climbed the circular stairs, Marjorie watched him thoughtfully and wondered if there was a way for her to be with the love of her life and still keep her son's best interests at heart. She wished Konnor would change his mind and come back to her. Mayhap he could bring his mother with him. She was sure they would be great friends.

But wishing wouldn't make it so. She needed to get used to living a life with a hole in her heart. Nothing to do about that.

At least she and her son were free, unlike Ian had been these past years. Thank God, her dear cousin was back from the dead.

CHAPTER 29

L os Angeles, two weeks later

"KONNOR, SON, DINNER'S READY!" HIS MOM'S VOICE CALLED from the kitchen.

Konnor screwed a bulb into the chandelier and stepped down from the chair.

"Coming," he said as he walked towards the switch.

He flicked it and light filled the room. He sighed, looking around. That was the last repair his mom needed. He picked up a glass with whiskey and downed the remaining liquid. Unlike the medieval moonshine, it tasted full and smoky. Just perfect. And yet he'd give anything to drink the rough uisge, because that taste would forever be connected to Marjorie for him.

He switched off the soccer match on TV. While he'd been doing repairs around the house, his mind had wondered, thinking of how else he could make a soccer ball in medieval Scotland. If he'd had more time, he'd have taken wood shavings instead of hay, made pentagons out of leather and sewn them together properly.

Yeah, right. He'd never get the chance to do that now, so what was the point of thinking of it?

He stood up and walked from his mom's living room into the kitchen. Her house was a two-bedroom bungalow, with a shed in her back garden that served as the studio for her painting. The living room was colorful, with walls painted in rich turquoise and wood paneling that shone almost golden. The brightest paintings hung on the walls—white orchids, and hibiscus flowers with yellow-and-pink petals, and orange and blue birds of paradise. The house stood on a hill, and Konnor could see the ocean over the roofs.

As he entered the brightly lit kitchen, the scent of freshly ground coriander and fried chicken filled his nostrils. Mom set two plates with burgers on the kitchen island, carrot and celery root fries on the side. Her tablet next to the plates.

She flashed a nervous smile, though her blue eyes sparkled. Konnor's stomach twisted in a nervous knot.

"Sit, sit," she said. "I went to a cooking class on Thursday. We made chicken burgers with a Thai coriander dressing. I thought you'd like it."

Konnor sat on the high stool and stared at the bun and the fried chicken breast that steamed between it. Mom poured herself a glass of red wine and took out a beer for Konnor. Then she took a seat as well. Her short hair was wavy today, something she hadn't done for a long time, and turquoise earrings hung from under her locks. She also had pink lipstick on.

Lipstick? She doesn't wear lipstick...

The light-gray blouse and big turquoise necklace matching her earrings were new, weren't they? And what about the makeup?

"Mom," Konnor said. "What's going on?"

She chuckled nervously. "Let's eat first."

His gut twisted. "No. Tell me."

They had a usual Sunday routine. He'd come in the morning, bring her groceries and cash. She'd cook lunch, during which he'd do whatever small repairs she needed. They'd talk, she'd show him her new painting, and they'd go for a walk on the beach if the weather permitted. She never wore makeup, as far as he could remember, and she usually had something cozy on, like a jersey.

Actually, he'd noticed that something was different ever since he'd gotten back from Scotland. When he'd reached the Keir farm, the first thing he'd done was call her. And she hadn't even missed him. She'd been surprised he'd apologized for not calling sooner, even though he was supposed to have been back the day before.

The Keirs had taken him to the hotel in Dalmally, where a pissed-off Andy had raged and yelled at him for an hour. Scottish search and rescue hadn't been able to find him, and they'd been really close to calling his mom to tell her it was likely he'd died.

He'd told Andy he'd gotten lost in the storm, fallen into a ravine, and injured his ankle and his head. He'd said a woman who lived in a cottage found him and took care of him, and he'd stayed with her for a couple of days. The phone lines had been broken, so he couldn't contact anyone. Andy had still been furious with him.

Andy had his bag with his passport and his phone, and they'd both flown back home right away. During his first week back in LA, Konnor had gone to see his mom daily, making sure she was all right. She seemed surprised, and maybe even a little annoyed, to have him visit so often. "You're like a mother hen, Konnor, for God's sake. I love you, but please stop, I feel a little suffocated."

His firm was doing well, and it seemed the world had moved on while he was gone.

Only he hadn't.

"Mom," Konnor said, "whatever it is, tell me."

She sighed and glanced at the tablet. "All right. But promise me you'll take the news calmly."

His heart drummed. News? Was she sick? Was she moving? What was going on?

"I met someone."

Silence. If silence could explode, it just had.

"You what?"

She sighed. "I met someone, and I want you to meet him, too."

"Mom!"

She shrugged. "He's an art dealer who went to the same painting class as me six months ago. About portraits."

Goddamn it.

"He loved my painting, and I showed him my collection. He said the same thing you've been telling me for years, that I should have an exhibition and sell them. And you know what, I'm doing it. He's helping." She giggled. "In New York, of all places!"

Konnor groaned. Fear gripped him in an ice-cold vise. "You're not serious."

She blinked. "All right, all right. Calm down. I'm not moving in with Mark or anything. But we've been dating for six months now."

"Dating for six months, and you're only telling me now?"

"Because I feel like it's only now gotten serious. While you were away in Scotland, we took a trip to Vegas. Mark's very respectful and sweet and..."

She'd left town with a man he hadn't even met while he was out the country? No wonder she hadn't been worried her son hadn't called.

His blood pulsed hotly in his temples. She was about to give him a heart attack. "Sweet? But after Jerry—"

She stood up and propped her hands against her waist. "No, Konnor. You don't get to bring up Jerry now. I learned my lesson. I went through therapy. It was fifteen years ago, son."

"And I still cannot forgive myself for letting him hurt you like that."

She stilled, wide-eyed. Something he hadn't seen on her face for a very long time appeared. Guilt.

"You? Forgive yourself? You were a boy, Konnor. Nothing about that situation was your fault. What could you have done?"

They had never spoken about it. Not while Jerry was alive, not after he died. But it hung on Konnor like a heavy weight. The guilt.

"Something. Tell someone. Call the police."

"I told you not to."

"Still. I should have been stronger."

"No, Konnor." She took his face in both her hands. "I should have. Do you hear me? It's on me. On the grown-up. I should have left him and protected both you and me."

Tears welled in her eyes, and his chest tightened. She let him go and sat on the chair, taking a big sip of her wine with a shaky hand.

"Actually, it's something I've talked with Mark about. He understands me because he, too, comes from a home where his father beat him."

A spasm contracted Konnor's stomach.

"But despite that," Mom continued, "he's a wonderful father, because he never wants his children to go through what he went through. I met his ex-wife. Actually, she owns the gallery in New York, and they're very amicably divorced. Mark and I, we're both victims of abuse." Her voice shook. "And so are you, honey."

Konnor jumped off his chair. It was too painful to listen to this, too shocking. He wanted to erase these words from his memory and not hear a word of it again. His mom was moving on. Either that, or she was making the biggest mistake of her life. Hadn't she learned that love only ended in pain?

He paced alongside the kitchen island, clenching and unclenching his fists in an attempt to relieve the tension in his shoulders and arms.

"But how do you know he's not going to be just like Jerry?"

She straightened her back and raised her chin. "You're right. I don't know it for sure yet. But I'm also not jumping into anything like I did with Jerry. I'm taking it slow. I'm looking after myself."

She glanced at the napkin with seashell patterns and shifted it on the table so that it lined up perfectly with the middle of the plate. When she met his eyes, Konnor felt as though a goddamn spear was ripping into his chest.

"I should've been strong enough to leave Jerry," she said, "and not put us both through hell. But I am stronger now. I will recognize the signs of a violent man if they appear." She lifted her brows. "Unlike then, I don't need a man. And I'm not in a rush to move in with someone or anything. My life is great as it is." She cocked her head and smiled. "I'm happy with myself, Konnor. I have you, my wonderful son. But you have your own life to live, and I'm closer to the end of mine."

"Mom! You're not even sixty."

"Yeah, and I'm sure I have many more great years ahead, and I want to enjoy them to the fullest. You're grown. You don't need me. Maybe my art show will be a hit, and I'll finally get out of your hair and earn my own money doing something I love. Wouldn't you like that for me?"

Yeah. His feeling had been right. His mom was moving on. Everything was changing. Except him. Was he clinging on to issues that were no longer there? Did his mom no longer need him?

A dark, bottomless wound throbbed in the middle of him. The only thing that would make the ache go away would be to get on the next flight to Scotland, find that ruin, and travel back through time to take his Highland queen in his arms and never let her go.

He leaned against the kitchen island top, the black granite cool against his heated palms. "Of course, I'd love for you to be happy. But I need to make sure the guy is good for you. I won't forgive myself if anything bad ever happens again. Safety comes before any infatuation."

"Infatuation?" she said, looking puzzled.

"Yeah. Infatuation. What else can be there after a couple of months of knowing each other?"

She smiled. "Six months. And it's more serious than infatuation. Here." She shifted towards the tablet. "Let me introduce you. Please?"

Konnor's nostrils flared. Everything within him screamed against it. He was worried for her. He hated the man already. He sighed. The guy was in his mom's life, and it was Konnor's job to make sure she was safe.

"Okay. But if I sense even a hint of violence in him..."

"Then what?"

"You'll break up with him, that's what. I'm not risking your health and your safety."

She rolled her eyes. "It's not for you to decide." She unlocked the screen and called a Mark Campbell on Skype.

Campbell?

While the tablet rang, Konnor's stomach roiled with a strange sensation of déjà vu. Campbell was no doubt a modern version of Marjorie's clan name, Cambel.

"Does he live in New York?" Konnor murmured.

"No, LA, but he's in New York to set up my exhibition for next week."

"Next week? Were you even planning to invite me?"

The screen went live. "Hello!" a male voice said.

Staring at Mark's face, Konnor sat completely still.

Tamhas looked back at him from the screen, only a sixty-year-old version, and with his long hair completely white. He even had the same white stubble on his chin, and intense gray eyes.

"Hold on," Mark Campbell said, and the background behind him shifted. "Let me find a calm spot. Ah here, the back of the gallery will do." He looked at Konnor and his mom and smiled. "Hello, Helen. Hello, Konnor. Nice to finally meet you."

He had a bright, pleasant simile. Wise eyes. Calmness and peace radiated from him.

"Hi," Konnor said, stupefied.

"Hi, honey," his mom said.

Konnor suppressed a growl. *Honey? We'll see about that.*

"So I hear you've been seeing my mom," Konnor said.

Mark nodded. "I've been fortunate enough to, yes. She's one of a kind."

Konnor cocked his head. "We can agree on that. What are your intentions towards my mother?"

He sounded like an old-fashioned prick, but he didn't care.

"My intentions..." Mark met his mom's eyes, and they warmed with such light and love that Konnor gritted his teeth. "My intentions are to make her deliriously, unconditionally happy. As long as she'll have me."

Yeah. We'll see about that, too.

Konnor's hand clawed around his fork. "When are you back in LA?"

"Tonight."

"Like soccer?"

"I do, actually."

Konnor was pretty sure the man said that because his mom had told him Konnor was a soccer fan. But at least he had the decency to pretend like he did.

"How about we go to see a game tomorrow. Have some beers. Talk man-to-man, not on Skype."

"Sounds like a plan. Just one thing. I don't drink."

"Why? Alcoholic?"

His mom gasped. "Konnor!"

Mark laughed. "It's a fair question given my upbringing. No, I'm not an alcoholic. I tried a beer once when I was sixteen and hated the taste and the way it made me feel. In combination with my childhood and my father being an alcoholic, I decided not to drink."

Ah, hell. Konnor just might like the man, even though he hadn't intended to.

"All right," Konnor said to the modern, older version of Tamhas. "I'll see you tomorrow."

CHAPTER 30

The stadium rumbled with the singing of thousands of voices. Konnor watched the brightly lit green grass, though he wasn't really interested in the game. The seats in the Midfield Box of Banc of California Stadium were amazing. Konnor wasn't a poor man, but he couldn't afford being a member here.

Mark really did like soccer and had enough money for the membership. They sat in the middle of the box, and a vendor brought them two boxes of nachos and two sodas.

"The preparation for your mom's exhibition is going well," Mark said. "I've seen many different artists in my years of doing business, but raw talent like your mother's doesn't come along often."

Konnor simply stared at Mark's profile. The resemblance with Tamhas was uncanny. Yeah, there were some differences, like Mark's nose was thinner and higher, and his eyes were a different color. But even the voice, save for the Scottish burr, sounded similar. Mark and Tamhas had the same pleasant baritone. Only where Tamhas talked fast and was always on the lookout for danger, Mark was calm and at ease.

"I've been telling her she should show her paintings to someone for years."

"Yeah. She told me. You were right."

"But are you sure you're not just trying to get her to like you more?"

He smiled sadly, his eyes watering. "I was afraid I could be biased because I'm so in love with her."

In love? Konnor's lungs contracted.

"But I asked my ex-wife, who owns a gallery in New York, and some of the art dealers I know and trust. They all think she's a gem. How many does she have? Hundreds? She's sitting on a fortune, my friend."

Konnor sighed. It was great to know his mom was so talented and could secure her future if for any reason Konnor were to disappear...

If he went back in time, for example.

Oh, how he wanted to see Marjorie. Take her into his arms, inhale her herbal scent.

But he couldn't. No matter how desperate and sad he was, how empty his life felt without her...

He loved her.

He, who knew love was an illusion and only brought pain, loved her. The Highland faerie Sìneag was right. Marjorie was the woman for him. He knew it in his bones. It fit so well. And he'd needed to cross hundreds of years and see his empty, pointless life to realize that.

Still, he couldn't abandon his mother. And he still needed to make sure Mark was the man his mother thought he was. After all, Jerry had been sweet and kind until Helen and Konnor had moved in with him.

"What do your kids do?" Konnor said.

"My oldest, Denise, is your age, and she's a boat captain. My middle son, Trevor, is a pediatrician in Chicago. My youngest son, Jack, is still in school studying psychology." He chuckled. "They say psychologists go into the profession to solve their own problems, but I hope we didn't do too badly of a job as parents."

Konnor looked sharply at him. He hadn't considered that until right now. Even though Mark was the victim of domestic abuse, like Konnor, he'd gotten married and had three children. Yes, he was divorced, but he didn't look like he was suffering or anything. He said he *loved* Konnor's mom.

"So what happened with your ex-wife?" Konnor said. "Why the divorce?"

Mark inhaled deeply, sat back in his chair, and sighed, looking at the players running around the field.

"Good question. What happened... I don't know. We were deliriously happy. I loved her. She loved me. We had our kids, did a great job with them, if I say so myself. I'm very proud of every single one of them. But then...something was missing. I suppose, Janet said it first. She asked what was going on. We simply...grew apart. There was no hatred between us, no drama. The whole divorce thing was really boring. We still have a good relationship. A lot of it revolves around work. She has her gallery, which was ours before, and I hunt down great art. We're comfortable financially, as you can see. I think it was a bit difficult for the kids, but in the end, they understood and agreed it's better for everyone."

Konnor felt it. The man was being truthful with him. It was in the ease of his words, in his relaxed pose, in his tone.

"So there was no pain? When you divorced?"

He narrowed his eyes thoughtfully. "Not pain exactly. More like sadness, I think. I did mourn our relationship. We were happy, and I'd thought we'd always be together. You don't marry someone thinking you'll be done with them one day, right?"

"That would be what I'd be thinking," Konnor mumbled.

"What was that?"

"Nothing."

"No. Tell me. Did you say you'd be thinking that?"

Konnor sipped his Coke, regretting his words, hoping he could distract the man. He had no intention of talking about his feelings and limitations. "Doesn't matter."

"No," Mark said. "It does. It's not my business, of course, but I do think you and I, and your mother, share something deep and unfortunate. That experience of being abused and helpless and being taught all the wrong things about life. I used to hate everything and everyone. I stole stuff. I beat the shit out of others. I thought bad things about myself because my father's fists taught me to do so. I think that's why I went to study art, to find the relief from pain."

Konnor nodded thoughtfully. For someone with a similar violent upbringing, Mark seemed like a normal guy now. Not broken. And he was a family man who'd raised three kids.

"Did your ex ever accuse you of being emotionally unavailable?"

Mark rubbed his chin with an amused half smile. "Is that what your girlfriend accuses you of?"

Actually, Marjorie had never said that to him. She was hurt he left, but she was the first person he'd opened up to. He'd told her his worst insecurities, and, surprisingly, she'd accepted him. Not only accepted, she'd kissed him.

For the first time in his life, he'd been emotionally available to a woman. And he'd loved it.

He loved her.

She'd believed in him unconditionally. She'd trusted him and hadn't been afraid of him. She'd said he could be a wonderful husband and father.

"What helped you be a good husband and father, Mark? Your dad, like my stepdad, was a terrible role model. What made you think you could do it?"

Mark chuckled. "Well, to be fair, I didn't think I could do it until the day my daughter was born. But the moment I held that little pink baby in my arms, the moment I heard her first cry, I knew what I didn't want to be. Him. That I'd do anything in my power to shield her from that. That I'd be the opposite of my father, whatever that meant. I wouldn't be violent. Wouldn't be a selfish asshole. And suddenly, I was thankful to him for showing me how bad someone could be. For giving me the choice of not being like him. And every day of my life, I wasn't. And it's because I know that darkness that I can choose light. And I can show my wife and my kids light."

Konnor blinked.

"I think your mother knows it, too. And so do you, Konnor. So do you."

Konnor stared at the soccer field but didn't see it. The sounds of the crowd yelling grew quieter and became echoey. He felt as if he were being lifted out of his body and flying up, staring at himself sitting next to Mark from a distance.

Mark was right. Why was he so fixated on not knowing how to be a good father and a husband? Of course he didn't know. But no one knew until they figured it out. And sometimes, knowing what you don't want to be was enough. It was everything.

And what about love leading to pain? Could it be any worse than what he'd gone through when he'd left Marjorie?

But he realized, as long as he didn't become his stepfather, he'd be all right. He'd make Marjorie happy. He'd teach Colin soccer and read him *The Lord of the Rings* and show him what it took to be a good man. Because, in a perverse way, that was exactly what Jerry had taught him.

"You are all right, aren't you?" Konnor said to Mark.

Mark chuckled. "I think I am."

"You won't hurt her? You'll support her and take care of her?"

Mark's eyes relaxed with understanding and shone with a calm, inner light. "Of course I will."

And Konnor knew that he would. His mom was ready to live her own life without his support.

And he was ready to live his.

With Marjorie and Colin. Even if it meant going back to the Middle Ages. He was ready to go back, forever, if that was what it took to be with the woman he loved.

He'd go back to the Highlands and wouldn't stop until he found the faerie or some way to open up the damn tunnel through time. He didn't know yet what he'd say to his mom, what he'd say to Andy, and what he'd do with his firm... But he'd figure it out, and as soon as he did, he'd take a plane to Scotland and go hiking, and somehow, he would get lost.

But he had to know one thing. "Mark, do you have any relations in the Scottish Highlands?"

"I think my ancestors were Campbells, yeah. Why?"

Konnor grinned. "It's just you remind me of someone. If you're anything like him, I think my mom will be all right."

CHAPTER 31

T *wo days later...*

MARJORIE WIPED HER FOREHEAD WITH THE BACK OF HER hand and put her sword back in its sheath. The sun burned her skin after a long training session. The courtyard around her swarmed with activity. Other warriors trained, too, and the air was loud with the ring of swords clashing against each other. She'd hoped regular exercise would take her mind off the constant, nagging pain in her chest that had been there since Konnor left.

But nothing did.

With Ian gone yesterday, she'd plunged into an even deeper darkness and despair.

"Good," Marjorie said to Colin. "Ye will be a great warrior one day."

The lad grinned and blushed.

"'Tis an honor to be trained by ye, my lady."

"My lady?" She chuckled. "Please."

"Aye, but ye are. Ye're a great lady and a great warrior who protected the castle all by yerself."

Marjorie took a sip from her waterskin. "I would never have been able to do that if nae for our clan. And our good friend."

Her voice shook a little as she said the last word, and her stomach twisted. She nodded to Colin and went to the well to wash her face. The cool water brought some relief and distracted her a bit from constant thoughts of Konnor. She'd dreamed about him every night, imagining how his life was, hoping he was well. She tried to picture the future, the houses and castles that people had, the horseless carriages that Konnor had described, the cupboards where food didn't go bad, the boxes with bards that played music whenever one wanted. The world where women were men's equals.

Her position was remarkable with the freedom her father and her uncle Neil had given her, but it was because they both felt guilty and wanted to spare her feelings. Any other woman her age would be expected to marry and run her husband's household, not wield a sword and protect their castle.

"Are ye tired, lass?" Isbeil said behind her back.

Marjorie turned around. The old woman's kind eyes fixed on her with sympathy and amusement.

"Aye," Marjorie said, wiping her face with her sleeve. "I've been training the lad since the midday meal."

"I am nae talking about that. Are ye nae tired from this waiting and sighing? 'Tis already been two sennights since he left."

Of course, Isbeil saw deeper. And of course, Isbeil was right.

Marjorie propped her hands against her waist. "Aye. But I canna do much about it, can I?"

Isbeil chuckled softly and shook her head. "If 'tis the story ye keep telling yerself, let us take a walk. Help me gather some herbs."

Marjorie really didn't want Isbeil to lecture her or point at any more painful spots in her soul. Marjorie was happy to help her, but the main reason for the walk wouldn't be herbs.

"Ma, may I come?" Colin said.

He suddenly appeared by Marjorie's side. The lad used every opportunity to go outside the castle walls.

Isbeil turned and walked towards the gates. "Come, Colin. Ye can help me, too."

Marjorie looked at the old woman's back helplessly. How was it possible that such a small creature had so much power? She sighed, nodded to Colin, and they followed her.

Passing by the gates, Marjorie marveled at how easy it had become for her to walk out of the castle on her own. Ever since the battle, she'd gone hunting and taken long walks in the woods by herself. All she needed was her sword and her bow. She felt safe in her own company.

They walked in silence for a while, as fast as Isbeil's aching knees allowed. Colin went to the side a bit, happily beating trees with a stick, as boys did. He leaned down from time to time and picked wild strawberries, bringing some to Isbeil and Marjorie. They crossed the flat meadow and walked into the woods, following the creek in the crevice that had the ruin that had taken Konnor away. Marjorie's stomach knotted painfully at the thought, and she took a lungful of the fresh scent of the woods and exhaled it to release the ache.

It was quiet here. Birds chirped, the stream murmured gently, and leaves rustled in the wind. From both sides, steep, rocky slopes descended into the ravine. Ferns and wildflowers grew around bushes and trees. Rocks and boulders lay scattered. Isbeil stopped and bent over.

"Ah, thistle." She carefully cut a violet floret with experienced fingers so that the needles didn't hurt her and studied it briefly. "For Malcolm's heart. Although 'tis yer heart that concerns me now."

"Found them, too!" called Colin from about twenty feet away.

Marjorie sank to her knees by another gathering of thistle and cut a floret with her dagger. She hissed when the thorns prickled her. "My heart? I'm healthy and strong. Dinna fash yerself about me, Isbeil."

"Hmm."

"Truly."

"'Tis nae yer physical heart I speak of. Dinna pretend like ye dinna catch my meaning."

Marjorie stood up and dropped the florets into Isbeil's basket. The old woman looked at her with reproach.

"What do ye want me to say?" Marjorie threw up her hands. "That I miss him? I do. That he broke my heart? He did. All that is true enough. And so?"

"And so?" Isbeil straightened up with a fleeting expression of pain. "Ye've lived as a shadow of yerself ever since ye came back from Dunollie. After Konnor came, I saw ye flourish and heal and come back into yer true self. And now that he's gone, ye're nae yerself again."

Marjorie turned away, her face burning, something stabbing between her ribs. "It'll pass. I'll forget him."

Even she heard the false tone in her voice. She'd never forget him. Konnor's name was branded on her heart, his presence on her soul, his touch on her skin. Forever. If she was supposed to be happy with anyone, it was him. She wanted no one else's hands on her, no one else's lips, and no one else's body.

"Hmm," Isbeil hemmed again and came to kneel by a big gathering of thistle near Marjorie.

"I'll try," Marjorie added.

"Ye will try. But ye will fail. How do ye imagine yer life from now on?"

Marjorie shrugged. "I'd go to war with my clan, but I canna leave Colin. Sooner or later, Da, Uncle Neil, and my brothers will come back. Mayhap we'll travel. I'd like to go see Ireland with Colin... Mayhap, France. Mayhap, Flanders..."

"Flanders," Isbeil muttered, her hands working efficiently on the thistle. "Ye want to travel all right. Only nae to Flanders. Were ye nae like an excited wee lass when he told ye all about the future? I dinna remember ye ever being as joyful about my Highland tales as ye were about Konnor's."

Marjorie stilled with the thistle in her hands. Travel to the future? "Of course, I'm curious. Who wouldna be?"

"I am nae curious. I am perfectly fine where I am."

"But I'd never go."

Isbeil scoffed. "And what keeps ye here?"

"Everything! My life is here. Colin's life is. My father, my brothers, my whole clan..."

"I dinna think they struggle up north without ye."

Marjorie pressed her lips tightly together.

"I'm Craig's only sister of whole blood."

"And?"

Marjorie threw the thistles angrily into Isbeil's basket. "Isbeil, even if I wanted to abandon everything here, he doesna want me there."

"And how do ye ken that?"

Marjorie frowned. How did she know that? He hadn't asked her to come with him, but he also hadn't said he didn't want her to come. Aye, he had things he needed to do in the future, but his main reason for leaving hadn't been that he didn't love her. It was that he worried he wouldn't be a good enough husband and father. That he couldn't give her the love and happiness she deserved.

But he'd been a good role model for Colin. And he could give her love and happiness. He was the only one who could.

And she loved him. Her heart thumped painfully against her chest at the thought. She loved him more than anything.

She loved him so much, she was half a person without him in her life. And it didn't matter where that life was—here or in a distant future.

She wasn't a coward anymore. She'd walked out of the castle alone many times. Could she be brave enough to go even farther than that—to go into the future?

But all that was completely useless.

"Even if he didna mind me there," Marjorie said. "Even if the Pictish magic works, and I can go, he didna ask me to go with him. How can I trust he'll want me there?"

"Ye canna trust he'll want ye? He risked his life for ye and yer son. If 'tisna love, I dinna ken what is."

Marjorie glanced sharply at her. "Love? Ye think he loves me?"

Isbeil laughed. "Of course he loves ye, ye silly lass."

"But he said... He said he shouldna have become close with me."

"'Tisna because he didna love ye. 'Tis because he does. And he doesna want to hurt ye."

Marjorie shook her head slowly, thoughts whirling in her head like leaves on the wind.

"But he doesna want to be with me because he thinks love is a lie. Because of his stepda."

"What of his stepda?"

Marjorie bit her lip. "His stepda is his ma's Alasdair."

Isbeil stopped plucking. "Oh."

"Aye. He's afraid he's going to hurt me."

Isbeil resumed plucking. "And do ye think he might hurt ye?"

"Nae. Never."

"Ah, dinna lower yer head so, lass," Isbeil said. "He's a man of honor. A good man for ye, lass. I believe the faerie didna send him through time for ye for nothing. If ye can be happy with anyone, 'tis him."

Marjorie exhaled sharply. The truth of those words sank into her. Her heart squeezed with a dull ache and longing for Konnor. She'd found her inner strength thanks to him. But was she strong enough to cross time?

Marjorie locked her eyes with Isbeil. "Am I brave enough to risk everything?"

"The question is, lass, how much do ye love him?"

Marjorie's eyes filled with tears. "More than life itself." As she said that, she felt like she expanded, as though her body became bigger and taller and encompassed the whole world, was connected to everything around her.

"There's yer answer," Isbeil said softly.

Marjorie looked at Colin. "But 'tis nae just my decision, Isbeil. 'Tis also Colin's. I canna leave him here, and I canna force him to go."

"Have ye asked him if he wants to? He's terribly in love with that... What does he call it? 'The ticker'?"

Marjorie studied Colin, who was sharpening a stick with his knife thoughtfully. She hadn't even considered that Colin might actually want to go to the future. He loved the clan, and it would be difficult leaving everything he knew behind—his grandfather, his uncles, his home...

"No. I'm sure he doesna want to. His whole world is here. He'd never want to leave the clan."

"Ye stubborn Cambel," Isbeil murmured. "Ye're even more hardheaded than yer father. And as long as I've lived, I havna met anyone as stubborn as he is."

Marjorie clenched her jaw tightly. "Ye dinna ken my son as well as I do, Isbeil..."

"Ugh!" Isbeil splayed her hands in the air, her face distorted in an angry mask. She was angry. Marjorie had never seen her angry in her life. "I swear, ye Cambel children will be the end of me one day." She sighed and watched Marjorie as though contemplating her next words.

"Lass," she said, "I havna lived all these years to watch ye crumble and darken and curl into a ball again. A part of my soul would die. Did ye ken yer son came and asked me why his mother is so sad? If there is something he can do to put a smile on yer face? He asked me if I have a magic potion that would make his mother happy."

A pain as sharp as the tip of an arrow pierced Marjorie's chest. She looked at her son, who'd now found a hazelnut cluster and was kicking it around, just like Konnor had. Her eyes blurred with tears.

"Konnor came," Isbeil continued with her index finger pointed in the air, "and there was no magic potion needed. Ye bloomed. And so did Colin."

Oh, Jesu, she was right! He had seemed happier and more excited. His eyes had shone when Konnor had told him tales of the twenty-first century.

Marjorie swallowed a painful knot. "But the clan is more important to him. He's a Highlander. He's a Cambel. I canna just uproot him from everything he kens."

"And how do ye see his future? He doesna have an inheritance. Ye dinna have land. When yer father dies, Glenkeld will belong to Craig as the oldest, aye? Domhnall has an estate already. Owen is entitled to land, as well, if yer father ever decides he's mature enough. There is nothing left for ye, lass, and therefore nothing for Colin. As long as yer father lives, ye live with him. But what's next? Will ye be forever at the mercy of yer brothers? Will ye leave Colin forever at their mercy, too? Will the lad have to bow down to that MacDougall scum and beg to be made his heir after all?"

Marjorie inhaled sharply. "My brothers will never betray me."

"Aye. Of course they wouldna. But will ye like to live forever at someone's mercy, for yer son, too?"

Oh, she hadn't even considered that. Isbeil was right.

Marjorie would hate it with every fiber of her soul. Konnor had told her that women were as strong and as rich as men in the future. They earned their own fortune and didn't need to depend on a husband to have a good life.

What world did she want to live in? And what world did she want Colin to grow up in? She was sure it wasn't as simple as Konnor described, and she had no idea if she could find her own place in that future world, but she liked the idea of equality. She liked the idea of being independent. And she wanted Colin to experience that, too. He was a bastart here, no matter how much her family loved him and treated him like he wasn't. He'd never have the same rights here as a legitimate child. He'd always be treated like an inferior man by those born in a legitimate marriage.

What would he become? A mercenary. A knight, mayhap? He could still have a good life here, but only if it was connected to war and full of dangers.

Or he could accept John MacDougall's offer to legitimize him. But Marjorie couldn't stomach the thought of her boy in their hands.

Though Konnor was a warrior, too, the twenty-first century he'd described sounded like a more peaceful and healthy time.

And yet there was so much she couldn't even imagine. How would she even find Konnor? How would she make sure she and Colin were safe? Would Konnor want them there at all? Would he send them back? What if Colin got his hopes up only to be rejected and hurt by Konnor?

She couldn't let her son get hurt. And yet she wanted to go. She wanted to dare. She wanted to see the future. Most importantly, she wanted to be with Konnor.

"Colin, son," she called. "Come here, please?"

Colin caught the hazelnut cluster in the air and came to Marjorie. "Can I help ye with something, Ma?"

Marjorie inhaled and looked at Isbeil, who chuckled a sly, satisfied smile and busied herself with another thistle plant.

"Tell me something, son," she said. "When Konnor told ye all those stories of his time, what did ye think of them?"

His eyes sparkled. "I enjoyed them very much."

She swallowed a lump in her throat. "Would ye like to see it?"

His eyebrows rose to his bangs. "Aye, I would. Of course I would."

She squeezed his hand. "Me, too. And could ye imagine..." She chuckled softly, not believing she was about to ask this. "Could you imagine living in the future?"

He stilled and blinked. "Living there? With Konnor?"

She nodded. "Aye. I hope so."

"And what about Granda? And my uncles? And Isbeil? What about Glenkeld?"

"They'd stay here. Ye'd probably never see them again."

She bit her lip, gathering strength for what she was about to say next. "There's one more question, Colin. The question of yer inheritance. Yer grandfather MacDougall wants to have ye. He wants to legitimize ye. That would mean ye'd have right of inheritance. Ye could stay here and get lands and status from him. I just want ye to ken all yer options."

His nostrils flared. "Never. Nae land nor inheritance will make me want to be related to the man who tried to harm ye."

The weight of a boulder lifted off Marjorie's chest. She beamed. "Oh, thank Jesu."

He frowned and looked at his shoes, thinking. "Ma, I've never been anywhere other than Glenkeld in my life." He gazed around the woods longingly. "And I really want to."

He glanced at Isbeil and sighed. "I'd be sad to never see my granda and uncles. But I'd be sadder to see ye the way ye've been since Konnor left."

Oh, her kind, brave, loving boy.

His eyes shone. "And I really want to see the carriages that drive themselves and the giant iron dragons that fly in the air..."

Her vision blurred with tears. "Are ye certain? Ye want to go?"

He nodded, a fervent smile on his face. "Aye. I want to play soccer with Konnor."

CHAPTER 32

F*ive days later...*

WHAT THE HELL WAS MARJORIE SUPPOSED TO DO WITH THIS godforsaken rock? It lay flat and round and as large as the seat of the great chair in the great hall. The carving of three wavy lines forming a circle and a thick, straight line piercing it brought a nervous shiver through her. By its side was an imprint of a large hand, right in the stone. It looked like someone had pressed their hand in clay, and it had dried this way.

Marjorie was no Isbeil, but even she felt something...like the air wavering over rocks in direct sunlight on a hot day, except today was as gray and as cold as this rock.

With a frown, Colin clenched "the ticker" in his fist and studied the rock. He had a shoulder pouch with only a few valuable possessions: some silver coins—enough to buy passage as far as China, the farthest destination Marjorie could think of—an antler comb, a waterskin with water, clean linen cloths, as well as several jars with healing potions and herbs. There was also a rope for making rabbit snares, a meat pie, cheese, bread, and bannock for the few days on the road. Marjorie had Grandfather's sword in the sheath behind her back for when Colin would be grown enough to be able to wield it, as well as her bow and a quiver full of arrows. She was dressed in her leather breeches, perfect for a long way. A woolen cloak hung from her shoulders, for the nights they'd need to sleep outside in the woods. She wondered how long it would take to find Konnor—a few moons? A year? Mayhap, more. They had to be ready for everything. Colin had Marjorie's dagger on his belt next to his wooden sword.

She'd said goodbye to the whole castle, explaining to them Konnor had proposed to her and they were going to be with him. The shock Marjorie saw in the people's eyes was overwhelming. Malcolm said she was clearly out of her mind and threatened to lock her in her room until her father came back. Muir said he'd come with her. Marjorie cried for a while over Tamhas's grave, and somehow, she felt supported and blessed after.

The whole clan was in turmoil, staring at her as though she'd lost her mind. Isbeil was the only one who actually looked at her as though she was sane, and she calmed the people down.

Marjorie considered going to Inverlochy first to see if her clan was there and to say goodbye, or if she should wait for them to return from the war. But she was sure that if she did, they'd never let her go. Her father was very capable of locking her in her room until she came back to her senses.

So no matter how much it hurt to possibly never see them again, to not be able to say goodbye, it was the best thing to do. But she did write long letters to Craig, Domhnall, Owen, and to her father. She only told the truth about time travel to

Craig. He had watched over her all her life and rescued her from Alasdair. She owed him the truth, whether he would believe it or not. He'd probably think she'd lost her mind, but by the time he read the letter, she'd hopefully be long gone. Colin dictated her his own goodbye to everyone.

With that done, and Glenkeld left under Malcolm's careful supervision, Marjorie, with Colin by her side, went through the woods with her stomach squeezing in anxiety. She was afraid that the rock would work, and that it wouldn't.

And now that they were here, she had no idea what to do.

"Mayhap ye put yer hand in the handprint?" Colin said, hugging himself.

"But what if I go and ye dinna?"

"Then mayhap ye take my hand?"

Marjorie nodded and sighed. She took Colin's palm in hers. His was warm and solid, hers was cold and shaking. She looked into his eyes. "Ready?"

"Aye."

She released a long, audible breath. "Godspeed."

"Wait," a female voice said behind her, and the scent of lavender and grass reached her nose.

Colin and Marjorie both turned their heads. A woman in a dark-green, hooded cloak stood nearby, copper hair cascading in perfect waves down her shoulders and on her chest. She came closer, her eyes studying both Marjorie and Colin with bewilderment.

Marjorie stood up and pulled Colin behind her back, her hand on the hilt of her sword. The woman may be a faerie or a queen, but until Marjorie was sure she meant no harm to her son, she wouldn't be calm.

"I'm Sineag." The woman smiled. "No need to be afraid, Marjorie."

"I'm not afraid," Marjorie said. How did she know her name? Knowing everyone's names must be among the faerie's magical abilities besides time travel.

Sìneag glanced at the rock, and her face gained a sly satisfaction. "Were ye trying to go through time? To Konnor?"

Marjorie raised her head. "Aye. We were."

"Usually 'tis just one person."

"Usually?"

Sìneag laughed. "Aye, ye dinna think ye're the only one this has happened to, do ye?"

"I did."

Sìneag shook her head. "Nae. 'Tis what I do. I match people through time. Yer brother Craig and Amy. I hope ye and Konnor... Who kens how much happiness through time I can create." Her voice rang with excitement.

Marjorie's mouth opened. So she was right about her sister-in-law's accent and some of the words she used, that she sounded like Konnor. Marjorie hadn't spoken with her long when they gathered the family in Inverlochy, but she remembered an odd feeling about the woman. Why would Craig not have told her? Maybe for the same reason she hadn't wanted anyone to know about Konnor's real origin. She wouldn't have believed Craig. She was glad she'd decided to tell him the truth in her letter, after all. He was probably the only one who'd believe her.

"Ye, too, lad?" Sìneag said.

Marjorie looked back at Colin, and he stared at Sìneag with an open mouth and eyes full of wonder.

"Aye." He stepped from behind Marjorie's back. "We both."

Sìneag sighed and pressed her mouth mournfully. "Oh, lad, 'tis wonderful that ye want to travel in time, too. But 'tis nae possible."

"What? Why?" Colin said, the wonder in his face replaced by disappointment mixed with anger.

"Because the tunnel of time can be opened only three times for *a couple*. Those are the faerie rules."

"He's part of the couple," Marjorie said. "I'm nae going anywhere without him."

Sìneag pressed her lips together, thinking. "Aye. A good mother wouldna leave her child behind, but the two of ye just isna possible."

"Can ye make an exception?" Marjorie said, something inside of her shaking with worry.

Sìneag mournfully tilted her head to the side and bit her lip.

Colin said, "In one of Isbeil's stories, the faerie asked for a sacrifice. All I have is Arthur, my sword."

"Do ye love it dearly?" Sìneag said.

"Aye. 'Tis like my great-granda's sword. 'Tis all I have until I can wield a great claymore like his."

"Aye. I can accept it."

Colin's hand shot to the hilt of his wooden sword. "Arthur..." he whispered. He looked down at the sword and swallowed. "Granda made it for me. Uncle Owen suggested the name and trained me with it for the first time."

Marjorie's heart bled for him. It was probably like leaving a part of his childhood behind. Colin took a deep breath, pursed his lips in a mournful grimace, and gave a curt, decisive nod. He took the sword and carried it in front of him ceremoniously.

"I sacrifice ye, Arthur, for passage to the future."

He came to stand in front of Sìneag, who watched him with big eyes that watered a little. She took the sword from his hands and held it before her like treasure.

"I will cherish it and keep it safe," Sìneag said, and it disappeared in her hands. Marjorie gasped. Colin blinked several times and looked at Sìneag with reverence.

"Yer sacrifice is accepted, lad," she said. "But before ye may go, I need something else." She smacked her lips a little like a hungry babe. "Traditionally, milk is left for faeries overnight. But I'll take any food ye have. I'm a wee bit of a glutton." She giggled. "Consider it a bribe."

Marjorie chuckled. "What's a piece of pie for the lifetime of happiness? Colin, please give Sìneag the meat pie."

Sìneag clapped her hands, and Colin went into his purse and retrieved a piece of pie wrapped in linen. Sìneag quickly unwrapped it and bit into it. She tilted her head back and closed her eyes, chewing.

"Mmmm. Ye mortals dinna ken how good yer food is."

Marjorie and Colin exchanged a surprised glance and watched her devour the pie in three large gulps. For a seemingly delicate woman, Sìneag ate like a blacksmith after a long day of work.

Finally, a satisfied smile bloomed on her face. Her cheeks looked rosier than before, her lips red. "Aye, that will do, my lovelies. Now ye both may go. But remember, this will be the last time, so think carefully. Ye may still stay."

Marjorie and Colin looked at each other. "We go," Marjorie said to Sìneag.

"Good. Then hold hands. Marjorie, think of Konnor and place yer hand in the handprint."

Marjorie took Colin's hand and sank to her knees by the rock. She closed her eyes and thought of Konnor, and her whole being felt like she were flying. Joy shone through every little part of her body, radiating warmth and love through her heart. She placed her hand in the handprint, but instead of a cold rock, there was empty air. And suddenly she was falling, facedown into waves of pure vibration. She swung her other hand, searching for Colin but not finding him.

With the thought of him and Konnor, she sank into darkness.

She didn't know how much time passed. It felt like a lifetime later, or mayhap it was just a moment. Marjorie opened her eyes. The painful sensation of being sucked into something and then falling through eternity was dissolving in her body like blood in water.

She wasn't falling anymore. Hard ground supported her. Her palms leaned on soft grass, and pebbles stuck into her skin. She looked around. There was the ruin and the Pictish rock. The brook burbled nearby. Familiar steep slopes stood on both sides of the crevice.

Colin! She looked around, and there he was, sitting and staring at her with an astonished face.

"Are ye whole, lad?" she said.

"Aye." He stood and looked around. She did the same.

Were they really in the future now? How could Marjorie tell? The woods looked the same. It sounded the same. There was the peaceful chirping of birds, rustling of leaves, and babbling of the water.

The pouch with silver and other things was still on Colin. They needed to be prepared in case the people from the future wanted to take her silver or harm them. Obviously, there were men with bad intentions in all times. Marjorie stood and drew her sword, feeling much less confident than she was trying to look. *What was that?* She looked around.

Someone moved up the slope between the trees. Alarmed, she put her sword back in the sheath, took her bow and an arrow, and aimed at the figure behind the trees. Her heart drummed in her ears. She followed the dark figure with her arrow pointed at them. Then the bushes moved, and a man stepped out from behind them, his brown hair catching the light, a travel pack on his broad shoulders.

Konnor.

A hot, happy wave rushed through Marjorie. Time stopped. So did her heart. Nothing existed except for the man who was more dear to her than life itself. He stared at her, as still as time was.

"Marjorie?" he said finally. "Is that really you?"

His voice. His dear raspy voice sounded better than the song of the best bard.

"Aye, 'tis me," she said and lowered her bow.

"And Colin?" he said.

"Aye!" Colin came to stand next to Marjorie.

Konnor scratched his head. "How did I travel back to you without touching the rock?"

"We traveled to ye," Marjorie said.

She looked back at Sìneag, but there was no one where the woman had stood. The scent of lavender and freshly cut grass was gone as well.

"You traveled to me?" He shook his head in astonishment.

Marjorie put her bow on her shoulder and her arrow in the quiver. Her hands shook, and her knees wobbled. "Aye, we did. And now it seems there's just this slope that separates us."

"Stay there. I'll help you up." Konnor removed the big bag on his back.

Marjorie shook her head and chuckled softly. "Isna it how ye injured yerself?" With her stomach both knotting and bubbling with excitement, she walked towards the slope. "Stay there. We're coming to ye. I'm nae a gentle lady who needs rescuing."

Konnor grinned. "No, you are not."

The way up was harder than she'd thought. Rocks and pebbles ran from under her shoes. She breathed heavily, and her heart thundered against her ribs. Was it from the climbing, or from seeing Konnor? She grasped branches and roots to keep from falling. She and Colin helped each other get up the hard places.

Finally, they stood before Konnor. Marjorie felt flushed, hot, and sweaty. She took in a lungful of air in an attempt to calm her ragged breathing. There he was, hugging her son with the brightest smile she'd ever seen on his face. The man who'd brought her back to life. The man who understood and cherished her more than anyone in the world. His blue eyes pierced her with the intensity of lightning, like he could look into her soul, like he could see her whole, naked, and vulnerable.

When he let Colin go, he came to stand before her.

"Hi," Konnor said softly.

She forgot how to speak. His presence melted her like fire malted a wax candle, so sweetly, so deliciously. She remembered his mouth on her lips, his hands making her body sing like a citole. Her mouth went dry, and a new layer of sweat broke out over her skin. Suddenly, she craved something strong to drink.

"Why are ye here?" Marjorie managed. "Isna Los Angeles on the other side of the world?"

"Yes, it is," he murmured, and his voice stroked her like a gentle hand. "I came to go back through time for you."

The ground shifted under her feet, and she needed a moment to find her balance again.

"For me?"

"Yes, my Highland queen." He brushed his knuckles against her cheek.

Highland queen. She let the words wash over her for a moment. They settled in her stomach, instantly setting a whole cloud of butterflies into the sky.

"Did ye change yer mind then?"

"I did. I don't want to imagine my life without you."

Those words were like freedom. Like running on the edge of a cliff without a worry in mind, jumping off and being caught by the wind and carried above the sea. She felt weightless. Expanded. Complete.

"And I dinna want a life without ye," she echoed. She looked at her son. She smiled to him, and he gave her a nod. "And neither does Colin."

Konnor took a step towards her, a mountain of a male, his scent the sweet mixture of unknown herbs and sea and his own musk.

"Come here." He took her in his arms and kissed her.

The world around her swam and shifted, and everything around her disappeared but Konnor. Only his lips stayed, the warm, soft bliss of his mouth, the gliding of his tongue against hers, the gentle nibbling of her lip. The iron rods of his arms around her waist was the best confinement in the world.

"Ma!" Colin gasped. "Konnor! Ye can lick each other's mouths when ye're alone."

With difficulty, Marjorie leaned back and interrupted the kiss. Oh, how she'd missed him. She hadn't even realized how much she'd missed him until right now. She belonged with him. In these arms, glued to this body, breathing the same air as him. Dissolving with him.

She smiled at Colin. "Dinna fash, son. One day ye'll meet a woman ye love like I love this man, and ye'll understand."

Colin blushed and mumbled something. Marjorie and Konnor exchanged an amused look. But there was still one question to sort out.

"Did ye want to come stay with me in 1308?" she said.

"Yes." Konnor chuckled. "I'd be happy to live in any time as long as you and Colin are by my side. I know your life and your family are in 1308, so the last thing I wanted was to take you away from them."

Marjorie chuckled softly.

"Well, I was hoping to stay in yer time. Sìneag told me this was the last time we could use the rock."

Konnor grinned the most heartwarming, sunny grin she'd ever seen. It transformed him from a somber warrior to a carefree boy. He picked her up, whirled her around, and kissed her again.

"I love you, my Highland queen, the love of my life."

"I love ye, too, Konnor Mitchell, warrior from the future. I canna wait to have this life with the two most important men in my life."

Colin grinned and hugged her waist, and Konnor put his arms around them both. As she swam in the ocean of happiness together with the man of her dreams, she knew he was the only one in the whole world, in all time, who could give her hope.

The hope that now grew and brought her the biggest adventure of all—a lifetime with the man she loved and her son. Finally, a family.

EPILOGUE

L os Angeles, October 2021

"OH, HONEY, YOU'RE SO BEAUTIFUL," HELEN, KONNOR'S mother said as she entered the room.

Marjorie met Helen's eyes in the mirror and bit her lip, trying not to let her tears fall. She looked back at her reflection, not quite believing that she was seeing herself in the mirror, and not someone like Sìneag, a faerie from another world.

The dress was modest compared to what Marjorie had seen in Los Angeles and was likely old-fashioned for modern tastes. It was, in essence, the dress of a medieval lady. The neckline ended just below the neck, and draped sleeves that reached her knees. The dress hugged her waist and her chest but fell in a free skirt down her legs to the floor.

The ivory lace was as delicate as the first frost on the loch. Her dark-brown hair had gained golden tones under the almost eternal California sun, and there were even freckles on her previously clear skin. A hair stylist had created large curls in her long hair, and a diamond circlet sparkled on her head, but even that couldn't compare with how her eyes shone.

Because she was marrying the love of her life.

"Thank ye, Mother," Marjorie said and wiped a tear that refused to obey her will.

She'd called Helen mother almost since the day she met her. Helen surrounded her and Colin with love and care that Marjorie had never experienced even with her stepmother. Together with Mark Campbell, they'd truly made a home away from home for her and her son.

Helen walked into the brightly lit hotel room. They had rented a small hotel called Glen Thistle, situated right on the cliffs of Malibu. The building had a roof with merlons, was made of rough, dark-gray granite stones, and had a three-story, round, ivy-covered tower. It reminded Marjorie of a wee castle. There were boulders on the property, and even an artificial brook that flowed into a pond in a small waterfall. There was no moss, no heather, and no lochs. But the hotel overlooked the ocean, and it was as close as they could get to the Scottish Highlands. Konnor and Marjorie had known at once they wanted to get married here.

And the exuberant price hadn't mattered because Mark Campbell, Helen's beloved, had booked the location for them as his wedding present.

"Honey, may Mark come in? He's waiting outside. He doesn't want to come in if you'd rather not."

Marjorie beamed. "Of course he can."

"Mark, come in," Helen said to the door.

Mark came in, and as with every time Marjorie saw him, a lump formed in her throat at the striking similarity to Tamhas. His hair was in a small ponytail at the back of his head, and he was cleanly shaved for the occasion. He was dressed in a kilt, something that would apparently become Scottish later in the history. As she learned, the blue-green-and-black tartan would become Campbell clan colors, and the sense of unity overtook her, expanding in her chest. It meant a lot to her that he'd chosen to wear the kilt. It was for her sake, to show her his support, and though the whole clan and tartan colors weren't something she'd experienced back in her time, she loved and understood the meaning of them, the significance, and she loved Mark for showing her they were one clan. On top, he wore a tuxedo with a crisp white dress shirt. A large magenta thistle was in his lapel, the flower of the wedding.

Colin's head appeared from behind the door. "A certain gentleman also can't wait to see you," Mark said.

"Colin, come in, son," Marjorie said.

Colin ran into the room and into her open arms, kicking the air out of her as he slammed into her embrace. He wore the Campbell kilt and a thistle in his lapel.

"Ma, ye look like a faerie queen," he whispered.

Marjorie pressed him closer to her chest. "Thank ye. But please, stop, or ye'll make me cry, and I'll ruin the makeup and will look like the queen from the vampire stories ye love so much."

"And Konnor would still marry ye," he said, stepping back and looking her over.

Seeing him now in a tuxedo jacket and the kilt, Marjorie realized how much he'd grown in the last year, ever since they arrived in the twenty-first century. He'd started going to school in August and was still adjusting. The new school wasn't without challenges. He spoke differently and thought differently from most of the children his age. Aye, some kids had tried to bully him, but he'd stood his ground and hadn't let anyone treat him with disrespect. He'd spent the first year learning to read and write in modern English, as well as math and other modern school subjects he was supposed to know by his age. Konnor had hired a private tutor who taught Colin every day, and the woman was amazed at how quickly Colin was learning math and science. English and the arts were the most challenging subjects for him, and only Konnor's love for stories and reading *The Lord of the Rings* and other fantasy and sci-fi stories made Colin want to learn to read faster.

Colin absorbed everything like a sponge, and Marjorie was sure it was because of Konnor's, Helen's, and Mark's care and warm welcome. However, in the last couple of months, ever since starting school, he hadn't been as happy. Marjorie wanted to pull him out of school and continue with the private tutoring, but Konnor had suggested they try to help him adjust with lots of emotional support. He suggested they find Colin friends who loved the same things he did: history, fantasy, and science fiction. He'd already found a couple of friends who Konnor lovingly called "nerds," and they came to the house from time to time to play Dungeons and Dragons and study together.

Thanks to Konnor's daily exercise with Colin, the lad was succeeding at soccer. She thought that Colin was happiest when he kicked the ball around, and so was Konnor.

Well...except when he was with her.

Colin had been accepted onto the school's soccer team as a striker, and after the school won their first game thanks to his goal, he'd quickly gained more friends on his soccer team. That had made him happier, of course, and Marjorie, too.

Colin looked back at Mark. "Now, Uncle?"

Mark nodded to him and winked conspiratorially. Colin went to him, and Mark handed him something. When Colin turned back to her, a white bouquet with a tartan ribbon stole her breath away.

"Something blue," Mark said. "And new."

Colin brought her the bouquet, and when Marjorie took it in her hands, she felt something else there: a box attached to a string that held the bouquet together. She opened it and gasped. An elegant diamond necklace sparkled there.

"No, Mark!" she said. "'Tis too much."

"It's actually not from me," he said.

Helen clasped her hands. "It's only borrowed, Marjie. And it's old, I bought it at an auction. I have more money from my paintings than I can ever need, and I want to spoil you. I'm so lucky I have Konnor, but I've always wished for a daughter."

Marjorie shook her head. "Nae, I canna."

"You'll give it back afterwards. Let me do this for you. Please?"

Marjorie sighed. Her clan had never been rich, and no one had ever spoiled her with anything, not because her father didn't love her, but simply because they hadn't been wealthy. Everything in the twenty-first century seemed luxurious to her. Miraculous machines that washed dishes and laundry, audio systems that played music, cars—the iron carriages that drove themselves, the vacuum cleaner that swiped and cleaned... Not to mention airplanes. Everything was cleaner than anything she'd been used to, except the air. It had taken her a while to get used to the constant scent of burned metal that hung in the air in Los Angeles. Konnor told her it was the air pollution.

"Thank ye, Helen." She took it out. "I dinna want to offend ye, but ye dinna need to do this to care for me. Yer love and acceptance is everything I've ever wanted in a mother-in-law."

Helen wiped a tear and came to her. "Here, let me help you, honey." She took out the necklace and put it on Marjorie's neck. It sparkled like stardust on her dress.

"'Tis wonderful. Thank ye."

"You're so welcome, sweetheart."

A knock sounded at the door, and Gina, the wedding planner looked into the room. "We're ready for you, Marjorie. The groom is awfully handsome and waiting for you."

Finally, she could go and marry Konnor.

When she and Colin had traveled in time and met with Konnor, he'd taken them to a hotel in Edinburgh. Both Marjorie and Colin had been completely overwhelmed by the future. The train, the houses, the cars, the noise of the city, the number of people, the scents, the lights, the buildings with huge windows.

They'd stayed in Edinburgh for a few weeks, and Konnor had helped Marjorie and Colin to slowly adjust to their new lives. One of the challenges had been creating documents for Marjorie and Colin. Konnor had taken care of that. She didn't really know how exactly he'd done it, but it had involved a lot of coin, hiring someone called a "hacker," something called "the dark web," and waiting for passports to arrive. The most difficult thing, apparently, had been to keep their real names and make it so that Colin was still Marjorie's son even in the twenty-first century.

The flight to Los Angeles had been the scariest thing she'd ever done in her life. Konnor had held Marjorie's cold, sweaty left hand, and she'd poured one whiskey after another down her throat, murmuring about why was it worth it to cross hundreds of years only to die in a giant, iron, dragonlike carriage that could fly. Colin had had the best time of his life, watching with huge, excited eyes the crystal-blue sky and snow-white clouds passing by out the window.

But they'd made it, and Marjorie had no intention to sit on a plane ever again.

All she needed now was to walk outside together with her son to find everything she ever wanted in her future—Konnor Mitchell.

Marjorie nodded to Gina. "Aye. I'm coming." She bit her lip, containing the burst of excitement in her heart. She looked around at her new family, thinking of her old one—her father, Craig, Owen, Domhnall, Lena, and Ian, and of her friend Tamhas, and Malcolm, and Muir, and Isbeil, and everyone she knew from Glenkeld. She knew even if they weren't here physically, they were with her in spirit.

"Let's go," she said and hooked her hand through Colin's arm.

He was walking her down the aisle.

They descended the beautiful stairs to the ground floor and went through a grand foyer with wood paneling and paintings of the Highlands. They walked out into the open air and the green meadow facing the ocean. Bagpipes started playing "Highland Wedding" when she appeared, and the guests stood from the rows of chairs and faced her. There were friends of the Mitchell family, including Konnor's best friend, Andy, with his wife and daughter. Konnor's aunt Tabitha was there with her family. Mark's three children were also there, as well as other more distant relatives Marjorie hadn't meet yet. Then there were her own friends.

Six months ago, she opened a sword-fighting school. Her students were kind and interested in her. They could probably also be what Konnor called nerds, and though Marjorie knew some people considered nerds boring, she loved them. They were the ones she could talk to the most. People who loved history and sword-fighting and medieval culture. Many of her students had become her friends, and she loved spending time with them.

Then she saw the man she loved at the end of the aisle. He was wearing a Campbell kilt and a tuxedo jacket, and the happiness in her chest truly bloomed, swirling inside of her in a tornado of bubbles. He stood watching her with such a glowing expression, as though everything he'd ever wanted had come true. As though he finally understood the meaning of life. As though he was finally happy.

Colin escorted her towards an arch made of white roses. When they reached the small white platform, Marjorie gave Colin her bouquet, kissed him on the cheek, and joined Konnor. His blue eyes shone brighter than the sky under his long eyelashes. Her heart squeezed in her chest at how handsome he was, and how solemn at the same time. He was so tall and broad-shouldered, and something about him wearing the kilt made her stomach flip in the most delicious way. There was a sprig of white heather in his buttonhole, a Scottish tradition for good luck.

He took her hands in his, and a jolt of lightning went through her, as well as a shock of pleasure.

"Marjorie..." he whispered. "God, you're so beautiful, it hurts to look at you."

Marjorie squeezed his large, warm hands that felt like home. The hands that had taught her body to sing, and love, and live. "Ye look like the man of my dreams, Konnor."

The bagpipe music finished, and the reverend, a beautiful Black woman with a short haircut, looked around. "Dearly beloved, we're gathered here today to join this woman and this man in holy matrimony. I believe the bride has something to say?"

Marjorie smiled to Konnor. "I will say a Highland blessing for us." She cleared her throat. "Let morning dew wash away any quarrel we may have with each other. Let the rowan tree keep away any people thinking harm. May white heather bring good luck to us. On this blessed day, let the boundaries of time dissolve, and the strength of destiny bring our family a long and happy life."

Konnor nodded and grinned, the special meaning of her last sentence apparent only to the three time travelers.

The reverend continued, "Do you, Marjorie, take Konnor to be your husband, in sickness and in health"—she cleared her throat—"in this century or another, as long as you both shall live?"

Marjorie looked into Konnor's eyes, and there was everything she'd ever wanted. Her prince who'd woken her up so that she could fight her own battles. The man who'd helped her be whole and herself again. The man who'd given her the life she'd never thought she'd have.

"Aye," she said, and a smile so huge that it hurt spread on her face. "I do."

He let out a small, happy exhale and smiled. God, he had a

beautiful smile. Her stern, brooding man became happy and carefree, and he looked young and gorgeous with those dimples under his well-groomed scruff.

"Do you, Konnor, take Marjorie to be your wife, in sickness and in health, in this century, or another, as long as you both shall live?"

"I do," he said, and those two words caressed her and planted the most delicious feeling in her stomach, as though her blood had turned to honey wine.

The reverend looked at Colin, who stood with a bright smile on his face. "I believe there's one more person who the couple wanted to ask. Do you, Colin, take Konnor as your father?"

Colin raised his chin and straightened his shoulders, his face serious and solemn. He met Konnor's eyes, and there was light in them. "Aye. I do, Da."

Konnor's blue eyes watered, and he blinked to hold off tears. Konnor was the first and only father that Colin knew. And Marjorie couldn't imagine a better one.

The reverend clapped her hands. "You may kiss the bride!"

Konnor stepped forward, took her into her arms, and kissed her. The guests around them erupted in cheers, but Marjorie didn't pay any attention to them. His mouth was hot, plush, and delicious. His lips caressed and worshipped her, and she forgot everything and everyone else but her husband as she swam in an ocean of happiness.

Her blood boiled, her breasts aching as his hands went up and down her body, and when he stopped the kiss and pressed his forehead against hers, he whispered, "That's it, my Highland queen. Our happily ever after is only beginning. You made me the happiest man in the world, and our family of three is all I want."

She smiled. "We won't be three for much longer. We'll be a family of four. I did a blood test, and ye miraculous modern medicine has already told me 'tis a lass."

He stilled and blinked and planted the most delicious kiss on her lips. He walked with her down the aisle as the guests showered them with white rose petals, and Marjorie thought of the moment he'd appeared in her life and given her hope. Hope for happiness. Hope she'd be able to come back to her true self. Hope that all the horrors in her life were behind her.

She knew just what their daughter's name would be.

Conceived by time travelers. Blessed by Highland magic. Born in a different time.

Hope.

THE END

Loved Marjorie and Konnor's story? Keep reading about the Cambel Clan, and read Ian's story in **Highlander's Heart.**

Get your free bonus epilogue to Marjorie and Konnor's story here: https://mariahstone.com/bonus-epilogue-highlanders-hope/

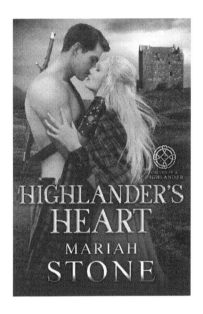

**She's a lost time traveler. He's a haunted Highland
hero. Can their romance survive the test of centuries?**

Scotland, 2020. Kate Anderson is desperate to keep her
restaurant from falling into ruin. But while soliciting the help
of a celebrity TV chef at a Scottish castle, she's injured and
suffers amnesia. Disoriented and lost, she touches a mysterious
rock that hurls her back in time where she encounters a handsome warrior.

Scotland, 1308. After years of bloodshed as a gladiator,
Dundail heir Ian Cambel swears he'll never kill again. Reset-
tling in his father's estate craving a peaceful life, he takes in a
charming woman with no memory and offers her a position as
a cook. But as the English army threatens his stronghold, he

fears for her safety and tries to hide his growing desire for the pretty lass.

As Kate's memories slowly return, she's driven to return to her modern world, despite her feelings for her noble protector. But Ian knows helping her get back home means waging war on the invaders, and when Kate sees the killer he really is, she'll leave him forever.

Will the two wounded hearts find their destiny across the ages?

Highlander's Heart is the entrancing third book in Called by a Highlander time travel romance series. If you like medieval adventures, tormented heroes, and Cinderella tropes, then you'll adore Mariah Stone's page-turning tale.

Read ***Highlander's Heart*** to remember love's identity today!

PROLOGUE HIGHLANDER'S HEART

Baghdad, Abbasid Caliphate, 1307

"HEY, SCOT. SCOT, WAKE UP."

Ian opened his eyes and lifted his head, ignoring the ache in his old wounds. Moonlight fell on the dirt-packed floor through tiny vertical windows up by the ceiling. It was warm, even at night. Around him, other slaves wheezed peacefully on the benches by the walls. The air smelled of unwashed bodies, dry dirt, and the orange tree that grew outside the windows. Even after ten years here, Ian missed the fresh, grass-scent saturated air of the Highlands.

Abaeze, the slave from Africa, whose bench stood right next to Ian's, raised his head, his eyeballs glowing white in the darkness.

"Yes?" Ian whispered back. "What is it?"

They spoke Arabic, the common language here. Learning it when he'd arrived had been the difference between staying alive and dying.

Abaeze glanced around, sat up, then slithered soundlessly to Ian, quick and efficient. A slender man even taller than Ian, he was as dark as the night, his hair a black cloud.

Abaeze crouched next to Ian's bench. "Abaeze hear a thing," he whispered, his accent thick. Since Abaeze had only arrived recently, his Arabic was limited, but he could get his point across. "You be careful today. You watch you."

A bad feeling settled in Ian's stomach. "For what? Something during the fight?"

The man nodded. "Abaeze sleep and see death. You watch you."

Fear gripped Ian's throat in its icy hand. With that final message, Abaeze left Ian and settled back on his bench. Soon, he wheezed rhythmically.

Ian lay on his back and stared at the lime-cured white ceiling.

Death.

Would it be so bad, to let it finally take him? What hope did he have with a life like this? He'd never see the Highlands or his family again.

He always asked this question before a fight. His opponent and he were needed to kill the other to live, to continue giving their masters the bloody satisfaction of power. The entertainment. The rush of a bet.

And on and on.

Every fight he'd won since he'd been here meant he'd taken a life. Ian had lost count of how many he'd killed. He'd become famous. The red-haired unbreakable beast of the caliph—the Red Death, they called him. Or simply, the Scot. Because the caliph valued him as a rare find—no other Scotsman had been captured.

Thank God.

He'd fought Germans, Spanish, Indians, Turks, English, Africans, and many, many Arabs. It didn't matter what skin color they had, what language they spoke, if they had a family back home, mayhap children and a wife. They all fell from Ian's hand.

Because he wanted to live.

But maybe Abaeze had seen the time for him to welcome his own death. Was he ready?

Ian asked himself that question repeatedly during the sleepless night and again in the morning. The sun shone into the room, and slaves brought food. The men were let out into the inner yard to clean and sweep. He was still thinking about it during the midday meal.

Other slaves were afraid of him. Abaeze, being relatively new, was Ian's only friend. He'd had friends here before. They all were dead now.

The fights were always in the afternoon and towards the evening, when the sun had already started to set, to avoid the main heat. As always, Ian and the others were given armor first, then led into a windowless chamber full of weapons— scimitars, spears, and shields. There were two doors: one lead to the courtyard where the caliph held the fights, the other— back into the small wing of the palace meant for slaves.

"You watch you," Abaeze repeated, taking a sword.

"You watch you, too," Ian said. "Thank you for the warning, friend."

The door to the courtyard opened, bright light blinding Ian in the darkness. They waited to see who'd be called first. But instead, many feet pounded against the dusty ground. Guards shoved the first of the men standing closer to the door, yelling for everyone to get out, then those behind them.

Abaeze and Ian exchanged glances. "Looks like we fight many against many," Ian said. "I will have your back."

"And Abaeze fights for Scot."

They shook hands. Then the crowd pushed them forward, and they were out in the daylight. Bloodthirsty shouts and cries filled the air. Warriors beat their weapons against their shields. There weren't many spectators for these things, just the caliph and his rich, important subjects and their invited guests. They all sat up on the second-floor balconies—away from the warriors, away from the danger of slaves turning against their masters.

But the yard, which normally held only two fighters, swarmed with slaves. They stood in two groups, beating swords and spears against their shields, ready to launch at each other, just like in a battle.

This would be quick and bloody and deadly.

They set off and the audience bellowed.

Shields and swords clashed. Spears flew and pierced live flesh. Blood sprayed and bones cracked. Taken lives disappeared in swirling clouds of dust.

A dark-skinned giant launched at Ian with a hammer. Ian raised his shield, which met the man's blade with bone-crushing power. He stabbed, and Ian jumped back. His opponent's sword slashed empty air next to Ian's abdomen. Ian stabbed from under his shield and struck right under the man's chin, sinking the blade into his head.

The next blow came from behind, someone's sword scratching against Ian's armor. He whirled to see a quick, slender Arab. Ian fought him, but more came from all sides. They all must have decided to finish him. Someone slashed his shoulder, pain burning him. Another went for his neck, but Ian ducked. A third attacked from the left side, and Ian barely managed to hit him with his shield. He fought for a while, losing strength, being chased back. As soon as he fought one, two more appeared.

Abaeze managed to rescue him once, but soon he had to fight his own battle.

Death looked into Ian's eyes and invited him to come along.

Maybe it was for the better. He deserved death. God knew, he'd taken enough lives. But his body kept fighting, kept clinging to life.

And then everything changed.

Screams rang all around—from behind the walls of caliph's palace, from inside it. Everywhere. Giant rocks began falling on the buildings. Arrows flew and hit the ground and the men.

Ian's enemies stopped fighting him, ducking under their shields, running for their lives. The caliph and his guests disappeared inside the building.

"Abaeze! Abaeze!" Ian cried, looking around.

Men lay dead, crushed under the rocks, blood soaking dry dirt. There were men Ian had been sharing a room with. Black, white, brown bodies with gashes and wounds lay around the courtyard.

Something shielded the sun, and a shadow was cast over Ian. He glanced up, seeing a rock fly right at him.

This was it. The great, bloody death.

Out of the corner of his eye, he saw Abaeze leap towards him. They flew to the side, the rock hitting the place where Ian had just stood. Dirt and gravel showered down on them.

"Thank you," Ian mumbled.

They stood up. The buildings around them were crumbled, corners destroyed. People screamed in pain, some crushed under the rocks, some suffering spear and scimitar wounds. Rocks continued falling from the sky, no doubt shot by distant catapults. Then the arrows flew. Masters, guards, servants, and slaves were scattered on the ground, wounded or dead.

An arrow swooshed past Ian, and relief flooded him at the near miss. Then someone yelped. He turned and froze as an icy wave of horror washed through him.

Abaeze sprawled in the dirt, the arrow protruding from his chest.

"No!" Ian fell to his knees by his friend's side.

Abaeze gurgled blood and reached out for Ian's hand.

"You watch you," Abaeze murmured.

His eyes locked with Ian's, desperation in them.

"No." Tears burned Ian's eyes.

"I am finally free," Abaeze said. "Go, Scot. Go."

His eyes stilled, and Ian knew then that his friend would never be a slave again. He pulled him to his chest and hugged him.

Then he saw that the gates were still open. No guards. None alive, anyway. Another rock flew at him, and he rolled onto his side.

"I'll watch me," he whispered. "Thank you, my friend."

He rose to his feet and hurried towards the gates. Mayhap, the dreams of green-and-brown Highlands wouldn't be just dreams, after all.

Mayhap, he'd finally get a chance to go home.

But if he made it through the dangers on the way, would his clan take him back once they knew what kind of man he'd become?

LOVED THE PROLOGUE? KEEP READING **HIGHLANDER'S Heart** now!

ALSO BY MARIAH STONE

CALLED BY A HIGHLANDER SERIES (TIME TRAVEL):

Sineag

Highlander's Captive

Highlander's Hope

Highlander's Heart

Highlander's Love

Highlander's Christmas (novella)

CALLED BY A VIKING SERIES (TIME TRAVEL):

One Night with a Viking (prequel)—grab for free!

The Fortress of Time

The Jewel of Time

The Marriage of Time

The Surf of Time

The Tree of Time

CALLED BY A PIRATE SERIES (TIME TRAVEL):

Pirate's Treasure

Pirate's Pleasure

A CHRISTMAS REGENCY ROMANCE:

The Russian Prince's Bride

SCOTTISH SLANG

aye – yes

    bairn - baby

    bastart - bastard

    bonnie - pretty, beautiful.

    canna- can not

    couldna – couldn't

    didna- didn't ("Ah didna do that!")

    dinna- don't ("Dinna do that!")

    doesna – doesn't

    fash - fuss, worry ("Dinna fash yerself.")

    feck - fuck

    hasna – has not

    havna - have not

    hadna – had not

    innit? - Isn't it?

    isna- Is not

    ken - to know

    kent - knew

    lad - boy

    lass - girl

    marrit – married

nae – no or not

shite - faeces

the morn - tomorrow

the morn's morn - tomorrow morning

uisge-beatha (uisge for short) – Scottish Gaelic for water or life / aquavitae, the distilled drink, predecessor of whiskey

verra – very

wasna - was not

wee - small

wilna - will not

wouldna - would not

ye - you

yer – your (also yerself)

ACKNOWLEDGMENTS

Highlander's Hope is officially the book that has undergone the most changes out of fourteen I've written so far. The idea to send a man back in time came from you, my readers. Initially, I wrote it as a novella, in which the male character was quite different and Marjorie didn't have a son. But it didn't quite work the way I've hoped it would, and seeing the book's potential, I decided to turn it into a proper novel, and it grew twice the size. It was quite a lot of work and it wouldn't have been possible without the support of my husband, my sweet baby daughter who let me write while she napped (thankfully, she was a great napper!), and my amazing team.

My brilliant editor, **Laura Barth,** helped me shape the story into its best version and held my hand through all challenges and encouraged through every doubt. If you enjoyed this book, this is really thanks to Laura who is the best editor and book coach in the world.

My copy-editor, **Heidi Shoham**, patiently helped improve the flow, the writing, and corrected all mistakes.

My proofreader, **Laura LaTulipe**, is the Sherlock Holmes of continuity. I've never met anyone with a sharper eye for inconsistencies, errors, and typos.

Finally, **Romance Refined,** and specifically, **Rachael W.** who bravely beta-read the rough, pre-edited version and helped me understand what a reader would love and what they wouldn't and saved me a lot tears.

My **my readers** who make it possible for me to not live the life of a business consultant and spend my life in hotels and airports, but to do what I love and be with my family every day.

Thank you!

Mariah

ENJOY THE BOOK? YOU CAN MAKE A DIFFERENCE!

Please, leave your honest review for the book.
As much as I'd love to, I don't have financial capacity like New York publishers to run ads in the newspaper or put posters in subway.

But I have something much, much more powerful!

Committed and loyal readers

If you enjoyed the book, I'd be so grateful if you could spend five minutes leaving a review on the book's Amazon page.

Thank you very much!

ABOUT THE AUTHOR

When time travel romance writer Mariah Stone isn't busy writing strong modern women falling back through time into the arms of hot Vikings, Highlanders, and pirates, she chases after her toddler and spends romantic nights on North Sea with her husband.

Mariah speaks six languages, loves Outlander, sushi and Thai food, and runs a local writer's group. Subscribe to Mariah's newsletter for a free time travel book today!

facebook.com/mariahstoneauthor

instagram.com/mariahstoneauthor

bookbub.com/authors/mariah-stone

pinterest.com/mariahstoneauthor

Manufactured by Amazon.ca
Bolton, ON

18571878R00166